HORSES of ANGER

HORSES
of ANGER

by JAMES FORMAN

FARRAR, STRAUS & GIROUX

NEW YORK

A Bell Book

This book is for three good friends,
all of whom fought in Hitler's war:

ROBERT S. FORMAN ✣ HANS G. ENGEL
REINHARD PAUL BECKER

From their remembrances has come the story.

Horses of anger trampling, horses of anger
Trampling behind the sky in ominous cadence,
Beat of the heavy hooves like metal on metal,
Trampling something down . . .

From *John Brown's Body*
by Stephen Vincent Benét

A glossary of terms begins on page 245.

ONE

"LET US THANKFUL BE." He sang the birthday song slowly to the end, and was thankful that he was still alive, that the night was silent. He might have been a choirboy at practice except for his uniform and the helmet which rested on the table before him. Beside the helmet was a small, damaged cake, on which one candle burned. Wax dripped onto the icing because Hans Amann, whose birthday it was, could not bring himself to put the flame out. It was April 20, 1944. Hans was fifteen, and he had been at war for a year.

Hans was tall and sturdy but curiously unfinished, as though his bones and muscles had not entirely meshed. Upon his earnest, eager face recent experience had etched a trace of bewilderment. His thoughts were brief and disconnected, without development or fulfillment. "Not tonight. Don't let the bombers come tonight." Then he thought of his family, or rather he saw them, himself included, singing the birthday song in lusty chorus. Gretchen gave him a kiss which made him smile, then just as quickly frown. He expected to see none of them again in this world and he did not believe in the next.

Hans blew the candle out, and as he did, K3 entered. K3

1

was Hans's loader, so asthmatic and spindly in the early days that he'd needed a Russian prisoner to help him load the ammunition. Hans and the others had not always been ciphers. Like all the members of the battery, they had once been classmates, and Hans made a conscious effort to call K3 by his school name. "Greetings, Ernst."

"Heil, and all that," replied Ernst Peiper, handing Hans a tin mug of war-watered beer and raising another to his lips. "May you live to grow old, Hans," he toasted, and Hans drank too, hoping for forgetfulness from one weak measure. "If you had a birthday wish, Hans, would you ask to be home with your mother? Would you like to be tucked into a feather bed, all curled up like a baby that hasn't been born?"

Hans managed a smile. "That's too good. Just give me a quiet night." Yes, a quiet night, he thought, with nothing louder than the hiss of a shooting star ten million miles away.

As he spoke, the barracks bell rang, that first warning from fighter command which regularly on dark nights sent Hans fumbling into his uniform to wait on his cot, staring into the blackness. Somewhere in the north a stream of bombers was flowing. Somewhere soon the pathfinders would drop their flares; then the big bombs would rip off the roofs to make way for the suffocating incendiaries. Across the frosted radar panels in the battle opera house the phantom flood would creep, south or east. The haggard men of fighter command must be already watching, thought Hans. Soon the warning would be sent. Should it arrive at Hans's barracks, it would mean the planes were moving against the cities of the south. They might fall short, hovering over Ingolstadt, or Regensburg or Munich, in which case Hans would not be needed. On the other hand, they might pass over to his home town—fifteen minutes' flight for a bomber, two hours by Autobahn, an interminable time by rail, the way a soldier traveled. If the bombers came that far, forty-eight schoolboys, Hans among them, would clatter up twelve wooden towers where heavy machine guns waited like strange telescopes to track the moving stars.

"Well," said Ernst, "perhaps you're to be honored with birthday fireworks."

In Hans's imagining, the second alarm had already rung, and the third. "I am K1," he repeated to himself, "the gunner who aims and fires. I am K1." And then, "Why tonight? Why on my birthday?" And then the old thoughts . . . "Take care of Gretchen. Take care of Mother and the house." It was his usual silent prayer, directed to no one in particular and followed by no amen.

The first alarm at length brought the other members of the gun crew into the room. First came Siegfried, skin as pale as his ash-blond hair, his small tight face buttoned together by two round, parrot-blue eyes. As K2, his job was rotating the gun. In task, as in stature, he was inferior to Hans. Bearing full equipment, Siegfried could not have weighed more than a hundred and twenty pounds, but Hans and others accepted him as the flak crew's natural leader. As Jungvolk troop leader, he had been an example of patriotism for them all. Now, in the antiaircraft, Siegfried seemed to live a life of terrifying joy which Hans could not understand and which had brought a rift into their old harmony.

As always, Heime arrived last, running and stumbling, his legs ensnared by oversized trousers that were half on and half off. A short, untidy figure, a coward at games and a failure at studies, he had been known as "Toad" from the first day of school. He had been drafted into the air-force auxiliary at the age of thirteen, but soldiering had not changed him at all. He remained as pallid and moist as his hated nickname indicated. In his role of ammunition boy, he was constantly underfoot. Still, he served a valid purpose as the battery scapegoat, a necessary outlet for their anxieties.

"What's this!" exclaimed Siegfried, confronting the cake as he might a six-legged dog. And then, "Ah, congratulations." Hans felt compelled to cut them all a piece. He shared his cup of watery beer as well. "To you, my dear friend," pronounced Siegfried in his clear cool voice. "And to our Leader on *his* birthday . . . Heil Hitler!" Siegfried spoke sparingly, but when he did, it sounded authoritative and final.

Hans echoed him, but Ernst lay back in his chair and made a grimace as if something had tickled the end of his nose. "Yes, to God and his little black mustache. May he never fall out of heaven." Hans studied him, but Ernst's spectacled eyes, magnified by thick lenses, were enormous as soap bubbles and completely unreadable. Once Hans had tried on these glasses, and it had been like seeing the universe through two marbles: round, brimming, unnatural.

"Ernst is being funny again," said Siegfried good-naturedly, but his face was redder than it had been. "I don't think he's ever serious." To this, Ernst readily agreed. "But don't you think some things are too . . . well, too sacred for that kind of talk?"

"But I mean it," said Ernst, tilting further back in his chair. "I like little black mustaches, all furry and caterpillary. And I never joke about God."

"If you'd ever met him—if you'd shaken his hand as I did, and felt his vitality—then you wouldn't joke. Listen, Ernst . . ." Hans knew what was coming. Patient as a preacher, Siegfried would begin again from the beginning. He would state his conviction that Hitler, who filled his life and occupied his thoughts, was beyond the judgment of ordinary men, a beacon lighting the way for humanity. Heime shifted in silent accord.

"Born into this Iron Age to restore the Age of Gold!" Ernst jeered. "We know, we know."

"Mock all you like. You'll see I'm right." Siegfried sat forward in his chair, hands clasped, secure in his faith.

Hans agreed with Siegfried. Whatever doubts Hans might have, he believed in their leader. Still, he had no intention of arguing with Ernst, whose frail body housed a sharper mind than his own, however misguided Ernst might be.

Ernst was about to reply with his usual sarcasm, but Siegfried gave him a glance like a shout at close quarters. Ernst held his tongue. Though Hans knew that his leader loudly aspired to a life of action, he knew, too, that Jericho would never tumble to Ernst's trumpets. Cowed, Ernst fumbled in his pocket, producing a large atomizer, with which he sprayed his throat. "Ahhh!" he inhaled asthmatically, letting his chair slap forward onto all four of its legs.

Heime gave a snuffling laugh. "Hear the dear old Toad," said Ernst. "You know, what a birthday party needs is colored hats. Shall we paint Heime's helmet blue with pink stars?" Heime protested. "No? Well, let's pile all the helmets on Heime's head. Won't you feel safe, then, Heime?" Grinning wickedly, Ernst began to make a pile of the helmets.

"That's majestic," said Ernst. "Isn't Heime majestic? Heime, you should always wear four helmets. You're an enchanted prince. You don't look like a fat little toad any more. Not a bit." Deliberately, or because his neck was simply not strong enough for the load, Heime let the helmets fall. "Now look at him, Hans. So ordinary. You could cut off his ears and he'd pass for a milestone. Oh, Heime!" Ernst began to whimper softly, overcome with helpless laughter.

Though seldom an active participant, Hans enjoyed Heime's silent sufferings. It was cruel and Hans knew it, but it helped somehow to exorcise the poisons that infused them all. If only Heime would resist! But he endured enigmatically, week after week, mirroring the gun crew's own helpless endurance. There was not even a show of rage, but Hans knew that rage was possible. He had once seen Heime drive his fist against the wall so hard it had remained black and blue for weeks. And he had heard the village rumor that Heime, in a fit of passion, had driven an ice pick clean through his father's hand.

Hans picked up his helmet from the floor, a birthday crown that would fit a million other skulls as comfortably. It would probably survive him. He handed Heime's helmet to him.

"Don't take it, Heime!" warned Ernst. "Without your helmet you might just end up with a nice, clean, little send-me-home wound. Oh, oh, oh, for a send-me-home wound," he began to sing. Hans's touch on Ernst's wrist and a whispered "That's enough, Ernst, let it go" failed to stop him. "You'd be with Mother, safe and sound. Even a belly wound isn't too bad; these doctors are amazing nowadays. And it's so rotten being scared to death every night. You are scared to death, aren't you, Heime?"

"We all are. All the time," said Hans. In fact, fear had been with them so long that it had grown old and died. Only hysteria remained.

A faint glisten of perspiration had appeared high on Heime's forehead. Siegfried began to lecture again. "You know, Heime, I'm concerned. We're a team, the four of us. I'm concerned about Ernst's foolishness, but I'm more concerned about you." Thoughtfully he relit the candle in the dismembered cake. "A team's like a chain, and when we're up there on the gun it's the weakest link, in a way, that's the strongest. It can break the chain. That mustn't happen. Whatever the pressure, we must control our fears, and we can. Let me have your hand. . . . Heime, let me have it. This is not meant to be cruel, Heime." And he forced Heime's hand over the candle flame.

Heime screeched. "You did that for fun!" Ernst fell back in his chair, shouting with laughter. Hans did absolutely nothing. He was too horrified.

"Heime, I assure you I didn't enjoy that at all," Siegfried insisted. "Look at me." He held his own hand close over the candle, palm down, fingers very steady—so steady that Hans could see that every nail was bitten down to the quick. It was the only unmilitary thing he had ever observed about Siegfried. "Pain is nothing if you are not afraid of it. You simply must control yourself." Each word was carefully articulate. Hans stared, hypnotized, until Heime lunged forward, knocking over the candle. Icing scattered.

"Look what you've done to the cake, Heime," said Ernst. "You'll simply have to put on your apron and bake another. Really, what a rotten party!"

Siegfried placed his hands lightly together in his lap. Hans knew he must be in severe pain. He knew also that he would rather die than give the slightest sign. The tableau held until Heime dug his Youth dagger into the table. The dagger often spoke for him. As Heime whittled, as he gesticulated, the dagger became the mouth of a secret Heime. Hans had seen him unsheath it, hold its shiny blade up to the light, and examine his noble posture in the mirroring surface of the dagger. Inscribed "Loyalty Unto Death," it was the living sign of whatever manhood Heime possessed, the imperishable proof that he was a soldier. It stayed with him always, on his body even in sleep. Hans watched him now, gouging at the tabletop, and wondered about them all. They had been schoolboys together a year before, good friends, and now they were lunatics sharing the same cell in an asylum that was the entire world.

Heime had managed to form a particularly small H with his dagger when the siren in the Polish work camp began to howl. Hans listened intently as the sound rose shrill and terrifying, shrill enough to crack the stars. Hans groped for his boots. Any minute the last alarm would ring, and K1, K2, K3, and K4 would go to battle the sky. The siren rose and fell in sorrowful loops of sound. "Heimdall's horn," Gretchen had called it. Was she hearing the siren now, trembling in her bed, clutching her battered teddy bear? "Don't be afraid, Gretchen. Don't be afraid like me." Then the alarm bell rang in the barracks, and Hans's birthday party, which might never have been except that his uncle, Major Konrad Wirth, was the commander of the flak battery, came to a clattering end.

TWO

WHEN HAD IT ALL BEGUN, this war that surely would continue until long after Hans's own life had ended? With Bismarck and his generals? When Cain first took a jagged stone in his hand? Its historical origins were too complex for Hans to understand, but it had begun for him five years before, in Munich.

On April 20, 1939, Hans was ten years old, a Gymnasium candidate, newly accepted into the Jungvolk. All the people he loved were still alive. They were celebrating this singularly happy occasion in the Bürgerbrau Keller, which the beloved Führer was expected to pass on his way from the airport to his apartment on Prinzregenten Strasse. Loud with talk and music and the clatter of beer mugs, heavy with the aroma of beer and sausage, the cavernous hall did not seem to be bounded by four walls but rather faded away into smoky infinity.

The day was hot. A waiter, with a protruding shelf of teeth that gave an effect of perpetual laughter, had brought Hans's elders great steins of Weissbier. Hans nursed a tiny mug, taking small sips because this was all the beer he would be allowed to have. An orchestra of rawboned Ba-

varian girls with fleshy arms and flushed faces struck up a
tune. For Hans it had all the screeching, squeaking, scrap-
ing effect of an endless traffic accident. He loved it, but his
grandfather stirred in his chair as though he'd just been
jarred from sleep and said, "Gott im Himmel! This is awful.
Something must be done." The music went on, a tempest of
fiddles, a barrage from half a dozen brazen trumpets. "God
in heaven!" said the old man again. Trying to get his fourth
glass of schnapps to his lips, he managed only to dampen
his floppy black tie and waistcoat. "That isn't music! They
are simply murdering silence. My eardrums will burst." It
seemed to Hans that his grandfather's ears must be particularly sensitive, for they were enormous, pendulous and red-
veined. His mother said they made the professor look like a
Volkswagen with both doors open.

"Herr Professor, please! You didn't have to come." It
was his mother speaking. She did not find the music too
loud. With her stein held before her, she tapped the floor
and moved her lips in silent song. Sitting beside her, Hans
could feel the bench moving. His mother was the most
lovable and at the same time the most comforting and
familiar of beings. Under the enormous feathered structure
of her hat, her eyes looked out, lively, scornful, and blue as
cornflowers. Her skin was milky white, a proud possession.
Even at the age of ten, Hans knew that the sum total of her
handsome features was not real beauty. The upward tilt of
her nose, the eyes a fraction of an inch wider than they
ought to be, the explosive laughter, a mind which frequently
tried to jump in five different directions at once, these qualities made him smile.

As long as the music played, his grandfather had gone on
mumbling and muttering. Just to keep the engine going,
Hans supposed. He loved his grandfather, though his

mother often treated the old man with patronizing embarrassment, as if he displayed some conspicuous deformity. "He's the dearest old thing in the world," she was saying now with rough affection, "but the way he hunches over his food, the way he spills . . ." The fact that her husband was only a small shopkeeper while the old man remained Herr Professor was part of it. As Hans watched, she attacked her father-in-law's vest as though he were an empty suit of clothes. Taking a comb from her purse, she began to comb his splendid head of rivery white hair, an attention the old man had long resented but against which he no longer raised a protest. In fact, he winked at Hans, and his eyes were bright and undaunted.

When the music came to an end, the relief was so great that Hans felt slightly dizzy. His father, Klaus Amann, had been squirming about, crossing and uncrossing his legs. Now he leaned forward over the table.

"Lore!" he whispered, as stealthily as a prisoner transmitting a message to someone in a neighboring cell. "Lore, will you stop that?"

"I've done it again! Look at my poor husband's face," said Lore Amann in a voice that carried.

"Lore, it isn't that I mind, or that he does. You mustn't imagine that . . ." That was the way his father always spoke, inconclusively, eager not to confront directly. "Must you treat him like a baby? After all, people are looking."

"I love him. I am simply making him presentable."

"Come along, Lore. Relax. Sit down, eat. The parade'll be here any minute." It was Uncle Konrad who spoke, crisply, emphatically. If not to her brother's tone, then because of the food, Lore responded. Like the rest of her family, she enjoyed food and lavished great care upon its preparation and consumption. Mealtime, for all of them, was a sacred ritual. "Lore, this sausage is good," Konrad commented. "Almost as good as yours. We'll all of us reek of garlic."

Uncle Konrad would be a hero in the coming war. He was already a hero to Hans. He had a profile stolen from Homeric myth and a manner that people and dogs could trust. Konrad had left Munich University and joined the army, hoping for an officership in the cavalry because he loved horses. In Dresden he took a rigorous course of training, supplemented by attendance at a school of dance, conversation, and the management of eligible young ladies. Konrad reached his objective—the cavalry—but he soon found himself in a tank, rather than on horseback. He became commander of a diesel Panzer II in realistic maneuvers on the Lüneburg heath. A year later, as a lieutenant in Guderian's Second Panzer division, Konrad had taken part in the Austrian Anschluss and the reoccupation of the Rhineland. Recently he had entered Czechoslovakia behind a crowd of cheering soldiers who in their jubilance had torn down the custom-house gates on the border. It had been another painless victory for Germany.

"So you're ten, are you?" his uncle said. "A pleasant age. They'll work you hard in the Jungvolk, believe me." But Hans thought being in the Jungvolk was fine. He'd passed the pimpfenprobe exams; only Siegfried had done better. Hans had sworn the blood-flag oath: "To the saviour of our country, Adolf Hitler!" Let them work him hard. He was ready for long marches, hunger, even death on the field of honor.

"Well, here's to Hans," said Konrad. "May he . . . may all of us have a pleasant, peaceful year."

"May England and France rest in peace," said the old professor.

"And Holland as well," added Konrad. Hans knew he was thinking about his ex-wife in Rotterdam, the beautiful dark-eyed riding mistress. They'd loved horses first, and then each other, and they had been married young, before the alien blood laws, before the terrible "night of broken crystal" when Jewish property had been pillaged all over Germany. The marriage had been simple, without the benefit of the usual Bund Deutscher Mädchen choir, the Germanic blood blessing, or a swastika cake, and as simply as it had been performed, it was annulled. After all, she was a Jewess. She could not live safely in Germany, and Konrad could not leave the Fatherland and keep his career. He referred to the political climate in Germany as a passing insanity. In time they'd be married again. In Konrad's heart they were married still. So he had spoken more than once, but Hans thought the only insanity was marrying a Jewess in the first place.

"I wish we could count on that," said the old man.

"On what?"

"On peace. We're heading for war, you know. I've seen the signs before."

"But things are getting better every day. Hitler's making progress," said Klaus. However much Klaus complained of the Party, he always spoke out for the Fatherland. Of all the anti-Nazi jokes he repeated in Hans's presence, not one touched derisively upon the Führer. In fact, Klaus had recently hung a rather fierce picture of their Leader in the kitchen, on a peg formerly reserved for Goethe, and if the eyes had not had an odd facility for following one about, Hans would have approved emphatically of the transfer.

"Progress that leads to the trenches and the insane asylum," grumbled the old man.

"I won't accept that," said Konrad. "He took Austria and

Czechoslovakia without a shot. Why, everywhere we went, we were cheered. Our tanks were garlanded with flowers." Sometimes the old man's mouth opened long before he could say anything. That happened now. When the words finally came, they were accompanied by a wry smile. "I've often thought that if the Romans had invented a decent combustion engine, they'd have built good enough roads for it from Khartoum to Edinburgh. They'd have motorized the Legions, and they'd never have fallen. They would have spared us a great deal of bloodshed. But things didn't work out that way. They turned a cow into a god, instead. Or was it a horse? Now we're doing the same thing, except in our case it's a wolf." He gave a little cough, which was his usual comment on the wittiest of his remarks.

"So you really believe war is coming," said Klaus.

"I'm afraid so. Every day it steals closer."

Konrad set his stein on the table. "Sometimes I've thought so," he admitted reluctantly.

Lore looked first at one, then at the other. "You're spoiling the party," she said. "All of you."

The old man maintained a dignified silence, but he looked strangely portentous, a prophetic apparition from another world. His daughter-in-law appealed to him. "And you, Herr Professor? You're too old to be a cynic."

"I am indeed, my dear. Actually, I'm just a sentimental old pessimist who worries about his family."

"Then will you please stop worrying?"

"Soon enough, Lore. That's one advantage of being eighty-three."

Lore gave one of her explosive sighs. "The things he says! Herr Professor, you'll outlive us all."

"I may," said the old man. "I've the secret of longevity. To live long, Hans, there's one philosophy. Be a coward, in deed if not in thought."

"He doesn't mean that," said Lore.

"Oh, I do. I tried to teach it to your father, Hans. I was ready to bribe a doctor in the Great War to certify your father as tubercular. That's true."

"Can't you manage to keep your voice down?" interjected Klaus.

The professor's efforts had had no effect, as Hans very well knew. His father had gone to war with a Lutheran hymn on his lips, leaving behind a promising career as a violinist. They put him into the Uhlan cavalry, where he'd received a leg wound; then for two years more into the Somme trenches as a deputy officer. "And what a Uhlan he was!" said Lore. She had a habit of glancing upward as she spoke, which made her look like a contrary madonna. In her voice was a trace of mockery. "You father's sword drew blood from the wind, only he didn't know how to ride a horse."

"Lore, don't go into all that again." His father looked embarrassed.

"He didn't know how to ride," she went on, "and he got himself stepped on. Your father's been trying to get even with animals ever since."

By this, Hans presumed she was referring to his father's trade. As a violinist he would have been ruined after the war, for the Weimar Republic had been too poor to subsidize veterans, let alone musicians. Under the Nazis, violinists had fared little better, so it had to be considered a lucky event that a British-flung grenade at Ypres had dispatched the town butcher's only son, Lore's brother, giving Klaus an opportunity to take over the business through marriage.

"Lore, if you're getting into one of your moods," said Klaus, "let's not inflict it on Hans. It's his birthday."

"I know it, I know it. Hans, I'm sorry. I apologize to all of you. I'm having one of those days." Hans wondered whether "those" referred to "bad" days or "old" days or, more probably, "bad old days," the time of the Great War. She had imagined herself triumphantly on the way to higher social circles, but her ambitions had not materialized. From butcher's daughter she had become butcher's wife, and this had remained a source of anguish, as disagreeable as having one shoulder higher than the other. "Shall we talk about what we're going to do after the parade?"

They considered the House of German Art, but the professor described the much touted gallery as a railway station and a cesspool of bad art.

"What about the opera?" asked Konrad. "The Merry Widow?"

Hans would have liked that . . . after all, Hitler might be there; but his parents decided it would be impossible to get tickets this late. Weiss Ferdl, the roly-poly, walrus-faced comic, would have been fine, but Ferdl had recently been sent to Dachau because of his jokes about the SS.

"Well, there's always the cinema," said Klaus.

"Actually, there's the film about the Führer, not far from here," Lore recalled.

"Must we see that man twice in one day?" the professor demanded.

But Hans, who had never seen the Führer in person, was enthusiastic, and so was his mother. "Herr Professor," she said, "you can sleep through it. It will do your heart good."

There followed an active silence as the professor pulled out an enormous meerschaum and then began blowing into the bowl. Its emptiness magnified the noise. The old man stuffed it carefully, grunting and puffing. The effort put lines from his nose to the corners of his mouth so deep and severe they reminded Hans of an iron bust of Bismarck. Finally, he puffed out a sigh of smoke.

A number of tables were empty now. The members of the orchestra were collecting their equipment and patrons were moving outside into the street. Hans listened for the parade, but heard nothing.

Klaus called for the check while Konrad reminisced about his brief career in the cavalry: the smell of the horses and of saddle leather, the sway and clank of troopers riding together, the razor-sharp second before the charge . . . a charge that for him had never come and might never come again for any man. "It's just as well," he said. "It isn't fair to make horses suffer for our quarrels." Hans seemed to hear the rattle of swords and the jangle of spurs back through the ages to the campaigns of Thor and the Valkyries.

"The parade's coming! The Führer!" he shouted, but Klaus knew better. It was only SA, the so-called Brown Army, clearing the streets. Bavarian though he was, Klaus's loyalties were to the old Prussian military tradition. He had no use for the new political armies: the ascendant Black Army of the SS, the eclipsed Brown Army of the SA. In fact, he had resigned from the Stahlhelm veterans group when it was incorporated into the SA, and it was his deepest fear that before long the Wehrmacht itself would fall subject to the SS.

When Klaus had finally found a waiter and paid the bill, Lore thanked him profusely. It was seldom she had the pleasure of sitting down to a meal she had not prepared herself, and now she said, "It does me good to get out of that house with all its musty books."

This comment was met with a look of sad reproach from the pale eyes of the old man. "My dear," he said thoughtfully, taking hold of his beard. "My dear, I don't mind your saying that unless you mean it . . . about the books."

She had often threatened to throw them out, particularly

those on Doctor Goebbels's forbidden list: the works of Thomas Mann, Helen Keller, H. G. Wells, and many others, not to mention, of course, Jewish writers such as Freud and Einstein. Countless books which struck at the root of German thought had gone up in smoke throughout Germany, though many of these same books remained in the professor's library.

"Listen," said Klaus, "now I do hear it. This time they're really coming."

The whanging beerhall band had vanished, but from the street came the muffled shocks and lingering vibrations of big bass drums. Hans felt hot and cold all over. The last few tables emptied, leaving the chairs and benches faced round in all directions as if a storm had abandoned them there. He pushed outside, ignoring the beerhall's iron hen, which returned cackles and a tin egg for a pfennig. He heard only the heavy rhythmic marching, saw only a bronze eagle flashing in the sun. The blood flags and the eagles passed, rank on rank, the black shirts and the brown.

"There aren't so many lads in brown," said his grandfather, but Hans hardly heard him. "In the old days, when the Kaiser held a review, the men looked like rare tropical birds. What plumage . . ."

Pimpfs were passing now, the young ones, whom Hans could afford to despise a little. They were too short for him to see except for an occasional flash of black stockings, black pants, and brown shirts with swastikas. "Hurrah, hurrah," they sang. "To the battle front march we!" Siegfried should be here. Hans had invited him, and of course he'd had to ask Heime, too. Hans didn't care much for Heime, but he and Siegfried were inseparable. They were like a couple of policemen on duty, with Heime having to take a frog jump now and then to keep up. But Siegfried's father had forbidden him to come, and had been called a Jew by his disappointed son. One didn't say that sort of thing to Herr Hellpack. Siegfried had received a savage hiding, which ended the argument.

The Hitler Youth stomped by, all boots and big young knees, strong shoulders and stronger jaws, and a *gruppen-leiter* who screeched commands like a peacock. Ernst would enjoy that. He'd say something like, "History in the making," and laugh his hyena laugh. Ernst was an odd one, like a plant raised in a humid cellar, shooting up too high. He collected stuffed animals and bugs. His mother had tried to get him out of the Youth program because of his asthma. He, too, had been invited to join the Amanns today, not by Hans but by Hans's grandfather, because Ernst often talked to the professor about Heine and Rilke, poets the old man loved. But parades were dusty and bad for his asthma, he had said. Hans thought it was just as well. He didn't know how to talk to Ernst.

The crowd became quieter, as though entering a church. In the distance a martial air, the Badenweiler march, throbbed like a hymn. Then through the press of flags and marching men Hans could see a stately car. "He's coming! Hitler's coming!" The crowd drew a collective breath. Slowly the car came on and with it the round-shouldered figure of a man. The jagged part in his hair, lit by the sun, gleamed like a scar. Hans couldn't believe it. Surely this wasn't Hitler. As the car approached, he saw a face, neither ugly nor beautiful, with a strong nose and a hard line of mouth. Then he felt the impact of those pale gray eyes from which sparked a lifetime of fury and naked power. The huge Mercedes paused for a moment, and the figure became animated. The right arm extended and was drawn back, the hand placed over the heart. "You are mine, and I am yours.

You are Germany! We are Germany!" And for Hans, standing in a crowd suddenly gone mad, that figure against the sun loomed as large as God.

"Sieg Heil! Sieg Heil!" the sea roared. Hans's mouth worked and his voice was already hoarse. He felt cold, afraid, exultant, and touched somehow with glory. Here was the greatest, finest, most magnificent man who had ever lived, and Hans longed to do something to show his devotion. He would die for him. If Hitler asked it, he would lie down and die.

As the car passed, a woman standing near Hans shrieked ecstatically. She revolved slowly, her eyes turned up so that only the whites showed. Then she sagged to the pavement. Konrad was cheering now in a deep voice. His father's lips were moving but no sound seemed to be coming from his mouth. No one bothered with the woman except the professor, and he was unable to lift her. "Give me a hand, boy," he said. Reluctantly, Hans complied.

"You ought to be cheering, Grandfather."

"I'm not a rooster. I can't crow loud enough to bother," said the old man.

They raised the woman to her feet. "Where am I?" she gasped.

"God only knows," replied the old man.

Louder and louder the marchers sang. "Zum letzen Mal wird zum Appell . . ." Hans scarcely noticed them. His eyes were inward toward a private sky, empty and open for his future deeds. His life's purpose had dawned on him. For the first time he saluted a world made for heroes.

"I'm tired," the old man had said, and he'd walked ahead to a park across the street. Hans and the others followed after the parade had passed. The park benches were crowded, except for the yellow ones.

"He would! Your father would sit down on one of those," said Lore. Beside the professor sat a wizened old man with a yellow Star of David pinned to his coat. He must have been very old and confused if he didn't know better than to appear in public on such a day.

"Will you get up from there?" Lore's tone, addressing the professor, was sharp.

"Why? It's a perfectly good bench. It's in the sun, even if the sun's not quite as hot as it used to be."

"Herr Professor, you know perfectly well why."

The old man with the star on his coat searched her face with bewildered eyes.

"At times, my dear, I appreciate the pleasures of growing old," said the professor.

A trooper with eel-brown eyes that matched his shirt strolled by. His foot fell heavily on the old Jew's foot. Moving swiftly, Konrad confronted him. He spoke very softly. Hans heard only the trooper's reply: "I don't go around molesting old creatures, human or otherwise!"

"Then get along," said Konrad. "And tuck your shirt in your pants."

Klaus gave a nervous little smile. "All right, Father," he said. "You've had your fun."

"Of course, if he thinks it's funny, that's perfectly all right. That's all there is to it. He can stay here. Herr Professor, would you like your ticket? We'll meet at the train." Lore began fumbling in her purse.

"He's just doing this as an object lesson for Hans. Humor him, Lore," said Klaus. "Don't make trouble."

"Trouble? Your father has only one trouble, and that's beyond curing. He's old."

The professor got up. He didn't answer Lore directly, but to Hans he said, "She's right, you know." It might have

been from the pain in his joints, it might have been something else, but Hans thought the old man's eyes were
moist.

Hans asked, "Are you all right, sir?"

"Fine. Fine. I'm quite indestructible." And he started off
with a brisk jerking pace, his cane tap tapping, block after
block.

There was a note of impatience and exuberant hatred in
the streets. Slogans, proud and patriotic, were scrawled in
paint on the rough plaster walls. A stormtrooper passed,
swaggering by, a brick in his hand, while a grocer apologized behind the shattered glass of his display window: "It's
only the people expressing themselves."

On the way to the cinema, they crossed the Königliche
Platz. Young men of the labor battalion strode ahead of
them, spades shimmering in the late sunlight, chanting the
trinity, "Ein Volk, Ein Reich, Ein Führer." In the center of
the plaza stood the Greek-style shrine for the heroes killed
in the 1923 Party Putsch: sixteen sarcophagi lit by eternal
torches, and a solemn troop of the Bund Deutscher Mädel
in white cotton shirts and shorts. Solemnly the girls dipped
their pennant while shouting out the names of the fallen.
"Alfarth, hier; Bauriedl, hier . . ." The anger of Hitler
pervaded the place, deep and trembling. It seemed to make
the torches flutter. ". . . Scheubner, hier; Richter, hier;
Stransky, hier; Wolf, hier. . . ." Hans had been told that
when Albert Schlageter fell before a firing squad, a skylark
rose singing to the sun. He could believe it now.

The mood was spoiled by his grandfather, saying, "Even
at eighty-three I don't see much pleasure in lying underneath a marble slab."

The old man walked on ahead. He stood straight enough,

but it struck Hans that he was aging fast. His heels hit the ground with hard jerks; there were cabbagy veins on the backs of his hands.

At the theater, the old man insisted on buying the tickets, and his unsteady hands spilled the contents of his wallet all over the sidewalk. Lore looked exasperated, his father embarrassed, but Hans saw only the sky and the first pink feathers of evening in the west. There too he saw the planes, too far away to tell if they were Messerschmitts or Junkers, but they were there as his imagination would have them, the daredevil pilots of the Condor Legion who'd taken care of the Red terrorists at Guernica, at places people remembered. He'd be a pilot all right when the time came. Then his mother was pulling at his sleeve and they were inside the theater.

Hans sat next to his grandfather.

First there was a preview of something called "In the Saddle for Germany." Then the feature picture began, with a blond young Bannenführer, leader of a youth detachment, telling his boys the story of Hitler's life. "In the sweetly intimate little town of Braunau on the shore of the romantically rushing river Inn, our beloved Hero-Führer first saw the light of day on the twentieth of April 1889 . . ." spoke the disembodied voice of the narrator. The professor pulled a linen handkerchief as large as a tablecloth from his pocket and blew a long ominous blast. Someone tittered in the darkness. The Amann family was rigidly silent. After that the old man, too, quieted down. He coughed once or twice, and when Hans looked at him, he saw his jaw moving up and down, but there was no sound. Then the boy concentrated on the film. He saw Hitler join the army as a young man, watched him leap from one shell crater to another, "fleet as a deer, brave as a lion, doing his sacred duty," as the narrator said. How had Germany lost the First World War? For Hitler on the screen, as well as for Hans, this was a painful question. But it would presently be solved by Hitler's chancellorship—this was the message of the film. A newsreel followed. His grandfather hated newsreels and usually went outside into the lobby, but this time he sat, his head bent forward. "Are you asleep, Grandfather?" Hans whispered, but he got no reply. The newsreel ended with Goering bestowing medals on his pilots who had put down the Communists in Spain. Then the image of Hitler was thrown on the screen, and everyone stood at attention, saluted, and sang, "Deutschland, Deutschland über alles." All except Professor Amann.

"Grandfather, wake up!"

Lore spoke sharply to the old man, but he didn't budge. The lights came on. "Such an amusing old man. Look at him, sound asleep," she said. "Wake him gently," said Klaus, and Hans whispered "Grandfather" softly, because he was close to the old man and something made him afraid. "I think he's sick," said Hans. Lore gave the professor a gentle shake, and he slid to the floor.

"Good God! He's had a stroke!" exclaimed Konrad.

Lore blanched, crouching to steady the old man with whom she had always fought. With her arms around him, she comforted him like a child. "You'll be all right, you'll be all right." Then she looked up, her eyes wet. "He's breathing. Thank God, he's breathing." In a moment the professor opened his eyes. An usher had come and then had gone to call the manager. "It's the hospital for you, old friend," said Konrad, but the professor said nonsense, he'd only fallen asleep. He was going home, a fiercely proud old man who always had his way.

And for once Lore took the professor's side. "He wants to go home," she said.

While the manager flapped behind them, they helped the professor up the aisle and out into the street. Cabs were a thing of the past. Not even the pharmacies had benzine. A tram, painted blue and white in a last salute to German monarchy, was their only means of conveyance to the station. The professor's legs had become so useless they had to carry him aboard and into a seat. Hans sat away from them, afraid of the way his grandfather was breathing, embarrassed by the way strangers whispered. He stared through the glass into the dark streets as the tram made its interminable, halting progress to the station. Some passengers disembarked at the Regina Palace Hotel and he could hear dance music. Hans tried to imagine the rich young crowd inside. Then they were passing the quiet of the English Garden. The professor's breathing had become almost as soundless as the mist oozing up from the nearby swamps. "Don't let the breathing stop, please!" At last Hans recognized the great steel-webbed railway station. Now Konrad and Klaus were helping the professor. Hans carried the cane the old man's hand had dropped. Sulfurous mists drifted up from the marshes and rolled like a yellow haze over the dark rooftops of Munich. In the distance, Hans heard the sounds of cheering and of glass splintering near the Marienplatz.

THREE

THE TOWN which Hans called home lay in the alpine foothills southeast of Munich. The new Reich Autobahn and the revitalized railway passing through on its way to Berchtesgaden had helped the town to grow. If the Amann family had owned a fast car, Munich would have been only an hour away, but the railway was roundabout and slow. It had never seemed slower than on the night they brought the professor home.

Some of the houses in the town were six stories high, half-timbered, with steep black-and-white-tiled roofs that looked at a distance as though they were made of corn. Above the gabled rooftops rose the knobbly church tower, and higher still the brewery and the castle with its eight towers and its square gate. His grandfather could remember a time when the town was entirely contained within the old walls, walls that had come under Swedish attack more than once during the Thirty Years' War. They had never fallen, though half the population had died of starvation and the plague before that war was over.

Now no one starved. The old brewery, built when his great-grandfather was a boy, had brought with it prosperity and had earned the steadfast loyalty of the townspeople. The brewery oxen had won the tug of war at the Dachau festival the year before; Hans had seen them do it. The Führer had further enriched the town with a new power-house, a tannery, and a factory that made ball bearings. His grandfather had told him it was because of the tannery smell that storks no longer nested on the rooftops, but there was enough fairytale atmosphere to attract a few German tourists, mostly soldiers with accents Hans could scarcely understand, Prussians who preferred hunting to skiing. They searched the narrow streets for cuckoo clocks and cheap violins. Hans had no use for them. He shared the local dislike of strangers and assumed a certain superiority toward all newcomers.

In fact, the superiority Hans felt toward transients was directed in milder form toward his fellow townsfolk. After all, his family tree was older. His house was larger. It had passed from father to son down the generations. Since when? He didn't really know. Since Barbarossa? Parts of it looked that old. A simple farmhouse to begin with, it had undergone expensive improvements during the lifetime of his great-grandfather, who had made a dubious fortune in Napoleonic antiques after the Franco-Prussian War. Perhaps anticipating a stray bolt of divine reproach, he had covered the roof with a forest of lightning rods. Hans's grandfather had added only books, and his father had made no improvements whatsoever, though it could be said of Klaus that he always kept meat on the table.

Little trace of what had once been a sizable farm remained. First the old drill field, then the Wagner-in-the-Woods Opera Company had nibbled away at the acreage. A small patch of beech and spruce was all that still separated the house from the rest of town. On the opposite side

there remained only the cemetery, where forgotten ances-
tors lay buried, and where his own grandfather soon would
lie. From the cemetery, hunters' trails led steeply up into
the mountains.

In former days man and beast had sheltered beneath the
great farmhouse roof which slanted over all with the protec-
tive wings of a bird. The kitchen still displayed enormous
ceiling beams blackened from the smoking of hams and
sausage. The cavernous stone chimney continued to be
scoured once a year by the sweep with his brushes and wire
snakes, but the stable had been partitioned into library and
sitting room. The hayloft had been divided into bedrooms
before Hans was born. A row of flower boxes marked
where the loft doors had opened. This was his grandfather's
home, soon it would be his father's, and one day it would
belong to Hans, who could imagine living nowhere else.

Hans fully expected, even welcomed, the prospect of
growing old in that ancient house; and yet, following that
April day in 1939 when the professor came home to die, it
had lost considerable attraction. Besides, there were many
preoccupations during that summer: collecting for the
Winter Aid Fund on Sunday afternoons outside the art
cinema in town, and many other Jungvolk activities. His
troop had missed the Mount Hesselberg rally with its fires
and singing at night, but there had been plenty of hiking on
the mountain trails. Hans loved those hikes, escaping the
smoky haze of the town, climbing above the blue-smocked
hog farmers and the shepherds. He didn't feel comfortable
among the peasants since they'd beaten up a troop of SS men
for trying to chop down a Maypole. Not that he was afraid.
His bunch wasn't a Sunday-school picnic group slouching
along but an army: vanguard, column, and rear guard on
the march. Up to the deep woods, up into the red-deer

country they plodded, and on the heights they sang the "Horst Wessel Lied" and other songs that were just for fun. "In Soviet Russland high up north, The long-nosed Jews go bravely forth: And plunder shops and rob the farms, And kill the Russki babes in arms . . ."

It was queer about the Jews. Hans assumed he hated them for their long noses and shifty eyes and the way they'd sucked the Fatherland dry with foreign money after the war. Not that he'd ever known one personally. You just didn't meet any foreigners up here. Only once had he seen an Oriental face, never a black African's. It was as if the surrounding mountains kept foreignness out. Maybe that was why he loved these long hikes, the feeling of belonging on the heights. The load on his back was never too heavy, the distance traveled never long enough. The mountains were always above and beyond, moving as he moved, brilliantly white under the blue sky which curved itself over the peaks like the roof of a cave. If they'd only had time to climb the Hochkaiter, or get up to Berchtesgaden. Berchtesgaden! What a magic name. "I live near Berchtesgaden. I guess you know where that is," was all he had to say to anyone. The higher he climbed, the more the mountains towered into the sky, the more the name "Berchtesgaden" sang gently in his head.

No matter how hungry and tired he was during that summer of 1939, Hans was reluctant to return home in the evenings. When August came, his grandfather was still alive, but Hans was painfully aware that he was failing. It was easy to forget the old man when Hans was among his comrades, but concern beset him when he entered the front door. Besides, there was the smell. The leathery smell of old, well-thumbed books, the sugary-bakery smell from the stone oven were the old smells, the good smells. Now home smelled like a hospital. When Hans entered the perpetual twilight of the big front hall, he would stand still in the dusk peering into the deeper gloom of the room beyond with sun-dazzled eyes. He longed to tiptoe by, but his conscience pushed him through the door. He would step quietly into the ancient clutter of dusty daguerreotypes and nameless souvenirs. There stood the battalions of books ranked to the ceiling. As a child he had used them as building blocks.

From an enveloping leather chair protruded a pair of slippered feet, two shabby boats abandoned at high tide. Often the old man was asleep, or so withdrawn that Hans had the ghostly feeling that he was dead, and he would loudly wind the great mantel clock in the hopes that his grandfather would hear the noise and awaken without being asked. Occasionally the professor would respond and be his old self, or at least an antique version, with skin shrunk back against his skull, his nose as sharp and hooked as a paring knife.

He had consistently repudiated the hospital. When they had brought him home from Munich, he had even refused to go upstairs to bed. He had stayed in his study, and Lore had made up a cot. "I'll die with my books," he had said. "Nonsense," Lore had told him. "We'll fix you up in no time." But the family doctor had admitted that the professor's condition was serious. It was all up to nature's marvelous powers of recuperation, which meant to Hans that his grandfather was beyond human help. Lore had taken charge as nurse, with tireless energy. "I will not be pampered and huddled over by a woman," the professor had protested. The two had argued constantly, rarely understanding each other, yet in a strange way loving and needing each other. Thus, spring had faded into the hot summer days while the old man's heart went on irresolutely fending off the inevitable.

Never once, however perilously he clung to life, had Hans heard his grandfather complain of pain or show any fear of death. Yet each time it was a terrifying effort to walk around the big chair to confront the silent figure. When the faded eyes finally focused on him, Hans had a hard time concealing his relief. They would talk a little, Hans impatient to go, the old man, with nothing to do, bent on holding him.

Every day his grandfather would ask him if he had wound the clock. "If you can hear time passing, it makes the day last longer," he would say. "I've come to appreciate a long day, Hans." The clock was a great brass affair surmounted by a wildly lashing charioteer. It was uniquely complicated, with separate hands for the minute, hour, day, week, month, and year. There was even one for the century. Across its frame were etched mysterious astrological signs. If Hans looked at it long, he would begin to feel that something might be going wrong with the universe. He would have to go outside and look at the sky. Somehow it seemed to him that the ticking of that instrument and the continued pulse in his grandfather's wrist were irrevocably linked, and so he conscientiously performed the daily ritual of winding the clock.

Sometimes Ernst came with him to the study. He never seemed bothered by the professor's condition, and the old man was always glad to see him. "If I were a building, they'd condemn me," he had said to Ernst, and the two had laughed together uproariously. For hours they would explore the old dog-eared volumes, each reading silently, yet seeming to share, like hunters in a game preserve.

"He's something, your grandfather. The last of his kind," Ernst said after one visit, and there was a warm and honest smile on his face.

So the summer of 1939 passed, full of excitement, exertion, and worry. Hans had no concern for the distant horizon where clouds built up and gradually moved toward them, a storm inevitable and unwanted. Yet the house seemed somehow to sense a change, with its timbers creaking and stirring like the joints of a person who cannot sleep. Often Hans heard soft footsteps on the stairs outside the door, water running in the kitchen, and the old clock chiming the hours.

One night when the room was particularly hot he'd gone out on the landing and met his mother there. "It's that clock of his," she had said. "Its striking keeps me awake and then I have to look in on him." Hans knew very well that she spent long hours every night with the old man, though she never mentioned it.

"How is he?"

"I don't know why he's still breathing," she said. "Well, maybe I do. It's will power. I think half of him's been dead for weeks, and still he has that will to stay alive." There was a note of admiration which Hans had not heard before. "But sometimes his mind isn't as clear as it was. It dims. . . . Funny. Your grandfather and I fought like cats and dogs over this house, over the changes I wanted and he wouldn't have. I never won those battles, Hans, but I wish he were able to fight back now. When your grandfather dies, it'll mean the end of something more than just your grandfather. Something I don't want to lose."

"Have you written Uncle Konrad?" he asked.

"No. They'd never forward the letter to him in East Prussia."

Hans did not sleep well that night and when the morning came it was gray and sultry and stirring with the Föhn wind off the mountains. It was Friday, September 1. He might have stayed in bed, except for his father, who routed him out. The radio was announcing something important.

"Since five forty-five this morning," came the passionate voice from Berlin, "the fire has been lighted." The Poles, it seemed, had launched a cowardly attack on the German radio station at Gleiwitz the night before, and the *Schleswig-Holstein,* fortuitously anchored in the Danzig harbor, had answered back with her 11-inch guns. Panzer divisions on field exercises in East Prussia had turned the tide of the Polish assault. The German people were to rest assured the situation was in hand. That meant Uncle Konrad! Hans wanted to shout, but from the way his mother's lips were drawn tight and tremulous, and from the way his father glared at the floor, he judged the occasion was a solemn one. "The Chancellor must know what he's doing," said his father rather hopelessly. "He's too crafty to let it start all over again." Then he added, perhaps for self-assurance, that a country was obliged to defend itself against aggression.

It was Hans who brought the excitement to his grandfather.

"I'm not interested," said the professor. "Your Uncle Konrad's old enough to take care of himself. . . . Hans, give me that book."

Hans stood crestfallen while the old hands roved over the desk. Finally Hans found the book he wanted. "Read it for me, out loud," said the professor, and he pointed with his finger where Hans was to begin.

"This?" Reluctantly, Hans began.

> "The Knight rides forth in sable mail
> into the stirring world.
> Out there is all:
> the friend, the foe, the valley, the day,
> the meal in the hall,
> the maid and the wood and the month of May,
> And the Holy Grail. . . ."

"That's enough," said the professor. "Does it mean anything to you, Hans?"

"Not much."

"Well, you haven't read it all. But suppose you were that knight, with so many roads to choose from. Which one would you take, boy?" Hans was caught up in his own excitement and distracted by the strong acid smell that permeated the room. He didn't answer the old man, who went right on talking as he usually did. "Do I seem like a demented old philosopher, boy? Worrying about poems when the world is going up in flames?"

"No, sir," said Hans softly. "I think you're a great man."

Hans surprised himself with his remark. The old man examined him piercingly, as though to unearth any sign of mockery in his face. At last he seemed satisfied. "Hans," he went on, "I'm talking to you because you're a boy, almost a man, and it's your job to take from the old. To take our places. I don't think I'm the sort who lives in the past, Hans. I like to see life moving ahead. I enjoy young people who can laugh at what I used to admire in my own youth. That's progress, or should be. But in our country, Hans, two thousand years of civilization have been torn up and flung away."

"We've a brand-new tradition," thought Hans, but it wasn't any use saying so. He stood and listened, eager now to get away.

"Germany's gone right back to the age of Teutonic myths. We're all trapped in a Wagnerian opera, each with a part to play. . . . Do you understand that, Hans? Am I making any sense?"

"Oh, yes," said Hans, who now was scarcely listening. Such thoughts had sent other men to jail, had led to his grandfather's retirement. The old man had called Dietrich Eckhard a "political rhymester." Imagine saying that of the finest living German poet! He had refused to include him in his lecture program, so quite reasonably the Studentenbund had protested and shouted the old man out of class. Not that Hans would ever think of reporting his grandfather's irregular statements. He loved the old man, and besides, he took his opinions for what they were, the sad protests of an old man who had slipped behind the times.

The old man had persisted. "I just wonder which road you'd take if you were that Knight. I think Rilke meant that Knight to be death, and death can take every road, but a man can't. I've led my life like Don Quixote . . . dreaming . . . taking no real road at all. No, no, don't go yet, Hans. I have one important thing to tell you. When I die, this library is yours. It would be of no use to your parents. They don't read, but I think you will one day." His voice was vibrant, ghostly, and his terrible eyes bored into Hans. "Read, read them, Hans, and live your life. Be a poet if you can. But live your own life, Hans. That's the only thing a child wants the moment it's born. That's the reason it cries for food, that's why the young corpse says, 'If only I were old again.' Look far and deep, Hans. Pick up that old telescope. Through one end you can see the stars. The other way, if you're lucky, you might see into your own soul."

Hans had sighted through the telescope often enough. Its fifty magnifications were trained on the mountains that rose to the south, rank on rank. He had seen all he wanted to see: Berchtesgaden, with Hitler's Berghof above, and, so small and mist-shrouded he could not be sure, the Eagle's Nest upon the summit.

"May I go now, Grandfather?" he asked. "Is there anything you'd like me to bring you?"

"No," said the old man. "Run along." He seemed particularly tired and sat so far back in his chair that the last Hans saw of him were his slippers and his thin ankles.

Sunday, the third of September, was hot and shimmering. In the morning Hans talked the political situation over with Siegfried and Heime. They'd all said it looked like war, but they couldn't really believe it. War? He'd walked home slowly for lunch, and kicked a single bright pebble all the way. His parents had been listening to Liszt's First Hungarian Rhapsody by the Hamburg station's orchestra when the music faded, and quietly, calmly, without flags or parades, the world had changed forever.

"The British government, in a note to the Reich government, has made the demand that the German troops which have advanced into Polish territory be withdrawn to their original positions. At nine o'clock in the morning," the radio explained, "the British ambassador in Berlin informed the Reich government in a provocative note that if a satisfactory answer was not received by eleven o'clock, England would consider herself in a state of war with Germany."

Then Liszt was playing again. It was now 1:45.

They were silent a long time. Hans was silent because his parents were, and because it was a solemn occasion. When his father said, "Maybe you ought to tell your grandfather," Hans went eagerly, thankful to be in motion. He paused for a moment in the open doorway, imagining a touch of autumn in the air. He heard the old clock wheezing as though oppressed by something in its throat. Shrill and irritable, the clock gave a double chime, and then what he took to be the sound of badly meshing gears turned out to be his grandfather pushing up from his great chair. In his hands was a book. He seemed to want to hand it to Hans, but the book fell open onto the floor and the old man settled back. "Grandfather!" The eyes stared at him so intently that Hans waited for his grandfather to speak, but the pause was interminable. Was it an old professor's trick of holding silent until the attention of his class was complete? Yet in this silence a certain vitality shot forth, a wise and human soul emitting a final indecipherable message. Then the glitter in the eyes dimmed, the lips parted with a sigh, and the tip of the tongue appeared.

Hans ran for his parents, but when they came the old man had already slipped into a timeless repose beyond sleep. His big twisted hands were limp at his sides and there was no sound in the library except for the ticking of the clock.

Hans bolted from the room, smashed open the front door, and ran, through the garden, through the briars beyond and up the steep hill, his legs scratched and bleeding. Before he reached the cemetery, he fell in the tall grass. For a long time he lay there, face down. When he finally returned to the house and the library, his mother was sitting among the books, her head resting on her arms. Her stillness was more frightening than tears. The big chair was empty, but there was something covered up on the cot. The windows were wide open and a breeze coursed through the room. Hans picked up the book. It was *Don Quixote*. The old man had been marking the book right up until the last, it seemed.

The old clock ticked off the minutes of afternoon with fearful serenity. Hans wanted to cry for his grandfather. It was a relief when the tears finally came and he resolved to write a poem that would make his grandfather live forever. If he were only Dietrich Eckhard, he would write a drum-tap and bugle poem, something majestic for the ages. But no poetry came. The sunlight played softly on the floor, over the book that Hans held for a time and then softly closed. He walked at last to the window. Outside, the day had become balmy, sunny and still. The hot Föhn wind breathed from over the mountains. The winter weather was still brewing far away in Siberia. But somewhere his uncle was fighting, and from the village came the eerie howling of a siren.

FOUR

THE SIRENS ROSE AND FELL, an interlacing of sound like a chorus of lonely wolves in the darkness. It was cold. Hans had forgotten his jacket and he knew it would be colder up on the open tower. Ahead of him, Ernst climbed the eighty-two rungs to the top. Hans followed mechanically, weighed down by the certainty that tonight he would die. With the stale cake of his fifteenth birthday undigested inside him, he would surely die.

He pushed up through the trap door. There was the gun—black, unfriendly, a glimmer of moonlight on its four spouts. He climbed into the swivel seat, the words pounding in his head: "I am K1, the gunner who aims and fires. Upon the command 'Air Raid,' I jump into the seat and adjust it to my height."

The sky was full of stars, needle sharp in the clear air. There was no sign of bombers. Maybe they were over Regensburg or Schweinfurt again. Maybe they weren't coming to Munich at all. But the sirens kept up their lamentations. The silence when it came was stunning. He strained to hear. There was a faint, far-off droning of flies. We'll be in it soon, he told himself, but it might be only the night fighters climbing outside the flak belt. Remembering his father's words, "When the stress is on you, breathe deep," he took five long slow breaths.

To the north the searchlights were coming on in clusters of twelve. Like infinite white spider legs, their beams probed the sky. Then their own lights came on, almost blinding him. They had originally been operated by school-girls, but he'd heard that lately prisoners of war were used instead.

Ernst began singing, "A mighty fortress is our God . . ." Fear must have helped his asthma, because his voice was strong. Lieutenant Rabbe ordered him in falsetto tones to be silent. Something was coming in over the headset, and the lieutenant quickly confirmed their fears. English Lan-casters, in force, were heading toward Munich.

Lieutenant Rabbe gave the command to load. Ernst cracked home the first magazine and Siegfried jolted the gun around as though he wanted to tip it from its mount. Hans glanced at him. He was grinning wildly, joyously. Frail as his body was, it seemed about to burst from the furious passion within it.

Still far to the north, over Munich's marshaling yards, the first marker shell burst, its contents sparkling down like the candles of an immense Christmas tree hung in the sky. "O Tannenbaum, O Tannenbaum," sang Ernst, and the others laughed, a foolish, hard ejaculation of the fear none could mention. Around the distant flare, searchlights began to congregate, feverishly colliding and intersecting.

"K4, get that ammunition ready. Snap to it!" The lieu-tenant's voice was high and thin.

Heime had been opening and closing his mouth in ugly trembling yawns. Now he lurched across the platform, fell, and sent magazines clattering. "Dummkopf!" shouted the lieutenant. The word was bitten off like the yelp of a drill sergeant. "Get up!" Heime crouched, seemingly unable to rise to his feet. The lieutenant advanced upon him with a step as light and nervous as his voice, but his hands were something else again. They were as large as shovels and as hard. Hands to keep away from, Hans thought, even when they were administering a comradely pat. Hans had never liked Lieutenant Rabbe. The man had a pallid face, with long jaws and a damaged complexion which tore easily under a razor. Ernst said that Rabbe's temperature was a couple of degrees above normal, like a wild animal's, but Ernst had no way of knowing such a thing. Ernst also said that he'd seen the SS blood-group marking under the lieutenant's arm. This was possible. Rabbe had used the barracks shower when the boys were there, but if it were true, why was he in the regular army?

Now the lieutenant took hold of Heime, pulling him erect, but there was no strength left in Heime's legs. He crawled after the scattered ammunition. "Is there anything more disgusting than a frightened man?" Siegfried said to Hans. But to Heime, who had finally collected the ammunition, he said, "Don't whimper, Heime, for heaven's sake! Get hold of yourself."

As though God had suddenly struck a match in heaven, the sky above them brightened. The stars vanished in the light of a marker shell.

"They're after the factory," Siegfried announced. "We'll have a chance at them this time."

"I hope to hell they bomb straight," said Ernst.

Ten thousand Polish and Russian laborers were housed in the factory compound, along with a detachment of works police. The factory itself was protected by reinforced concrete because jet-fighter components were being made

there. But the workers were expendable, and had only slit
trenches in which to hide. Hans prayed that the bombers
would do an accurate job, for the preservation of one eighty-
two-foot tower from stray bombs meant a good deal more
to him than the lives of ten thousand foreigners.

The lieutenant had the gun elevated until its twin
muzzles pointed straight up. When the signal came, Hans
would simply push his foot down on the firing pedal and the
bullets would soar up, as high as they could. That was some
12,000 feet, according to the manual. The raiders flew at
twice that height, so no matter how many little lead kernels
were sent spouting heavenward they would never reach
their objective. The young gunners might kill themselves a
thousand times over with their own gravity-driven shells
before a single bomber would even hear the chattering
protest of their guns. Then why were they here? Wasn't it
all useless? Hans had dared to ask this once, and Rabbe had
told him to stop thinking. His Uncle Konrad had explained
it was to bolster civilian morale, and to force the bombers
to operate at a higher, less accurate altitude. He'd accepted
this in the sunlit compound, but now, in the dark, with the
sky beginning to crack into a thousand sharp pieces, was it
good enough? Was it worth the flutter in his legs? The fear
that was creeping higher and higher? Soon it would take
him entirely, skin, blood, bowels, marrow. Don't think, he
warned himself. He tried to imagine the Führer's eyes
looking at him. He tried to imagine a medal being hung
about his neck, and he slapped his legs with a closed fist to
keep them from trembling.

No longer faint droning flies but a rolling throbbing sea,
the raiders massed layer upon layer. It was agony, waiting
for the bombs. In the Ruhr, planes were said to mass for
hours before letting go a single one. But why didn't the

command come to fire? The tower trembled. Down below, the ground must be moving, and Hans held tight to his gun. His uniform had grown too small for his heart and lungs. His saliva tasted rancid. He tried to spit, but his mouth was dry.

Heime had crept up against the gun platform like a mouse under a toadstool. Now he began to sob. Lieutenant Rabbe shrieked at him, and Heime stared wildly around, a small animal at bay. "You've all got to die eventually," the lieutenant told them. "You will very likely die on this tower, but probably not tonight. So don't think about it."

The lieutenant was obeyed because he was cruel, but he was unable to inspire confidence or respect. His painstaking thoroughness had produced only a deep sense of insecurity in his gun crew. When he ordered them to take care of their uniforms, he explained that a bomb fragment passing through a clean uniform would be less likely to carry with it infection and gangrene. It was such advice that made the gunners on the first flak tower an unstable group.

Perhaps it was an awareness of this failing which made Lieutenant Rabbe spring savagely at Heime. "You cowardly little pig!"

He raised the boy by a twisted left arm, and Heime gave a squeal of pain. As though the cry had brought him, a figure pushed up through the trap door. His hands a little out from his sides as if ready for fight, the lieutenant turned on the intruder. His arms dropped as he recognized his superior officer. He made a great business of the salute, smashing his heels together. The major nodded calmly, completely omitting to return the Nazi salute.

"Lieutenant, must I remind you, the enemy's up there?" said Major Konrad Wirth, and he lifted his eyes toward the sound of the bomber engines.

The lieutenant's face darkened. He tried to explain.

"Don't ever do anything like that again," interrupted the major. "Do you want to revisit the eastern front? It can be arranged."

Lieutenant Rabbe stood a little straighter, but he said nothing more.

Major Wirth showed no more interest in the lieutenant. He turned to the cowering boy, speaking in a quiet, chastening tone that was barely audible above the gathering roar of the raiders. "Here, boy, don't carry on before your comrades." He began walking Heime about the tower. "They're all keyed up and tired too." He spoke directly to Heime, but his voice, unmarked by any range of emphasis, reassured them all. It seemed suddenly impossible that at any moment bombs would begin to fall, that they would be opening fire. "You've a job to do, and so have the raiders. They've risked their lives to reach an objective. You know about that factory. You know how important it is to Germany—far more important than any of us. That's the very reason you're perfectly safe. They aren't going to waste their bombs on you. So do your job. When our friends up there have had enough, you can go to bed."

Hans had always taken it for granted that his Uncle Konrad was a hero. Twice wounded, bemedaled, the figure standing there in the greatcoat had a mythical splendor for them all. Along the Marne, at Austerlitz, on the red sands of Marathon, wherever soldiers were in need of courage, the same figure must have moved and spoken, rallying faint hearts.

Konrad's direct address brought Hans's attention back. "Heime's a good lad. You're all good lads . . . you'll do the job."

Hans wanted to perform bravely, but he knew he was

almost as full of fear as Heime. There was an imaginary beast behind his back. If he turned his head, he would see it crouching there. He would start to run, and once he started to run he would never stop. "I won't be a coward. I'm not a whimpering little animal like Heime." As he had many times before, Hans tried to build up the image of a super-Hans who would die uncomplainingly for the blood flag. But he could never bear to leave himself dead. He always revived at the end, to be thanked and decorated by generals.

Lieutenant Rabbe gave an exaggerated salute as the major departed. Further talk was impossible. In the north, the sky over Munich had gone mad, and now the "Raiders overhead" signal came to them over the earphones. "Fire!" The lieutenant's command was shrill. Hans pressed down on the pedal and the gun jarred against him. Up rose the tracers, an endless lashing necklace of fiery diamonds. The other guns opened fire, their projectiles forming a theoretical cage about the factory below. Again and again the searchlights converged, divided, crossed, until Hans could see pinpointed a dozen or more metallic moths moving languorously overhead. A torrent of bombs now rained upon the workers' compound and the factory. The separate sounds merged into a single roar, so uniform and constant that it became a kind of silence. It pressed against the sides of Hans's head with giant hands. He could feel the air shaking in strokes, the tower reeling and staggering like a drunken man, his seat vibrating with the spastic lurchings of the gun. Spent shells spilled almost continuously from the breech.

Doggedly the young gunners hurled their useless stream of tiny projectiles into an immensity of sky. The bullets soared into the clear night, straight toward the enemy, but never all the way. Hans fancied them wavering up there in the moonlight, beginning to fall back. There was more chance they'd bring down a careless angel than one of the raiders. At first he'd looked hopefully for telltale black smoke, for a wobble in their flight, but the great moths flew in and out of the searchlights, immune and unperturbed. Worst of all, they were probably ignorant of his efforts. If he were lucky enough to live through the war, would his right foot be larger than his left? Would he have to buy mismatched shoes to accommodate a foot grown large from tramping on a pedal?

Suddenly a procession soared over the trees and into the rays of the searchlights, unbelievably low, flying straight for the factory. Hans sat bolt upright. The lieutenant sprang about the tower on the balls of his feet, shouting, "Give 'em hell! Give 'em hell!" and striking the rail with a closed fist. Hans felt the world exploding around him. His thoughts became disconnected: "Enemy!" . . . "now" . . . "now" . . . "again" . . . "oh, God, please don't let me die" . . . Then his thoughts became confused with the words that were pouring out of Siegfried. "Jesus, please get me out of this! Please . . . please . . . Christ, I'll believe in you if you get me out of this . . ." Then the thunder overwhelmed them completely. Hans was only a dry throat, a pumping foot, and a head full of crashing bells.

The planes were gone as abruptly as they had appeared, except that one of them turned into a white streaking star that curved downward and vanished. Below the place where Hans had seen it, an incandescent flame shot up into the sky. They cheered with hoarse croaking voices. He heard cheers from the other towers, and this was his first awareness that the raid was ending. More suddenly than it had begun, the spectacle died away. Hans could hear the scratchy metallic voices of the loudspeaker down below in the camp. For a while the last detonations vibrated in the air and in the ears, more felt than heard, like a heartbeat. A rain of spent bullets cracked through the forest trees, battering like hailstones across the corrugated roofs of the barracks. Then it was over. Hans slumped in his seat. His eyes were red with fatigue and gunpowder irritation. The air smelled of cordite, and the platform was covered with hundreds of cartridges crushed out of shape by trampling feet.

"Well, Hans, happy birthday," said Ernst. His asthma must have caught up with him, because he began wheezing horribly.

"Ha-ha-ha," laughed Heime. "Ha-ha-ha."

"Ha-ha-ha," laughed all of them, staring at one another through the smoke.

"We got one! We really got one!" cried Siegfried.

It was a proud moment for everyone but Heime, who continued to laugh and stagger about. He was hysterical.

"Stop it! Will you stop it this minute?" shouted Siegfried.

When the laughter went on, he slapped Heime ringingly across the mouth. Still Heime laughed, and Siegfried hit him again.

FIVE

HANS DROOPED BEHIND THE GUN. His arms hung down and he took a slow, trembling breath. They'd celebrated his birthday with a victory on that spring night in 1944, but the joy of it did not last. However much Hans longed for a medal, part of him hoped that the plane that had flamed overhead had fallen to other guns.

In the old verses, in the rhymes of his childhood which sang of Napoleon and Bismarck, soldiers died neatly. They died politely, as good tin soldiers should. They did not scream or protest. They did not have human faces. The old-glory poets would never have peeled away the bullet-tattered shell of the falling bomber to see the fliers screaming inside. Yet Hans could not help seeing them, their fine leather jackets coming apart, their strong young bodies separating along no surgical lines, but bursting, splattering and finally burning into unrecognizable lumps.

Well, he'd try to believe they'd fallen to other guns. Maybe they'd bailed out. Anyway, hadn't they been asking for it? He wasn't going to have nightmares over it the way he had the first time he went hunting, four years ago.

It had been April 9, 1940, the day of the duel and the partridge hunt. The family was celebrating his birthday

48

more than a week early because Konrad's leave was running out. They all wanted to be together for a last long weekend in the mountains.

Hans remembered leaving the inn early in the morning while it was still dark. Konrad had a camera. He himself had a gun, the first he'd ever held. They'd asked his father if he wanted to hunt, but Klaus had refused. "The birds don't attack me. I don't attack them."

Hans shivered with the cold. Once the climb began, he knew he'd warm up, and when the sun came out he'd be hot. It was still misty, a vacuum between night and day when the sky and the mountains no longer seemed to exist. Everything was iridescent and blue.

Konrad looked well. The campaign in Poland had branded him with a flesh wound across his left wrist, but otherwise Hans thought war must agree with him.

They entered a beech and pine forest just as the sun came up. A flood of golden light oozed through the trees and sank into the river pools so that every colored stone and pebble glowed. The forest's enchanted, Hans told himself. It's turned the stream into wine. He wouldn't have been the least surprised to see Rhine maidens swimming by.

Near a small lake which was only one in a chain feeding Lake König, they stopped for breakfast. Hans unlimbered the shotgun and sat down with his back against a massive tree, its huge serpent roots coiled under his legs, entwining the moss and mold of seasons before he was born. Konrad had the food. From the big pouch pocket of his jacket he took flat spicy hunter sausages, almost too tough for the teeth, a thermos of hot coffee, and a flask of schnapps. Hans gnawed a sausage and gazed up through the branches with his eyes half shut. There the wind was stirring. Higher still, it tore the last shreds of cloud away from the mountains.

How good it was to be growing up, to be out hunting with a gun!

"Have you been here before?" he asked Konrad. "It's a marvelous place."

"Lots of times on horseback," said Konrad. "When I find a view like this, I could sit and look at it forever."

Little brooks poured out everywhere, some no bigger around than his wrist. Except for the ceaseless chords and musical notes of water falling from high places, there was silence. As Hans and Konrad sat, hardly talking, the skittering life of the place, of holes and burrows, began anew. There were winged hunters overhead. Rabbits lobbed softly through the brush. Hans actually thought he saw a deer, a rust-colored buck stretched out at full speed, vanishing into the pines.

"We're wasting time like a couple of field marshals," Konrad told him. "Let's follow the bridle path."

The path grew rapidly steeper. Occasional ledges of rock provided helpful steps. The silent tunnels through which they had been passing were no longer silent. Hans could hear the wind. When they emerged entirely from the trees, the mountains piled up against the sky, still snow-capped. For Hans it was unknown country.

"We used to leave our horses and hike from here on, Astrid and I," said Konrad. "Sometimes we'd stay at a lodge and do some skiing." He sounded sad when he spoke of Astrid. It had been two years since they'd seen each other.

"What a queer feeling, being up here," said Hans. "I'm trembling . . . but I'm not afraid."

"It's awe, I think," replied Konrad. "Can you see how easily a man could get lost in all this?"

Perhaps awe was part of what Hans felt, but there was love as well. He remembered the professor standing at the end of the garden, peering through his telescope, and calling them his lovely mountains. The old man had climbed here as a boy, his meerschaum belching smoke from between his clenched teeth. By the time Hans knew him, he was too old, or Hans was too young, and the mountains seemed fearful and inaccessible. When Hans had finally gotten his hiking boots, the professor no longer went outside with the telescope but kept it on a tripod in his study, the lens sealed with a little rubber cap. He told of those bold hikes, though, and Hans would long to be standing up there, overlooking the world. At last he was here, and only a thin mist like skimmed milk kept him from seeing the whole world.

"It's not so very far to Hitler's Berghof. But with that gun of yours, we'll stay well clear." Hans had never seen Hitler's retreat. "Strength through Joy" hotels had sprung up near the Obersalzberg, but now the Labor Front buses were out of fuel and Hitler walked there alone with his three wolfhounds behind barbed wire. Practically no one saw him any more. There was only his voice over the radio.

"Keep your eyes open. This is partridge country," said Konrad.

Here there were still traces of winter. The sheets of ice were thinner than window glass, but up to the very edge brilliant little mountain flowers were blooming: violets, crocuses, and bright orange flowers for which Hans had no name.

"Do animals feel pain? When they're shot, I mean."

"Not if it's a good shot," replied Konrad.

"Suppose it's a bad shot?"

"I don't know. Descartes said that animals were like clocks. The noises they make don't mean anything more than the ringing of an alarm."

"Wouldn't you like to try the first shot?" asked Hans. But

Konrad said that the Polish campaign had spoiled his appetite for destruction, so Hans kept the gun. He broke it open once to make sure. Both barrels were loaded.

It was already afternoon. Hans hadn't seen a partridge even in the distance. He was beginning to think they were up too high, or that it was too early in the season, when a flurry from underfoot made him take a startled step backwards. With wings purring, a partridge hurtled off in erratic flight. "Take it," said his uncle, and more on command than through his own volition, Hans fired the first barrel and missed. The second barrel seemed to fire itself. The bird pinwheeled in flight and settled gracefully, like a dropped handkerchief. Hans ran to retrieve the prey. It lay on the ground, wings spread, without any sign of a wound. Hans bent to stroke its feathers. The bird floundered forward.

"It'll have to be put out of its misery," Konrad told him. Hans wasn't able to finish the job himself, so Konrad took the rifle. Hans closed his eyes before the gun went off, and when he opened them, the bird wasn't beautiful any more. The feathers were mud-splattered, and the head was no longer attached to the body. Hans felt ashamed and a little sick. He knew Konrad felt the same, though he didn't show it.

"That was a fine shot," his uncle said, but Hans noticed he didn't look at the dismembered creature, still warm and dripping, when he put it into the game bag. They went on for a while, not talking. Another partridge flew up, but the gun wasn't even loaded.

"It'll taste fine, Hans." Both of them knew without saying so that the hunting was over. They started back toward the forest trail. Except for the headless bird, it had been a lovely day.

"Next year, we'll try skiing," said Konrad. "The war

ought to be over by then. You know, Astrid and I . . ."
but he didn't go on with it, not aloud, and Hans did not
press him. Silently they padded through the forest.

His eleventh-birthday dinner took place that night at the
hunting lodge, in the small dark room full of wine bottles
and beer in kegs. The kegs were piled right up to the
ceiling, and where there were no kegs the walls were
paneled with after-the-hunt paintings. Dead rabbits, dead
pheasants, ducks strung up on a thong, all heavily varnished
and dark with smoke.

"I wouldn't call this the friendliest room I've ever dined
in," said his mother. Hans was proud of the way his mother
looked that night, her hair in ringlets piled high on her
head, no wrinkles around her eyes, and her skin as clear
and fresh as a girl's. She'll never get old, he thought. His
father looked old, though, and rather bitter, a man to whom
life had promised much and given little.

"Well, I like it," said Konrad. "It's out of the way. It's
private. You can sit here and sip your schnapps and be
completely indifferent to the fate of the world. There's no
better medicine."

In April, the lodge was between seasons. Only one
couple was in the dining room besides them that night: an
apple-cheeked cartoon of a man who wore the Bavarian
lederhosen and green monkey jacket, and his wife. She had
an untidy fiery neck and hair, and cheeks like red rubber
balls, and she laughed loudly and swayed her head to and
fro.

"Let's keep away from that pair," said Konrad. "They're
the cozy, jovial Gemütlichkeit sort I can't stand."

The inn employed no help in the off-season, and the
proprietor cooked and served the meal himself. Fat white
Weisswurst sausage, red cabbage, fried potatoes, "and par-

tridge for the young man." The partridge, on a separate platter, was placed in the middle of the table. Konrad ordered wine, and it came in a heavy pewter pitcher.

"What's become of the gypsies?" he asked the proprietor. "I came expressly to hear them play." The proprietor told him they couldn't afford entertainment in the off-season, and went back to the kitchen.

"It isn't that at all," said the man at the next table, who had been watching them closely. He turned his chair around and leaned forward confidentially. "They've gone with the Jews," he explained, grinning through a set of ill-fitting dentures. "It doesn't have a thing to do with seasons, believe me. This place depended on Jewish trade. It's lucky it wasn't closed down. Now the Jews are on permanent holiday, so to speak, and the gypsies have been sent right along with them. You can't say Hitler isn't considerate!"

Konrad gave a polite little laugh, acknowledging a jest in which he saw nothing funny. "So we're getting rid of the gypsies, too," he said softly.

Hans remembered the shaggy-haired gypsy in the bright-colored rags who had come through town with a hand organ and a monkey on a chain. The monkey had jumped at the children. It had taken hold of Hans's leg and frightened him. He wouldn't miss the gypsies or their alien music. Its foreignness seemed to mock his world.

"I have a present for you," said Konrad. His voice sounded strange, as though there was something stuck in his throat. "I'll get it." "Not in the middle of dinner," Lore protested, but Konrad went anyway. It took him a long time, longer than it ought to have taken to go to his room and return. What he brought was a sword, an old one, with a carved hilt and a blade that looked to Hans like the blue-bright edge of a fading moon. With a mixture of embarrassment and longing, Hans stared at the sword and uttered not a word of thanks.

"Well, haven't you something to say to your uncle?" asked his father.

Hans couldn't look at it any more. He glanced down at his hands, and whispered incredulously, "Mine?"

"It belonged to an officer in the Pomorska cavalry. He gave me quite a whack with that thing, but now he doesn't need it any more."

"Konrad, I'm disappointed," said Lore. "All along I thought that mark on your arm came from a woman's fan."

"Did you kill him and take his sword?" asked Hans.

"I don't know," said Konrad. "In a fight, you're not sure of anything. Afterwards, people tell you what happened, and you say, yes, I guess that's how it was. Anyway, it's a souvenir. Happy birthday." Clearly he did not intend to say more about it.

Hans ate very little. He refused to taste the partridge. His parents finished it, along with two bottles of wine. They ate and drank as though this were the last feast of its kind they would ever attend. When the stout gentleman bellied up to their table, they greeted him affably. Red from laughter and full of wine, he asked to look at the sword. When he found out it was a birthday party, he yelled at the proprietor, in a voice without volume control, to bring another bottle of wine. Konrad tried to dissuade him. They'd had plenty to drink. It had been a long day.

"Surely you're staying up for the speech," said the man. Something important was due over the radio. A speech by Goering, he believed. He'd arranged with the manager to have a radio. They could all listen.

"No, thank you. We're not interested." Konrad's manner

was discouraging, but the stranger wouldn't leave. An uneasy conversation began at the table, as though they were actors reading from a script.

"I wonder," said Klaus, "I just wonder whether I ever told you about that time on the Somme, right after my leg . . ."

"I think you did," Lore interrupted. "Wasn't it just after you became a deputy lieutenant?"

Klaus turned quickly to her. "That's right. I guess I have told Hans that story."

"We've all had battle fatigue from listening."

"I'd like to hear it," said Hans softly.

"Did I ever tell you how it rained for a whole month when I was still in the Uhlans?" Konrad and Lore remained silent. Hans said, "Tell us that one, Father," but the stranger, who had been meditatively moving his mouth like a sheep chewing gum, interrupted. "You? In the Uhlans? This calls for a toast!" It turned out that he, too, had been in the Uhlans, and had joined the Stahlhelm after the war. "To all the old fighters," he said, lifting his glass of wine.

"To all of us: dead, buried, and alas, forgotten."

"Forgotten? Never!" cried the stranger. "Why, friend, it's the same war we're fighting today."

"It's over and won, if Hitler can only realize that," said Konrad.

"The war isn't over," said the stranger. "For a soldier, you really are out of touch." Summoning the proprietor, he had the radio plugged in and placed on a chair beside the table. Presently, a voice volleyed from within with hysterical vigor.

"Turn that thing off or take it back to your wife," said Konrad.

"Wait a bit, Konrad," said Klaus nervously.

"You'd better listen, find out what's going on," said the fat stranger. "There may be great news for Germany."

Konrad hunched over his drink. "I am not interested. I am not interested in your radio." His tone was deceptively affable. The stranger stood for a moment, seeming to fill his clothes more tightly, as though the slightest inhalation might burst the leather britches that engirdled him. Then he unplugged the radio. He took it back to his wife, plugged it in again, and turned up the volume. The little radio was unequal to the sounds that besieged it. . . . "Because Nazi Germany!" . . . a roar from the crowd . . . "I say, Nazi Germany" . . . a roar . . . "will never be defeated! We shall conquer" . . . a roar . . . Through the static, through the wild cheering, came the scalding voice. It didn't matter whether they could understand him or not. It was Hitler, and to Hans his voice was martial music.

"Don't do anything, Konrad," begged Klaus. "If we ignore him, he'll turn the thing down."

Konrad moved his chair so that his back was to the radio and centered his attention on his nephew. "Hans, I don't want you to think that I have any pleasant memories of Poland. That sword . . . Do you know I have bad dreams about horses?"

But their neighbor was unwilling to leave them in peace. Aware that they had not been listening, he filled in for the radio. Did they know that this morning Denmark had been taken without a shot, that Norway had been invaded and would fall within hours?

The excitement was contagious. Klaus was the first to speak. "It's a great success," he exclaimed.

"More than that! More than that!" exulted the stranger. He held up his glass. "To our Führer! Guided and guarded by Providence!" He drained his glass. Klaus and Lore drank with him, while Hans, choked with pride, downed a second and forbidden glass of wine. Only Konrad did not drink. He paid not the slightest attention. "Hans, listen to me. I want you to know how I came by that sword. It was in a great yellow meadow surrounded by a forest of green trees. It was a beautiful picture, all those sun-tipped lances, half hidden by trees, and then the brigade breaking out to ride us down. Not one sway-backed plow horse among them, not one Spanish knight in chamber-pot armor, but all gallant men, riding the finest steeds and longing to push their lances through two inches of armor plate. Perhaps they did mistake our tanks for windmills, but an eighty-eight-millimeter shell is very hard on a horse's classic lines, and fifty tons of steel rolling over a man's back tends to squeeze out the last drop of poetry. There are some things harder to look at than a dead partridge."

"War may be terrible," said the stranger, "but don't mislead the boy. Hitler didn't want this war. Germany didn't either. It was thrust upon us."

At last Konrad pivoted his chair around to face the stranger.

"It's amazing," he said. "Whenever Germans feel they're in the wrong, their only recourse is cant." Klaus put a restraining hand on Konrad's shoulder. It did no good. "I suppose you'd say it was thrust upon us by an international conspiracy of rich Jewish capitalists."

"Of course," agreed the stranger, the round blue eyes in his plump face looking as astonished as a china doll's.

"Have you ever considered," said Konrad, "why Jews are thought to be so wealthy?" The man only stared, his eyes narrowing. "Then I'll tell you. It's because in Germany they're made to pay for everything."

"Don't misunderstand me," replied the stranger. "I have nothing against the Jews, personally. I'd like a satisfactory solution to the Jewish question all around. But when you get down to it, it isn't a matter of politics or morality. It's more a question of delousing. It has to do with hygiene. The Jews aren't your worry. Or are they? Let me ask you something. Have you any Jewish blood?"

"I wouldn't know," said Konrad. "My father used to keep a bottle of something up in his room. Maybe it was just cherry brandy."

"You're amusing," said the stranger. Yes, Uncle Konrad was being amusing, and also quite shocking.

"I'm delighted you think so," said Konrad. "Wouldn't it be nice if we could provide some amusement for the others?"

"For instance?"

"For instance, we might fight a duel. Yes, we should fight a duel. Right here and now."

The stranger's wife, who had been resting her thick arms on the table, sat back with her mouth wide open, displaying a gold tooth. The man himself, equally astonished, pursed his lips into a pink, moist suction cup.

"I've come to the conclusion," said Konrad pleasantly, "that you're nothing but a pasteboard puppet. You have insulted my entire nature, and I am about to cut you to pieces with a sword. No, no, please don't go. Don't let me frighten you. I'm just having a little fun. Did you ever watch Charlie Chaplin fight a duel?" Here Konrad hollowed his back and wriggled in a Chaplin-like pose. "Did you know his movies have been banned?"

The stranger retreated backwards to his own table. He groped for a chair and half sat, half fell, into it. But Konrad had not finished. He snatched up the sword, and like a dangerous and shuffling Chaplin began to attack. He pursued shadows with awkward glissades, stopping at last with his sword very close to the stranger's nose. The action froze briefly like a film caught in midprojection, then it accelerated, with the stranger toppling backwards, chair and all. His stricken wife shrieked for the proprietor, who made a bewildered appearance only after the routed couple had vanished from the room.

By this time Konrad had retaken his seat, and except for a very evident and rapid pulse in both temples, he appeared absolutely calm.

"What was that shouting?" asked the manager.

"Only Daniel," Konrad assured him. "He found himself in the wrong den."

Shaking his head, the proprietor went back to his pots and pans.

"I will now apply myself to getting drunk," said Konrad.

"Anyone who didn't know you, Konrad," Lore admonished him, "would take you for a lunatic."

"That canting pig!"

"And if you go around wagging that sword at anybody again, I'm going to hide it. It shouldn't be within reach of irresponsible people."

"This has been a hell of a night, Lore. Don't needle me, please."

"He was rotten about the Jews. I don't honestly blame you," she assured him.

Konrad downed a glass of wine without even seeming to swallow. Refilling the glass, he said, "I used to think I was as patriotic as anybody. Oh, the concentration camps and the Nuremberg laws . . . I knew they were bad, but still I thought this national revolution of Hitler's was on the right track. But we ought to be over our birth pangs by now. I don't know where we're headed." He was speaking very softly. "There are things going on in Poland you wouldn't believe. 'Fear thy neighbor as thyself.' Put *that* up on your wall, Hans."

In the end, they had to help Konrad off to bed.

"He'll ruin himself if he keeps this up," said Klaus, and Lore added, "I suppose people have a right to dispose of their bodies as they see fit."

"I don't mean his body. I mean his reputation," Klaus replied.

Hans would not forget his eleventh birthday party, his uncle's duel, the partridge with its bloody neck. He had not gone hunting again. He had not fired a gun again until he'd come to the tower.

One week after the birthday trip, Konrad had reported back to the Second Panzers. A month later Hitler was proclaiming, "The fight beginning today decides the fate of the German nation for the next thousand years." Most of Europe had been brought to it knees in six glorious weeks. There had been plenty of food in those days, and all the theaters had stayed open. The Wagner Opera Company had played in the woods, and the victory in the west had been more of a shopping tour than a war. It seemed to have nothing to do with what was going on now. It had nothing to do with bombers, nothing to do with a hammering gun that deafened his ears, nothing to do with the beast licking its chops behind his back, the beast that sooner or later would devour him.

"All right, boys, bedtime." The lieutenant's voice brought him sharply back to the flak tower. "For all we know, the Americans'll be here for breakfast." This had not happened yet, but the possibility was sobering.

Hans climbed down slowly, rung by rung, because his knees had begun to tremble again. "If only this were the last time," he thought, but he knew that it was not.

SIX

LIEUTENANT RABBE stood at the foot of the gun tower, the white glare of his flashlight directed into the eyes of his gun crew. He would have preferred to march them off to bed directly, according to the book: "Place your clothes in the regulation place, go to bed with your right arm under your head, left arm over the blanket, and fall asleep immediately." Since this was the worst raid they had so far endured, however, this would have been futile, and Major Wirth had put all gun crews at liberty within the theoretical confines of the installation.

Clearly the lieutenant disapproved of the order. "You'll report by 0900 hours," he told them. "And keep away from the searchlight batteries."

"He means the girls," said Hans. Alone in the darkness, he and Ernst strolled off toward the quiet pines. "He's a queer fish, that Rabbe," Ernst replied. "You have to know him well to really dread him. He was laughing last week in the shower, all by himself. It was eerie. You know what I heard? That he's a reject from an action squad in Russia. Death's Head SS and all that. It's true, Hans. You know . . . torture, mass murder, fun like that. Ah, just breathe that night air."

"It's smoky."

"I thought we'd had it tonight," said Ernst.

"Be glad you're not one of those poor devils." Through the trees Hans could see the factory town. In the distance, the flames seemed motionless. "All the windows are lit up like a Fasching party. Fires are really beautiful." El Greco clouds were piling up, under an El Greco moon. "There'll be mosquitoes before long." But for the moment it was perfect. Hans was drunk on survival. Giddy and feeling slightly immortal, he couldn't keep still. How strangely remote the fighting seemed now, childishly spiteful and without plan.

As children, Hans and Ernst had had nothing in common. As schoolmates they had been rivals for marks. More than anyone else, Ernst had brought Hans to the dismaying realization that there were distinct levels of intelligence. Friendship had emerged suddenly one day when Paul Giesler, Gauleiter of Bavaria, had addressed the student body. The fatuous little Nazi had looked brutal when he was serious, insincere when he tried to smile. From behind an oily brown cigar he'd made an illiterate speech full of throat clearings and painful pauses. Hans and Ernst, as members of the Gymnasium orchestra, sat opposite each other, their faces turning purple with the pressure of re-strained laughter. Finally Ernst had begun to whimper, infecting Hans. The speaker had stopped in midsentence, his cheeks as fat and firm as a glass blower's. The subsequent disgrace was the first bond between them.

"Remember that Giesler speech?" Hans recalled. "Honestly, Ernst, you've got the wickedest laugh. What a time we had in those days, and we didn't even appreciate it."

"You know what I'd really like, Hans? Better than the Gymnasium would be a chance to hibernate for the duration in your grandfather's library. The last of his kind, your grandfather."

"And then what?"

"Oh," said Ernst, "I'd hang in a large golden bird cage in a sunny window."

"What a bore. If you're going to be a bird, why not an eagle? Something majestic."

"Heavens, no. A canary . . . tame and cared for."

"I don't know, something's wrong somewhere." Hans was conscious of a real disharmony inside himself, as nebulous and intangible as a shift in barometric pressure. It wasn't just homesickness. It wasn't despair, though he'd lost his taste for heroic poetry—death on the field of honor, all that childish stuff. Hans was still patriotic, he told himself that; ready to win a medal if he had a chance. But hell! And now he said it as he would have to none of the others: "I wish I were out of this. I wish we were back in school."

"There are ways of getting out of a war," said Ernst. "I don't mean shooting off a couple of toes; nobody gets away with that. But what about taking a few sugar injections to start up diabetes? Things like that. My mother keeps trying to get me a medical discharge. She won't give up, and she won't get it, either. No imagination. Well, it keeps her busy. But we'll get out before long, Hans. Crated and labeled, if you want my opinion."

"It's you that said that, Ernst, not me."

"No skylarks. No Valhalla. Just one big bang. I'm not Siegfried. I don't fancy myself laid out by Valkyries on the field of honor. When we go up, there won't be enough pieces to feed the cats or make into soup."

"Don't talk that way, Ernst. We're going to win this war."

"You know better, Hans, only you won't admit it. Listen, even Jesus Christ needed a few loaves and fishes. Hitler may be clever, but he's not going to keep us alive on hot air forever."

Hans refused to be taken in. His feeling for the Führer was still the profound sentiment of his life. Never before had there been such a man: brave and perfect from the start.

"We're going to get our jets soon," said Hans.

"Oh, yes? What about those fires, Hans? Do you suppose it's only the workers going up the chimney?"

"If it does come to a last fight, we'll be up there in the mountains. A few good divisions could hold them forever against the Allies."

"Up there? It's a blank on the map. Maybe that's a good place for the Thousand Year Reich. But they won't ever get me up there."

"Well, I'd go," said Hans. "And you know Siegfried would."

"Poor Siegfried. I used to think he had a good mind, but he makes it up too easily. He's the kind who'd look you in the eye and say, 'Hans, I know this to be true: the sun does go around the earth. I see it happen every day.' And you'd be inclined to believe him."

"He'd rather die than see us beaten."

"He'd die for a medal," said Ernst, and Hans agreed. For the Knight's Cross, Siegfried would happily exchange his life, as his older brother Reinhard had done. Reinhard had been tall and broad-shouldered and blond, and he'd charged a Stalin tank with a grenade in each hand. "I'm proud to die for the Führer"—the newspaper had quoted his last words. His parents kept the clipping and the medal under glass, loving them more, it seemed to Hans, than they had ever loved the living Reinhard. Perhaps that was right, after all. Until Konrad had gotten his award, it was the only Knight's Cross in town.

"And what about you, Herr Amann? For the mammoth cross of the greater cross of the knight's cross of the iron cross, will you jump out of an airplane at ten thousand feet?" Ernst held his glasses away from his eyes like a monocle.

"No, Herr Peiper, but I have a volunteer for you. Heime Kinderman." Hans clicked his heels. "You know he'd do it too, for Siegfried. The way he crawls around on his belly, it's a wonder there are any buttons left on his tunic."

"I wonder if he would," mused Ernst. "As far as I'm concerned, he's got all the qualities of a dog except loyalty. I wonder. He ought to hate Siegfried. But he just hangs around him, picking his nails with that knife and waiting for his daily dose of insults. It's like a tonic for him. Poor Heime, we ought to be kind to him, but he's such a complete zero. Even a Knight's Cross wouldn't add a decimal to his memory."

"Well, I don't think it'll come to a last fight up in the mountains. There's still Fortress Europe. But just suppose it does come to that? Those mountains are like one enormous fortress. They'd never get us out. I've been up there skiing. I wouldn't want to take them by storm. Ernst, I wish you would come skiing with us some time."

"I'm no skier," said Ernst. "Too brittle."

"Konrad could show you. He's the best . . . well, he was until he got it in the leg."

"I'm more of the walking-tour type—you know, over the mountains and down to Rome in time to advise Michelangelo how to touch up the Sistine Chapel."

"All right. I'm for a walking tour, then."

To this, Ernst gleefully assented. "With Goethe under one arm and Schiller under the other."

"That's agreed," said Hans, and they shook hands as though a projected holiday beyond the war might help anchor their lives in the midst of a storm that promised to drown them both.

SEVEN

HANS LONGED TO FEEL THE MOUNTAIN SUN through his clothing and the skis beneath his feet. He longed to hurl himself down endless slopes of Ice Age snow, but aside from short runs on the cemetery hill, three years had passed since he'd been skiing. Three years.

Konrad had called it a birthday treat, but it had been too early in the year for that. Poland, France, the small countries that didn't matter had all fallen by the winter of 1941. The war was over, if only England would admit it. Who could worry about a few nuisance raids when the mountain sky was brilliant with reflected light and fresh with a breeze from the peaks?

They both wore the white, aqua-striped skis of the Norwegian mountain battalions. They had tried them out the day before on the easier slopes. Now they stood high above the lodge, their faces red with windburn, catching their breath before the downward flight. Hans could see the unaccustomed happiness in Konrad's eyes. He felt joy throughout his own body. Laughing, they pointed out the various peaks to one another. Then Konrad was off, his sticks trailing like the thin legs of a wasp, throwing up streamers of snow. A rise concealed him. When he appeared again, he was smaller. He was flying. At least while he was in flight, he would forget about Rotterdam and what had happened there. Hans had heard from his parents how she had died, but Konrad had never spoken of it.

Digging in his poles, Hans shoved off. The lodge dropped suddenly behind him. The wild rush plucked his thoughts away and left him only with a sense of motion and a vision of whirling snow. The sky was clear and luminous. He felt like shouting aloud, "Nothing matters! Nothing matters!" The slope would never end. He would be young and wild-hearted forever. Now pine trees were flashing by. Take care! He crouched low, almost sitting on the slender skis. He was going much too fast, but he didn't care. He was no longer touching the ground. He was delivered to the winds.

Suddenly, in an explosion of soft snow, he rolled over and over. Then he lay flat on his back, his skis crossed and up in the air. If he was hurt, it was badly, for he felt no pain. He imagined a spinal fracture, and was afraid to move. But when Konrad failed to appear, he rose gingerly, feeling his legs with anxious fingers. He started down again, watching for the pockets where the wind left patches of soft snow.

Konrad was waiting for him at the bottom. "You look like a snowman," he said.

"I took a spill." Hans began slapping snow from his jacket.

Their skiing lodge wasn't first-class. There was no ski lift, but Konrad maintained that a skier who walked up had legs fit to slide down. What was far more important, there was privacy. No clubs or party organizations took their outings here, and that was why Konrad had chosen it. This suited Hans. He resented strangers in the mountains, and since the night of the duel he dreaded his uncle's public outbursts.

Climbing like penguins was a small price to pay for having the place to themselves. After the last run at dusk they would return to the lodge, relaxed to the point of exhaustion.

The pines and the bare windblown rocks soaked up the last light. "There's a fire going," said Konrad. They could see the smoke before they could see the nestling lodge itself. The roof was shingled and covered with stones. It looked more like part of the mountainside than something built by man. Against the side of the lodge, they stacked their skis. There was only one other pair, and that belonged to the owner's daughter. They took turns slapping the snow from each other's trousers, stamping their boots hard before the door. They entered an equatorial warmth. "Ah, this lovely, lovely place," said Konrad.

Snow-blinded, Hans could see only the crackling fire at first. Slowly, like the developing of a photographic print, the room appeared: low, heavily beamed ceiling, dark wine-stained tables, wooden benches polished by use, and a black stove with a porcelain top.

In another room, the proprietor's daughter was singing. She must have heard them, for the singing stopped. A slim, pretty, deeply tanned girl, she came into the room wearing a red apron.

"Ah, Herr Wirth and young Hans."

How fine it would be, thought Hans, if she and Konrad were to be married. The logic of such an arrangement had evidently not occurred to Konrad, who ordered a Steinhäger to warm his stomach. He asked the girl to go on singing, but she was too shy. Instead, she turned on a radio in the next room. The pom-pom-pompity-pom of a beerhall band assailed their ears.

The girl came back with the Steinhäger and began to

prepare potatoes and Braunwurst at the little stove. When she brought the food, Konrad ordered some wine. Except in out-of-the-way places like this, good wine was becoming scarce.

Konrad carefully examined the label. "That's all right," he said. The girl had forgotten glasses, so he drank straight from the bottle.

"You drink a lot," Hans said.

"A bottle's good company." The radio began playing "Bomben auf En-ge-land." It was noisy and patriotic, and Hans liked it. "Besides, it's the best medicine there is."

"Medicine for what?" Hans asked.

"Oh, for anything. For fear. For bad dreams. . . . I wish we had another day up here."

"Another month," said Hans.

"I think it's going to snow tonight. Hear the wind."

The radio music had ended. An announcer's voice was followed by the moist vowels and rolling consonants of the Führer.

"Can't we ever get away from that Austrian accent?" growled Konrad, and Hans feared another scene. "Let the war last as long as it will!" the voice was shouting. "The last battalion on the field will be a German one!" Konrad shoved his chair back noisily. Then, mysteriously, the radio stopped in midsentence. Softly, as though not to be over-heard, the girl began singing again in the next room.

"She shouldn't have done that," said Hans.

Konrad smiled. "I'm beginning to like that girl. She has a nice voice." Then, gently, rather sadly, as though musing over a familiar disappointment, he said, "I used to like Hitler's voice . . ."

"But not any more?"

"Hans, I'm patriotic. I've fought for Germany, and I'll probably die for her. But that man Hitler . . . I used to deify him . . . until he started throwing his shoes." For Hans, Hitler and the Fatherland were one, but his uncle went on thinking aloud. "Maybe it's this place. It reminds me of your grandfather. He used to come here. I remember so many things your grandfather used to say. He made a lot of sense, your grandfather."

But Lore had once said the professor was in possession of all the facts that no longer mattered, and Hans agreed with his mother. He had his own opinion of why Konrad was so changed, but he didn't dare to speak of it.

"I wish I didn't have to go back to school. I wish we could try the Zugspitze tomorrow," said Hans.

"There're lots of good places you haven't tried. I like this country. I like to get away from people. Maybe next year we'll do it again. We'll go farther back."

"I hope that's a promise," said Hans. He wanted to believe they would come back and try one mountain after another, going farther and farther back. He had never seen the Austrian Tirol except in pictures. Innsbruck—that green and pastel town with the blue stone hills behind it. Chamois country, and the white and deadly fogs of the Hungerburgbahn.

"We'll try," said Konrad, "but I can't promise. I might be in Africa next winter."

Konrad's eyes were beginning to look sleepy and moist. Hans talked about skiing in hopes of bringing his uncle back. "I bet nothing can touch those really high slopes for speed. Up there, I guess you're really taking your life in your hands."

"Especially in the spring, when the crevasses are covered. Of course, there's always some risk. That's part of it. Hear that avalanche in the distance? A good clean way to go, I think. Buried forever in an instant."

"You wouldn't talk that way if you didn't drink so much," Hans told him.

"Don't listen to me. I'm playing for sympathy. I said that for effect."

"Still, you drink too much. You do."

When he next spoke, Konrad's voice was soft and husky. He had the detached air of one who has given up the struggle. "I dream about horses every night."

"You should enjoy that," said Hans, but Konrad told him they were not ordinary horses, but a furious herd, like the legendary hosts in the sky, with upreared heads and hollow sockets with darkness where the eyes should be. "They look like horses from an old frieze . . . their striking hoofs, and their teeth. . . . And sometimes, I dream about her . . ."

The genie was out of the bottle at last. If Hans pretended not to see it, perhaps it would go away. Perhaps something of the pleasant evening could be saved.

"Astrid . . . Astrid . . ."

There was no hiding from it now. Hans knew from his uncle's voice that he was suffering and he would not interrupt him until he had talked his heart out. "Before we were married, I was lonely, you know. Sometimes I wasn't even sure I was quite real. If it hadn't been for your family, I would have left Germany long ago. Then with Astrid . . . While it lasted, it was so good. I used to be critical of women, but with her it didn't matter that she was too thin, or too sentimental. I loved it. She was such a good rider, she made me look silly riding beside her, but I loved it. I was a fixed star for her, too, and I sent her away. She wouldn't have gone if I hadn't sent her. And now . . ." Konrad tilted the bottle straight up before he drank, so that Hans knew it was almost empty. He also knew that the monologue was ending as the reality behind it had ended, in Rotterdam, where German dive bombers in advance of German motorized columns had ended the life of a young woman who had been driving a herd of riding-academy horses to safety.

Konrad set down the empty bottle. It toppled and rolled along the floor. He called the proprietor's daughter.

"What would you like, Herr Wirth?"

"You," he said. "I would like you to sit with me."

"This isn't a cabaret, Herr Wirth. I'm a working girl."

"All right, then I'll settle for another bottle of the same."

When the bottle came, Konrad insisted that Hans drink with him. Hans tried to refuse, but Konrad insisted, like a small boy who is afraid to be left alone in the dark. They drank to next year's skiing and to the end of the war.

"Do you think it'll be over by then?" asked Hans.

"You're too inquisitive, old man. You want to know everything. I can only tell you it will be over eventually."

"And of course we will win."

"We have many enemies in the world, and there are things in the wind that make me wonder. I wouldn't be surprised if a year from now we're involved in a far greater war. It'll make your father's war seem like child's play. I'm speaking of war with Russia." The remark was dropped absently, like a secret too unimportant to keep.

"Russia?" Hans echoed. "Our allies?"

Konrad wagged his head with a curious motion as though the tendons of his neck had suddenly loosened. He gazed at the half-empty bottle as if puzzled by its function, and then began to quote, "And yesterday the bird of night did sit, even at noonday upon the market place, hooting and shrieking." With Konrad, Shakespeare was the last thing before oblivion. Hans decided to get his uncle to bed, but all he accomplished was to move him off the chair and onto the floor.

He called the girl from the kitchen to help. She had been a skier all her life, and she was strong. Konrad's heels dragged along the floor. "Poor Herr Wirth," she said. "He's such a handsome gentleman. I remember his pretty wife." They managed to get Konrad up into his room and onto the bed.

"I don't need any more help," said Hans. "Thank you very much."

"You are both leaving tomorrow, yes?"

"In the morning. But we'll be back next year."

"Good, I hope so," she told him.

Hans assured himself that they would return the next year, but they had not. A month later Konrad had been assigned to the Balkans. He'd hoped all along to go to North Africa, where the army operated without any interference from the SS. A few letters from him arrived, and a bottle of slivovitz from Sarajevo. Then on July 22 the news had come: "Barbarossa," the surprise attack on the Soviet Union, had taken place, and Konrad had been part of it. The summer brought stunning victories: 600,000 Russian prisoners at Kiev alone. There were victories in the autumn, too, at Vyazma and Bryansk, but the winter was cold. There were no victories in the snow, and there had been no skiing. Now Konrad, with his stiff leg, would never ski again.

EIGHT

THE NIGHT WAS DARK. The aircraft factory worker's compound seemed only a scattering of embers. Above the mountains where Hans had skied with his uncle three years before, clouds were building up, hiding the stars. And suddenly the stars seemed cold, the clouds threatening, the mountains too steep to climb. Weariness had overtaken him, and he felt that if he closed his eyes, he would dissolve into the vastness. He told Ernst he was returning to the barracks. Ernst followed him reluctantly with his awkward jaunty step, rising and falling from his toes, whirling his arms. A mist rising from the marshes muffled everything except the coughing of a steam locomotive in the valley. Hans shivered. Trains had always been for him the carriers of separation and death.

"I think there's someone else out here," said Ernst. There had been no sound, only a nebulous sense of intrusion. Hans turned. He saw what he thought was an oddly shaped boulder. There were some gurgling, sucking sounds. Then a figure rose unsteadily and swayed toward them.

"Uncle Konrad!"

Collar open, buttons undone, the major looked anything

but the tower of strength which had rallied them only hours before. In his hand was a bottle. "Hans! Ernst! Well met, young friends." This was not the soldier talking, but the lonely drinker in need of companionship. "Hear that train . . . what a sad sound! Stay away from trains, boys. People get lost on trains. They never come back. You know, Hans, I haven't been on one since the day I came home . . . remember? But I was safe, of course, being a cripple. Cripples and corpses get where they want to go on trains. But a healthy soldier, beware. And a Jew . . . Hans, a Jew can't trust a train. The only way it'll bring him back is in a bar of soap."

Hans protested.

"Hans, old man, I know about trains. It was a train that stole my wife away."

Hans couldn't argue about that, but the rumor about the treatment of prisoners . . . this soap business . . . that he'd never believe. Naturally, a country at war had crowded prisons, but the so-called extermination camps in Poland . . . They couldn't be. Hitler was a man of conscience, a lover of children and dumb animals. Hans said as much to Konrad.

"Oh, yes, of course he's a man of conscience. Why else would he destroy the Jews except to prove to himself that they're wicked creatures? The sort a man of conscience ought to destroy."

"Life is really so quaint. Sad occasionally, but oh, so very quaint," said Ernst.

"I'm going to bed," Hans informed them. "You ought to get some sleep too, Uncle Konrad. Lieutenant Rabbe would enjoy reporting you for drinking. And for the things you say."

The major looked thoughtful. "You're right, nephew.

Some day Rabbe will fix me up. Hans, we've an ugly job tomorrow. We'll be going down to clean up the factory. It's not a job for youngsters . . ." He took a long swig from his bottle. "Good night, boys. Sleep tight."

"You too, Uncle. It's going to rain."

"I'll be along . . . Have you ever noticed the sound of rain on a barracks' roof? Like hoofbeats. Have you noticed?"

They left him conversing with himself.

"If he goes on like this, the lieutenant will get him for sure."

"He's a great soldier," said Hans, though a heavy cord seemed to kink and knot in his throat.

"But, Hans, just the way we call him Uncle Konrad, instead of Major Wirth . . . You can see that."

Hans could see it all right. What was worse, he knew his uncle didn't care. He'd gone to Russia careless of life. The fact that he'd collected nothing worse than a legful of shell fragments was simply a postponement of the inevitable.

"You know what happened to his wife. I don't think he's cared for anything since then."

Ahead loomed the gun towers, like giant skeletons against the murky sky. Soon rain would be falling on the barracks, on the fires left by the raiders, on the mountains where Hans had skied with Konrad, on the house where, he prayed silently, Gretchen and his parents slept peacefully, on the lonely train, on the station where two years before he had waited for Konrad.

It had been raining then, too, a soda-bubble rain that oozed down the cracked glass roof of the station. Hans had waited a long time on the platform, watching the station-master as he paced up and down in his little red cap.

There'd been only one letter from Konrad, and that was from the hospital. He was coming home on sick leave, and he emphatically didn't want a town reception just because he had won the Knight's Cross. So Hans was there alone. He thought of Siegfried's older brother, who had also won the Knight's Cross. Hans had come to the station to meet that train too, but that had been very different. It was sunny and summer then, and the Hitler Youth had stood in ranks, the girls all carrying flowers. And Reinhard had been carried off the train in a coffin. Hans had expected a moment of truth when he looked at it. He had been envious when he read the short heroic life story of Reinhard Hellpack in the paper.

Now the stationmaster waved his signal baton and a train broke through the veils of rain. Fuming and roaring, it sucked at his hair and was gone.

Hans examined some long wooden boxes that looked like coffins. Their labels indicated that they contained clothing for the eastern front. He walked quickly up and down, thrusting his hands deep into his pockets, but the cold was inside him.

Another train materialized out of the rain and the mist. It stopped, jolted forward, stopped again. Freight cars; the doors were locked partway open, enough for some air to get inside, enough for eyes and mouths and parts of faces to fill the narrow slit. Under the scrutiny of those eyes, he was a bug being scorched by a magnifying glass. There were voices, too, but the words weren't German words. A cadaverous hand probed through the opening, palm up, followed by a skeletal arm, but the elbow could not pass. Then the train jogged forward again. Hans's eyes were drawn along by the spectral hand until there were ordinary coaches passing and faces of convalescent veterans, smiling from behind the glass. When the train stopped, streams of smoke gushed from the engine. A soldier got off, lowering his body from step to step like a child, his hand clinging to the rail. The stationmaster waved his baton, the train exhaled and moved slowly away. The passenger approached Hans awkwardly, leaning to one side, straightening, then leaning to the other side, his right hand gripping the head of a cane.

"Uncle Konrad, you're back!" The two embraced. Hans had wanted to say, "You look fine," but all he could honestly manage was, "You're alive."

"Death gave me a nibble this time. I didn't taste good, it seemed."

There were two captain's stars on his uncle's coat, but no sign of the medal Hans wanted to see. Otherwise Konrad looked crumpled, his face as faded as his uniform. "Hans!" he said. "You've grown a foot, at least. Don't hold back. Tell me what's been going on."

They sat down on one of the wooden boxes to give Konrad a chance to recover himself.

"Oh, you know, nothing much. I mean, we're busy, collecting scrap . . . cans and iron fences, rags, that sort of stuff. Everything's getting short."

"How's school?"

"I don't know. Fine, I guess." He didn't really concern himself with school any more.

"And food, Hans? Are you all eating well?"

"Well enough . . . we're not starving," replied Hans. But it wasn't like the early days of victory any more, with chocolate from Holland, butter from Russia, bacon from the Balkans. His mother was queuing up for potatoes now. The official paper, *Das Schwarze Korps,* had criticized this practice at first, calling the women "nagging, fault-finding shrews." No more. It was a paper cemetery now, page after page of obituaries marked out with black iron crosses, and the women stood on longer lines and came home with less. Yet this wasn't the real change that Hans wanted to tell Konrad about, the change he himself wanted to understand. It wasn't even the raiders bombing Munich night after night. It was something more subtle that Hans couldn't describe. It was as if there had been a slow shift in the specific gravity of things, a growing consciousness of being at war that permeated everything.

They began to walk toward the trolley stop. Konrad limped badly, raising one shoulder higher than the other. Hans carried his bag. "Who were those people on the train?" he asked.

"Wounded going home," said Konrad.

"I mean the ones up front in the freight cars."

"Those poor devils? I heard they were Polish and Russian prisoners on the way to build a factory not far from here. They'll build it, those that survive, and work in it, and probably be buried in it. Poor devils. . . . How's your mother?"

"She's fine. Tired, though. Keeping the house and doing war work, too. You'll hear about it. Don't worry."

"And Klaus? How's the butcher business?"

"A butcher was executed for selling meat to a restaurant without stamps. Father's a nervous wreck from thinking about it."

The trolley stop swarmed with factory workers. Konrad said he'd rather walk; they could go slowly. "After all, what good's an old wound if you can't show it off?" They passed the war memorial, taking the short way along the river and around the mill diversion. Here there was snow in patches, soot-flecked, pocked by rain, and slashed by sled runners.

"The sledding was fine a week ago."

"How's your friend Siegfried? Keen as ever?"

"I guess."

"I was sorry to hear about his brother. Not that I knew Reinhard very well."

They passed the old water mill with its abandoned stork's nest. There was the new turbine mounted in concrete, and the club rifle range, unused now that civilians had no bullets. There, too, was the Catholic church with its high bell tower. No one paid any attention to the church except for a few forlorn old priests, and the Hitler Youth, who splashed its walls with obscenities.

"Witches were burned there once," said Hans.

"And may be again. Smell the tannery! Good Lord, you couldn't fish in that water." It was full of wood pulp and chemical residue and fragments of melting ice. Beyond the bridge, there was a steep hill to climb.

"Will anyone be sledding today?" asked Konrad. "I'm not sure I could get out of the way."

"I don't suppose the army will want you back," said Hans.

"I wish I could depend on that. Well, for a time they won't. I suppose I'll take a few courses at the university in Munich. I have friends there. Do you know the Scholls? Hans and Sophie . . . No, there's no reason why you should . . ."

"There's a sled coming," warned Hans.

They moved to the side of the path, and none too soon. A sled, with Siegfried steering and Heime hanging on for dear life, came sawing round the bend. Abruptly the sled swerved, caromed over, and came to a stop. Heime floundered on his back; Siegfried jumped to his feet. "Herr Wirth! Herr Wirth! How are you?" His eyes were roving for a medal that he supposed must hang about Konrad's neck.

"It's with my soiled underwear," said Konrad. He helped Heime up. The boy was rubbing a bruised knee. "Let's have a look at that," said Konrad.

"It's nothing," said Siegfried.

"It's a nasty bruise," said Konrad. "I'd get home and soak it in hot water if I were you, Heime. . . . All you boys have grown."

"Heime never grows," said Siegfried.

"Hardly at all," admitted Heime.

"You really slaughtered them in Russia," said Siegfried.

"But are they defeated?" retorted Konrad.

"In every engagement."

"And yet they fight on."

"Only skirmishes."

"You can win all the battles and die with your hands full of victories," said Konrad.

"Have you killed many Russians?"

"I've killed everything," said Konrad. "I was sorry to learn of your brother's death."

Siegfried seemed to stand a little straighter. "His death was in every way worthy of his life," he said, as if repeating a formula. "He was an example of how a hero should die."

"Yes, I'm sure he was," said Konrad. "I think I'd better go home and rest this leg. Heime, take care of your knee. And if I were you, I wouldn't wear that knife when I went sledding . . . Could cause a nasty accident. My best to your parents, Siegfried." When they were out of earshot, he added, "A pity Lieutenant Hellpack couldn't have been an example of how to live . . . Hans, I'm giving out." He looked old and weary by the time they reached the Amann's house.

Hans threw open the door, and Lore appeared from the dark hall. She looked tired too, until she recognized the limping stranger. "Konrad!" she cried. She clasped him in her arms and kissed him, pressing her face against his shoulder. "I thought you and Hans would never get here." Konrad turned to Hans's father. "Well, Klaus." They shook hands wordlessly. Hans saw that his father's eyes were moist.

The weeks that followed were happy, busy ones. Hans had school and his Hitler Youth activities. When the spring really began, he and Konrad took short walks. "Next year we'll be skiing, wait and see," Konrad would say with the sweat pouring down his face, but every time the walks were longer. Good news came from Russia; a spring offensive had finally been launched.

Most time-consuming of all was moving his grandfather's library to the cellar. The books belonged to Hans now, but Lore had threatened to destroy the books that were on the forbidden list unless Hans hid them. Besides, Konrad predicted that the new ball-bearing factory would attract bombers sooner or later, so for the sake of the books as well as to provide more padding for a makeshift shelter, they moved the entire library. Only the astral clock, the telescope, and his grandfather's black shako with the white death's head were left behind. Konrad surveyed the cellar when the job was done. "Your grandfather came down here when the SA were outside," he said.

Hans remembered that too. His grandfather had refused to vote in the elections of 1936 because the voting was controlled, and the SA had threatened him from the garden for three days and nights. The police had refused to help, and a drenching rain had finally driven the SA away.

Raiders had bombed Munich once or twice, and Lore had become concerned about the safety of the house. Her family laughed at her when she worried aloud about the condition of the lightning rods, which had stood on the rooftop for thirty years, unmolested. "Don't be silly," she said. "Of course I know they're no use against bombers." And still she was adamant, so Hans climbed along the roof and followed the wires down to the ground. Konrad checked all the locks because Lore wanted to be sure every one was secure. He even put a padlock on the front door, saying, "Now, Lore, those planes'll never get inside."

The early, lush spring made the garden get out of hand. "What can I do?" said Lore. "Those poor flowers. What can a woman do who's away all day making bullets?" So Konrad looked after the garden too. But he couldn't stay with them forever, no matter how much they all loved him. The medical report on his leg was favorable, and before long the army would have him back at work, in a position suited to a man with a stiff leg. It wouldn't be tanks again. "Probably antiaircraft," said Konrad. "In antiaircraft, you just sit and wait." He was still with them in late April, though, when Hans had his thirteenth birthday.

There had been a strange little celebration that Hans would never forget. Lore was still at the factory, so he and Konrad prepared the supper: a leg of lamb that his father had smuggled from the butcher shop, literally at the risk of his life, and potato cake.

"What pan shall I use for the cake?" asked Konrad.

"The one hanging on the wall beside the Führer."

"As long as he's hanging," said Konrad, "my mind's at rest."

They had a good time. Konrad laughed out loud now and then, such a rare phenomenon that it made Hans feel good. And Konrad looked better, too. He moved about the kitchen with a curious gliding limp that suggested his leg had made its final adjustment to a crooked tendon. Then

Lore came in. "Those streetcars! It's worth your life simply to get standing room. I don't know what we're coming to. Look at this kitchen. It doesn't even smell the way it should." Hans knew what she meant. It should have smelled of butter and sugar melting together, but if it smelled at all now, it was a rancid, secondhand smell.

"And I'd like to know what we're going to do with this refugee," Lore went on. "Another mouth to feed. I don't know how we'll manage. She'll be here any day." They even knew her name: Gretchen Schnabel from Bremen. The Allies had missed the submarine pens there, killing her parents and some chickens instead. Hans had studied her picture and been disappointed: a pale, sad face trying to smile. "Just what will we do for food? I'd really like to know." Lore's question was directed at Klaus, who had come in unobtrusively with a newspaper and now seemed to be hiding behind it. "It's just a pity she didn't go along with her parents. That's the truth." To drown out this unkind remark and her own feeling of guilt, Lore began knocking pots about noisily in the sink. Klaus folded his paper deliberately.

"We'll manage," he said. "We did in the last war. I remember a birthday party then. I came home on leave with the present that was the success of the evening. One hard-boiled egg. One hard-boiled egg for six children, and those faces as I cut it up—so serious and intent . . ."

Lore put the food on the kitchen table, as the dining room was closed to save heat. "I suppose it'll get worse before it gets better."

"It will," said Konrad. "Until we use up our stock of credulity."

"That sounds like something you picked up at the university," Lore told him. "Hans, eat while it's hot."

He ate, wondering how it could get worse and knowing very well that it could and would. The radio talked of home-front warriors now. It talked of sacrifice and salvation and no more of final victory.

"It's simply impossible for a woman to work all day in a factory and take care of a household," said Lore with a genuine air of discovery.

"You'll have the girl," said Klaus.

"At home, yes. I'd rather she'd take my place at the factory. Doing the work of two men . . . getting up at the crack of dawn . . ." Lore maintained that she was never at her best during the morning hours of male vigor and noise. "And I will not work Sundays! They can't make me. And those 'voluntary' meetings, and that 'people's car' we were supposed to get and never did. After that tram ride we all ought to be hospitalized, not put on an assembly line. Looking after a house is enough to expect of a woman of my age."

"Oh, go on, Lore. You always used to pray for a chance to get out of this house. That wretched place, you called it," teased Konrad.

"For heaven's sake. I live here. I don't live in a factory. We're a family, Konrad. We're a family!" She cleared the table furiously and began again to punish the plates.

"Sit down, Lore. Relax. This is a birthday party."

Lore smiled suddenly at Hans. "Many happy returns, liebchen," she said, and she handed him a flat package. "It's not from me. The air warden gave it to me when I was getting off the tram." She referred to a neighbor, Wilhelm Müller, whom they had always disliked and who was now feared, as a corresponding member of the Gestapo. The package contained a slender booklet printed on glossy paper. Hans found himself staring at a fine Nordic youth and a hearty blond girl in shorts sitting on a swing. The facing page offered a slit-eyed, pock-marked Asiatic, a repulsive specimen of that Mongoloid horde which the youth must hold at bay if the girl were to go on swinging. There were pictures, too, of black cannibals from the United States of America, their faces and arms tattooed with hideous caste marks and voodoo signs. Hans shuddered. When every other motive for fighting had passed away, that picture alone would sustain him.

There were other presents which were more welcome: socks knitted by his mother, brand-new shoes from his father, and from Konrad a bottle of 1937 wine. "Good enough to be opened at Hitler's funeral," Konrad said, and drank most of it himself.

Far into the evening they sat around the kitchen table. Hans listened to the men as they idly licked at the universe like children at lollipops. Lore broke up the session when she saw a cockroach on the tiled floor. She made a fuss, and Konrad put his foot over the bug. Hans had never seen one in the kitchen before, and its presence was provocation for Lore to begin to scrub down walls and floor. "You men can solve the problems of the world somewhere else," she told them. They went, single file, to the cellar, where men could smoke and talk and listen secretly to the B.B.C.

There the air was thick and furry. It seemed twice exhaled, but the warmth was satisfying, as was the companionship of the professor's books. When Hans had time, he read those he could understand, particularly the poets that his grandfather had loved, whose works he had underlined in his stiff firm hand. More and more Hans's thoughts turned to Rilke, the favorite contemporary of his grandfather's youth, and to Rilke's black knight, facing all the choices offered by life and by death. He'd be like that one day. When things settled down, he'd take the knight's road. He'd make the choice, one day . . .

His father turned on the radio, more from habit than anything else, and the voice of Deutschlandsender came on hysterically. There was optimistic news from Russia. "Lies," said Konrad. "I've been there. If you want the truth about Russia, I can tell it to you. Why don't you turn on the B.B.C.? They may tell lies too, but they do it calmly." Klaus fumbled with the radio. There was jazz playing from the Savoy Hotel in London, and he turned it on low. Konrad turned it up again, saying, "What's bothering you, with the Gestapo protecting us? What is there to fear?"

Hans looked up. It was not a joke for laughing. The local police were innocuous enough. They did little more than direct traffic. But the party members, the secret Gestapo men like Müller the air-raid warden, the party blockleiters who called themselves "men of confidence," were always on the prowl. Listening to the B.B.C. or to the Atlantic sender was taking a chance. The Amanns's dentist, Herr Kater, had spent six months in Dachau for listening, but Klaus continued the practice, though nervously. He sat now searching his pockets, clasping his hands over his knees, shifting about, crossing one leg, then the other, standing up, sitting down again.

Lore arrived in time for "Annette, the Mystery Girl," a silly show that did not seem to Hans worth the risk of one's life. Still, why not; after a dreary day Lore was entitled to relax. Following "Annette" came the midnight news.

"Churchill hasn't spoken in some time," said Konrad. "I hope he's well. What a lovely voice the old lion has. Calm and firm."

They never heard Churchill that night, though, or the news. Instead there was a knocking at the great front door, and Konrad lunged for the radio, turning it off and sending a book smashing to the floor. A solitary sheet of paper settled gracefully in the silence that followed.

"Could it be a friend?" whispered Lore.

"At this time of night? Here . . . the door's locked, isn't it?"

No one knew.

"Maybe they'll go away. Don't make a sound."

Again the knocking echoed above, and Hans heard an answering beat at his heart. There was no more rapping, only the stealthy sound of the heavy door swinging open.

The sole recourse was to go upstairs. They hid the radio behind some books and fearfully climbed the stairs. Hans expected to see men in black with the Tötenkorps' death's heads shining on the uniforms, but at first he saw nothing at all in the unlit hall. Then Lore turned on the light. There stood a dark, slender girl in an old, shapeless fur coat.

"Hello," said Konrad. "We won't bite you until we know you better."

"I . . . the door was open. I came in." Her voice was low and vibrant. She looked at them all with a questioning smile as though she didn't believe one half of what the world told her.

"I have papers," she said, and she fumbled for them in a string bag that wasn't much bigger than a purse. "This is the Amann house?"

"You're Gretchen? Gretchen Schnabel?" asked Lore. "Of course you are. Come inside. You're tired, I can see that."

She didn't have to take off her coat for Hans to see that she was skinny. She wasn't very graceful either, but it was her face that really bothered him. There was no color there except for the brown smoky circles under her eyes.

Lore escorted them all into the kitchen, and she made the girl sit down at the table and poured her a big glass of milk. His mother's remedy for every ill was food. Gretchen didn't touch the milk. She was thankful just to be here. The trip had been hard—that was all she had to say. Hans said nothing at all until Lore instructed him to show Gretchen to her room.

"I'll carry that," he told her, taking the string bag. It weighed practically nothing, but it was the only baggage she had. "Watch your step." He led her up the stairs.

"This'll be your room," he told her, turning on the light.

"It's a big room, isn't it?"

"It belonged to my grandfather." He stood for a few seconds looking at her. She looked up again, puzzled. "I was wondering," he said. "You are German, aren't you?"

"I'm from Bremen," she explained. "Actually, my father was French and I was born in Poland."

"That makes you German?"

She offered no reply. Somehow her high cheekbones looked to him vaguely Slavic, quite possibly Jewish, and certainly foreign. She was far from the blond, apple-cheeked perfection of the B.D.M. journals.

"Do you mind if I unpack?"

That didn't take long: a few rags of clothing and a battered teddy bear.

"A teddy bear?" He couldn't believe it.

"I've always had it."

"And lugged it across half of Germany?" he said, but the sad grave mouth and the evasive eyes seemed to implore no further penetration.

"I thought girls from Bremen were the laughing ones."

"My mother once scolded me for laughing too much."

"And that's why you stopped?" Then he added, "I'm sorry. What's there to laugh about, really. . . . There's an extra feather bed in the closet, and the bathroom's one door down." There seemed nothing further to add. He said good night and left, feeling annoyed with himself. They were off to an even more dreary start than he'd expected.

"What a rotten birthday," he told himself. A rotten dinner, a rotten book, and now this uncongenial intruder. It was after midnight. He ought to be asleep, but for a long time he stood by the window, resting one hand on the pane and staring at the grayness outside. When he finally did go to bed, he hadn't lain there long before he heard a cry in the darkness, a lonely, muffled cry. "It's the girl," he thought. "Can't she let a person sleep?" Then, when the cry was not repeated, he felt sorry for her. It must be hell coming to a strange house like this, after what she'd been through. Softly he went down the hall. After all, she might be asleep. The door was ajar and the lamp was still burning. He saw the girl, huddled against the back of the bed, resting stiffly on her elbows. Drops of perspiration shone on her upper lip and on her temples. Her eyes were tightly closed, the lashes shuddering.

Oh, lord. It would be easier to go away. He could call his mother. He didn't know what to do.

"Hello," he said. "Are you all right?"

Her eyes stared back at him, the confused eyes of a person shut up in the dark.

"Can I do something for you? Do you want some water?"

She made no answer but turned away, pressing her face into the pillow. Her shoulders were shaking.

Hans frowned at the floor. It might be best to go off on tiptoe. Whatever he said was bound to be clumsy. Still, he put out his hand and touched her damp hair, stroking it gently with the flat of his palm.

"All right?" he said. "You're safe here, you know." She

made an inarticulate sound. "Shh . . . shh . . . You're safe in this house," he went on. "You always will be. One can't go on grieving forever."

"I wasn't grieving," she whispered. "I was remembering . . . I was remembering in a dream."

"Sad things?"

"Horrible, horrible things . . . But I'm all right. You needn't . . ." He would have left her then, but she said, "Please, I'm sorry . . ." He gave her a handkerchief from the bedside table, and she blew her nose. "I guess I just felt so alone."

"Is that why you hang on to that teddy bear?" She was holding the bear in her arms now.

Gretchen looked down at the bear. "Sometimes I feel so alone I wonder if I even exist . . . I wonder if I'm in the world at all."

"It's funny you should say that. I mean, that's what my Uncle Konrad says."

"The man downstairs with the limp?"

"Yes. He lost his wife. He has dreams like you . . . about horses. I don't dream, myself, not any more. But I used to dream about wolves, and witches hiding in closets. Kid stuff . . ." Not for years had Hans had such dreams, yet he could still feel the formless terror, the shadowy menace that never quite withdrew when he awakened.

"I dream about Heimdall's horn," said Gretchen. "That's what I call the air-raid sirens. Half the time when I wake up they're really blowing."

"You couldn't have dreamed that when you were small."

"No, then I dreamed about being lost in the forest."

"Like Hansel and Gretel."

"Yes, like Hansel and Gretel." For the first time she smiled, a quick and artless smile that did not last. "Of course, they had to put Grimms's stories on the forbidden list."

"Perhaps it's for the best," Hans said. "After all, Snow White may be harmless enough, but the glorification of freaks . . . I don't know if you like Grimms's stories, but I have a fine old copy hidden in the cellar. What frightening pictures! You should see them."

"I want to," she said. It was amazing how a smile could transform her face. Her eyes struck Hans as unusual. There seemed to be little streaks of gold in the iris. It wasn't polite to stare, but they reminded him of the dark, veined stones he used to search for in shallow streams.

She said, "Remember how in the story Hansel keeps looking back and thinking he sees his little white cat on the roof? He doesn't want to go into the forest. Deep inside, he knows he won't come back, that something awful's waiting there. That's like my dream."

"I was always scared when they found the gingerbread house and heard the witch inside. Remember? 'Munching, crunching, munching, who's eating up my house?' "

"And the children say, 'The wind, the wind, only the wind.' "

"You really do know it," said Hans. "I think we're going to get along. I didn't at first, you know." She was silent. He looked up to catch her eyes breaking away from their regard of him. She was prettier than he had thought, and younger. In repose, she had the face of a child.

"You're a good person," she said. "I want you to like me."

Hans was pleasantly embarrassed by her frankness. "Don't worry," he replied. "How do you feel now? Dream all gone?"

"I'm fine. I'm perfectly all right now."

"Really? Then I'll go along. Shall I put the light out?"

"I'd like a light, please . . . good night, Hansel . . . and thank you for rescuing me from the forest."

"That's all right, Gretel. We'll cook the witch together. Sleep well."

He went away touched and very pleased, with a warm sense of responsibility for another human being, something he'd never felt before. Funny. Of course all he'd done was help talk away a nightmare. He hadn't really killed any witches, not even the sort that lurk inside a lonely soul. He hadn't rescued anyone from the forest. But Gretel was here to stay and he was glad, though she had given his world one more jolt. It was not the girl or her dream that had worked the change, but the reality which preceded her dream, a reality which for him was still no more than a wisp in the air.

NINE

Hans remembered the summer of 1942 as a happy oasis. He heard the radio reports of raiders in the north, but never the sound of bombs. The eastern campaign was going well. The Russians were bound to surrender soon. Konrad was still living at the Amann house, though he'd been assigned to a local flak battery. He would return to duty after he completed certain courses at the university. He came home every night in his little green Adler car to tease Lore and Gretchen, to listen to the B.B.C., and to read in the cellar. When he was discovered secretly reading a clandestine pamphlet, *The White Rose,* Klaus persuaded him to burn it in the stove.

From that summer Hans would remember Gretchen best of all. She was a great help to Lore. She helped Hans, too, when he began to paint the house, holding the ladder, handing up buckets of paint. "When you get finished, it'll look like a gingerbread house," she told him, and that was all right with Hans. For years the place had needed paint.

One Saturday in early June, Konrad invited Hans and Gretchen for an outing in the Adler. "If they provided captains with Mercedes staff cars, I'd take the whole family," he explained, but the little Adler had to back up some of the steeper hills as it was, and Hans and Gretchen had to hold the picnic basket on their laps. Konrad had brought the car around early, slamming the door as he got out, and he had crossed the drive swinging his hands high, no longer limping, but rolling nautically on his bad leg. He was all the hero Hans could ever wish.

With a mock display of heel-clicking courtesy, he helped Hans and Gretchen into the car. "You're wearing your uniform," Hans said. He was even wearing his Knight's Cross for the first time.

"Official business," was Konrad's cryptic reply. They drove off into a spring day escaped from Eden.

"It's lovely!" exclaimed Gretchen. It seemed to Hans that she had a perpetual flirtation with everything that was green and growing.

"*You're* lovely," Konrad told her. She denied this, and he assured her he wasn't a flatterer. He was simply stating a fact as one might state a fact about the ballistic properties of an .88. He seemed to Hans to be full of charm and wisdom, and for the first time very elderly. His gentle teasing brought an air of lightheartedness to all of them, and Hans, looking at the tall dark-haired girl beside him with her soft white skin and friendly eyes, saw that she was beautiful. The whole world was beautiful.

The sun was already high when they passed through Marzoli. Dew still sparkled on the leaves. At Aufham they got on the Reich Autobahn. Wild violets, broom, and rosemary made the whipping air redolent of early summer, and they drove with the windows open. You could tell by looking at Gretchen that she had known sorrow, thought Hans, but she really was lovely in her pale secret way. Hers was not the Nordic beauty which you saw all at once, but that of a strange painting which he had come to like after long and close viewing.

Konrad finally explained his errand. Work had started weeks before on the flak battery to which he would be assigned, and he wanted to see it. Two guards stopped them before they reached the site, but the Knight's Cross was enough to get them through. Tractors had been at work, and with the spring rains the road farther up was a slimy yellow sea of mud. "We'll have to walk, I'm afraid. You can wait here, Gretchen, if you'd rather."

"Don't be silly! I haven't come all this way to be left behind!" She went ahead, setting the pace with an intense swinging stride. She'd like the mountains, thought Hans, where walking is hard. Konrad couldn't keep up and Gretchen waited for them, pretending to be tired. Hans knew she was only pretending, and he was grateful. She even let Konrad take her arm as though she needed help.

Presently the muddy path entered the woods. "Brrr! It's cold," said Gretchen. "You can see your breath." •

Through the dappled shade prisoner workers moved slowly, as though their ankles were fixed with invisible chains. Dreamlike, they dumped lumber on a pile. Their guards could not speed them up. Farther on were the barracks. It housed guards now; the flak battery would live there in the future. "They'd never spot this place from the air," said Konrad.

"You can see the mountains from here," Hans observed. Transparent and serene, the mountains sparkled in the distance, a moving haze under the sun. "I'll teach you to ski some day," he promised Gretchen. "Maybe next winter."

Beyond the barracks, where the woods had been cleared, they came upon the flak towers. Laid out in a rough star pattern, the towers were not as Hans had imagined, but spindly and black, casting long dark shadows.

"They look like giant crosses," said Gretchen.

"That's a queer idea," replied Konrad.

"What's so odd about it? Just look at them."

"Do you know what the farmers around here call this place? They call it Golgotha, Place of the Skull. Judging from what archaeologists have pieced together from bones and beads and metal, the Roman legions crucified some German chiefs up there in the woods somewhere. Of course, that'd be nearly two thousand years ago." Konrad had slowed down as he talked, and now he stopped entirely and glared at the towers. "How do they expect to get .88's into those things?" he growled. He limped off to find the man in charge.

Hans and Gretchen waited silently. Everywhere the ground was muddy and torn up. There was no place to sit down. A bumblebee sped by, discovered its mistake, and buzzed away again.

Konrad came back, cursing. He'd been right. The towers weren't designed for .88's, the only decent flak guns Germany had. At best, they would hold the Swiss machine guns, which lacked the range to reach a modern bomber. "Take a look," he told Hans. "If there's anything to the rumors, you have a good chance of ending up in one of those things. Unless the war's over, they'll be drafting children into flak next year." Konrad was grim, but Hans felt ready for the call. If there was any choice, he'd prefer the Luftwaffe. He'd relish a chance to be like Joachim Marsaille, the "Pilot of Africa," whose picture was always in the papers.

"If you have any plans for the future, Hans, don't try to be a hero," said his uncle. "Marsaille'll be dead a year from now, a condition even the best poets haven't overcome. Why get yourself killed, old man? Don't you want to be a poet?"

"I didn't know you wanted to be a poet, Hans," said Gretchen.

He admitted it rather grudgingly. Beneath those grim towers, as the prisoners watched them with empty eyes, it seemed a frivolous and unreal ambition.

"To be a poet! How wonderful . . . Will you dedicate a poem to me?"

Hans thought she was teasing, so he did not answer.

"What do little girls want to be?" asked Konrad.

"I used to want to be a princess . . . like Cinderella."

"What a happy world, full of poets and princesses. I'll be a politician, myself, or maybe a banker. The Russians gave my body just enough lead to lend it weight."

Back at the car, they cleaned the mud from their shoes. Konrad took a rag from the glove compartment and made a fuss over Cinderella's slippers. Actually, Gretchen wore the heavy Jungmädel marching shoes, but he polished them as though they were glass.

"I suppose we could picnic somewhere around here," Konrad said.

But Gretchen didn't like the place, and neither did Hans. They drove off, looking for the right spot along the way. Konrad turned on the radio.

An orchestra played "The Red Lamps of St. Pauli" and "The Stars that Shine on Germany"; then the "Kuk! kuk! Raiders over Germany" signal interrupted the program. Gretchen drew a sharp breath.

"Don't worry, Gretchen," Hans assured her. "It must be a mistake. It's broad daylight."

"I wouldn't be too sure," said Konrad. "These days, the

world is too much with us." He pulled the car off the road. A year ago they'd been able to boast of lights on their Christmas trees while all England was dark. A month ago, a thousand planes had bombed Cologne in a single raid. There was no sense taking chances, and it looked like a nice stopping place.

Hans took the picnic basket in one hand and drew Gretchen along with the other. "Don't be afraid, Gretel," he told her, half in fun. Underfoot, the dry litter cried an alarm as they padded into the woods, but the smell was a good one. It was a smell he liked, stronger than the smell of books. At the stream's edge not far from the road there was a hint of laughter in the water. "Here!" Hans told them triumphantly.

He unpacked the picnic basket. There was every reason to be happy, it seemed to him, but Gretel still looked worried and sad. "Gloom is a punishable crime in this country. First offenders are hung," he chided her. She continued to stare at the water and he knew that for her the lights that played in the current were really flames remembered. "Talk about it, Gretchen. People ought to be able to share sadness."

Her first words of response were almost too faint to hear. Then Hans realized she was telling her story, talking about the bombings she had never been willing to mention before. Her voice was fragile, like the threading of a phonograph needle down the worn grooves of an old record.

"The first raids were just entertaining, like distant fireworks. When they got worse, I slept on a cot in the cellar. My parents' bed was too big to move downstairs, they said, so I would lie there at night alone." Her voice was hypnotic. Tone and cadence were more essential than the words, and Hans was with her in the cellar waiting for the bomb he knew must come. "They'd been bombing the docks as usual that night. The raid was really over, but a plane must have been lightening its load to fly home. Anyway, without the slightest warning the ceiling fell on top of me. I was buried for three days. If it hadn't been for my teddy bear, I'd have been asphyxiated. It was pressed against my face. They wouldn't let me see my parents. I wouldn't have recognized them, anyway. So I packed up in the best tradition of your fairy stories, Hans, and . . . well, here I am. That's all there is. Not much to tell, really." Her expression had changed suddenly in a manner very surprising to both Hans and Konrad. Somberness gave way to a radiant and com-pelling smile. "So I have every reason to be happy," she explained, "because no matter what, nothing worse can ever happen to me."

"Don't worry," said Konrad. "From now on, only good things will happen to you."

"That's right," said Hans, wishing he had spoken sooner. "Like this picnic. Like this brook." Sitting on its bank, he took off his shoes and socks and dipped his feet in the water. It shot exquisitely painful needles deep into his flesh. He made a face. Gretchen dipped her toes in the water and drew them out again, laughing. The sun through the leaves wove a light pattern in her dark hair. Hans felt himself overflowing with life, extraordinarily vigorous, strong, and perfectly happy.

"If only Hitler were here," said Konrad. "I mean it. If only Hitler were here, all alone with us, enjoying this picnic, I'd give him a nip of schnapps and then Gretchen could pick him a bunch of flowers. And you, Hans . . . maybe you could get him to take off his shoes. We'd get warm and sleepy. I'd tell a couple of stories, and finally, you know what he'd say? He'd say, 'Pfui on this war!' Imagine! We'd save Germany."

"Germany doesn't need saving," said Hans. Everywhere

the armies were victorious. In Russia, the Caucasus and Stalingrad were about to fall. In Africa, Rommel had taken Tobruk and had pushed the English back to El Alamein. Final victory could not be far off.

"I remember last year our tanks had 'On to Moscow' painted all over them," said Konrad. "But we'll never see Moscow, you know. There are too many Russians. It got so that the peasants we rolled over in the afternoon looked like the ghosts of those we'd slaughtered in the morning . . . Well, no more sad stories about the death of kings." But Hans urged his uncle to continue, and half unwillingly Konrad tried to make the facts credible. He told of endless roads, numberless prisoners, the broken machinery of war cluttering trackless plains like a neolithic burying ground. Frostbite came with November, and fires were lighted under tanks to get them going in the morning. Moscow with all its comfort was within sight when the counterattack came. "That last day is as vivid as a tattoo inside my head."

"The day your leg . . ."

Konrad nodded. "It was snowing right into our faces, and they came out of the snow all in white like phantoms. We would have run, I think, only there was nothing behind us but a frozen cemetery a thousand miles long and just as wide. So we stayed and fought, and most of us died there." The Siberian cavalry with their tough little jogging horses had come incredibly at night, stitching the surprised tank crews with tommy-gun fire. Konrad had been rallying his men in the flame of a dying tank when he saw a horse rise over him, a frozen scream full of flying hoofs. He'd spun away too late, and the hoofs had caught him along with the bullets.

Still, Konrad had been lucky. His comrades had envied him the trip home. For a time the war was over for him, except at night, when he dreamed of a great rushing stream of equine fury. It would trample him with the thunder of a train in an endless tunnel. "At first I couldn't control my teeth. I'd wake up and ask the nurse for some water and I'd bite right through the glass. I had to have a special tin cup."

"Don't talk about it any more," pleaded Gretchen, and she put her hand across his mouth to stem the flow of words. "Remember," she said, "pfui on the war."

He laughed. "You're right, Miss Elf Ears." And he began to unscrew the flask of schnapps. He took a long drink. "Well, Hans," he said, "since this is a day of revelation, what gives you bad dreams?"

Hans seldom dreamed about the past. He dreamed of an invasion to come: fang-toothed Siberians, howling cannibals pursuing him relentlessly like the hobgoblins of childhood. "I dream about things that won't happen," he told them. The real war would pass him by entirely. "I wish I could believe that," Konrad said, "but God and destiny take the side of the big battalions." When Hans asked what he meant by destiny, he replied unsatisfactorily that it was the relentless logic of each successive day.

"Hans . . ." Gretchen laced her hand in his, and laughter slanted from her eyes. "You look saddest of all just because you haven't anything sad to say. Let's walk. We'll pick flowers. Lore would love a bouquet."

Under the spell of the humidity and the warmth, nature seemed to have gone wild. A furious competition in living and growing was in progress. Insects buzzed continually and plunged into one flower after another.

"If there were bombers about, we wouldn't hear them, with all this droning," said Konrad. They talked no more of war. Each one gathered a huge bouquet of flowers, more than the house could ever hold.

"Smell," said Gretchen. She held her flowers up to Hans and then to Konrad, who reached out and gently stroked her cheek. The gesture was quick and delicate and very surprising to them all. "You remind me of Astrid . . . my wife," he said.

"Thank you. That's a lovely compliment," replied Gretchen, and that was the end of it. Hans felt a rush of joy at seeing these two people being good to one another. Of course Gretchen was too young to be like Astrid. There was little physical resemblance, as far as he could remember, beyond the fact that they were both tall and strong, yet delicately made. Astrid had been Jewish, descended straight from Joshua for all he knew. And Gretchen? She had seemed all Jewish when he had first seen her, and later, perhaps, a mischling, according to the Aryan codes. And now? After a few months she was simply Gretchen, a name he repeated to himself, a name for secret rhyming. The dark pharaohs of Nubia might sleep in her blood and it would no longer matter. Why? She wasn't terribly pretty, and she was older then he was by a year or more. He wanted reasons for the way he felt, but the only answers that came were confusing.

"Listen," Gretchen said. "They're bombing somewhere." And she looked afraid.

"It's only thunder," Hans reassured her. "See those clouds? A little thunderstorm. It will pass."

There was no storm that afternoon, but the thunder went on ringing softly inside him. On a sunny June day with summer drenching down around them Hans had fallen in love.

TEN

His BIRTHDAY in 1942 had started badly, but it had ended with the coming of Gretchen. Hans remembered that summer as a time of flowers and of falling in love. He'd composed sonnets and then thrown them away.

That was two years ago, and the good times were gone along with the sonnets. Hans was not an aviator, but an airforce auxiliary, without much glory. He'd fought a fight and been more terrified than ever before in his life, but he had survived into the first early morning of his sixteenth year. Now, with the fear walked out of him, he would try to sleep.

He would have gone straight to his cot, uniform and all, had not a chair been shoved back noisily and a figure planted itself across his path. Lieutenant Rabbe, a man one always had to walk around, turned the white beam of his flashlight directly into Hans's squinting eyes. Then the light glanced off Ernst's glasses so that the boy seemed to have electric light bulbs glowing in his forehead.

The lieutenant was slyly curious. Where had they been so long? It was impossible to guess what he was thinking or what action he might be going to take. "Could it be that you were over near the searchlights, I wonder?" They denied this. "I hope not, after my warning. I certainly hope not." He spoke softly. "If I ever catch one of my boys talking to the girls over at the searchlights . . . if that boy ever lied to me, I would have to whip him. It would be a whipping like none you've ever had."

Finally he let them go. Hans thought he would fall asleep instantaneously, but when he closed his eyes he felt the world spinning inside his head. On the roof above, the rain drummed down. Hans's fingers traced over his face, nose, chin, mouth; the rough blankets wound round and round him. Blood thumped in his ears and his eyes ached. He tried to lie quietly on his back, his arms crossed on his breast like a hero of old upon his shield, a hero who had died a thousand years ago, who could not be disturbed. In his ears rang the cosmic din of destroying armies, and through it all a voice shouting at him.

"Wake up, everyone! You, Amann! Wake up!"

His eyes blinked in the dull cold light of dawn. A bird twittered somewhere.

"Let's go . . . everyone up!"

For a moment he lay watching the slow revolutions of the ceiling fan. There was no beginning to its rotation and no end. Then he sat up. In the center of the long barracks room, Lieutenant Rabbe was going through a formalized series of exercises. "Let's—go—everybody—up!" His commands were in cadence.

Outside, a thunderstorm had left puddles and a pale opal sky. The window was open. Hans sucked at the fresh air gratefully. It would be a lovely spring day, yet something gnawed at his mind. Then he saw the truck outside, and remembered. It made him feel sick to remember.

Lieutenant Rabbe marched them out. They received hot

breakfast rations as they went and were told to eat them in the truck. There were enough trucks to transport the whole battery. Uncle Konrad was there with a motorcycle, his face flushed. He was addressing Lieutenant Rabbe in an emphatic voice, but Hans could not make out the words. "Yes, Herr Major," said the lieutenant, and Konrad replied, "Thank you, Lieutenant." Rabbe hesitated before he replied, "You don't demand it of the others, Herr Major," to which Konrad explained that the others did not think about it. Hans could not guess the object of the exchange. He could only see the dislike between the two erect and formidable figures.

"Carry on, Lieutenant."

The lieutenant grew another inch. "Very well, Herr Major," he said through clenched teeth. Konrad gunned the motorcycle, seemed to lose control of it, splashed through a puddle, and threatened to capsize. As Hans watched with horrified expectation, he regained control and shot off down the road. The trucks followed under the brightening sky.

Ernst sat beside him. His asthma was worse this morning, and he breathed like a leaky bellows. "If only they'd given us a decent hot meal," he said. Each had been alloted a pair of fat, congealing sausages. "They aren't even warm."

"They're fine if you like fat," said Hans.

"I don't mind a little lean as well."

"There's a bit of lean. Roll it over. There. The lean shrinks in the cooking."

"That's not lean meat. It's rust off the skillet." Ernst had no use for early mornings, particularly active ones.

In the valley toward which their convoy was descending they could see the geometric pattern of the new airfield. "I bet we'll see jets taking off from there this summer," said Siegfried. They all were proud of their part in preparing the secret weapon that would save the Fatherland. "You know, Hans, we haven't had much chance to get together lately, and really talk. Not like we used to."

"I guess not," said Hans. This had not occurred to him before.

"Listen, I want you to be honest, Hans. What's your opinion of me, anyhow?"

Hans was taken aback. His mouth was full of sausage. "Well, Siegfried . . ." He spat out some particularly tough gristle. "I don't know what you mean. We've always been friends. I mean, I like you."

"I don't mean that. I mean as a soldier. What I wouldn't give for a real chance . . . to be an officer . . ."

"When the time comes, you'll probably . . ."

"I know it," interrupted Siegfried. "We're a family of fighters. Look at my brother." Reinhard had been an officer in the SS at twenty. "It's a good life, Hans. It really is."

"I don't care for this sort of job," replied Hans.

"A soldier's got to know how to handle both the living and the dead. This is one of the bad parts, I have to admit it. But mostly it's been wonderful for me. Getting away. Of course war's terrible and all that, but it tests a man. It brings out his best qualities."

"Either of you care for my sausage?" interrupted Ernst. Hans shook his head, but Siegfried put out his hand. They were army issue and had to be good, although even he admitted, "I haven't had a real feast since that time last year at your house, Hans. That lamb!"

"Siegfried, I didn't think you believed in God," said Hans.

"No, of course not. Why do you ask?"

"I thought I heard you praying last night," said Hans.

"During the raid? Don't be silly. My mother goes to

church all the time. She'd drag me along. But you know, once you're in the Jungvolk, you haven't the time . . . Hell! You can't be seen doing that sort of thing." Siegfried hunched over his food. "This sausage could certainly have gone through the grinder a couple more times." He kept on chewing cheerfully, and he told Heime to clean his plate. "Oh, that birthday dinner of yours a year ago, Hans. I won't forget that. Your father was taking a devil of a chance. I told him so at the time."

On that sunny April day in 1943 the whole troop had been out on a military exercise, twenty-five or more boys with Siegfried at their head. Hans had operated a machine gun made from a ratchet. A tin can produced the proper noise, and he'd used a leather strap for an ammunition belt. They'd had a good time and taken a hill. He'd invited Siegfried to come for dinner. Siegfried was always glad of an opportunity to stay away from home, but Hans never invited him back after what happened that evening.

They'd had lamb, freshly killed by his father: a rare feast when a kilo of meat cost 200 marks. Of course the lamb hadn't come to the table through the usual channels. No ration stamps represented it, but that was a butcher's privilege. Any guest would have kept a grateful silence, but not Siegfried. At first he was delighted, then suspicious, and finally righteously shocked. "So soon after Stalingrad!" Anyone else would have laughed it off. But Siegfried's eyes blazed with indignation. After all, dealing on the black market was a capital crime. "It's black market, isn't it?" Hans stared at him with disbelief. "But it is, isn't it?" Siegfried persisted. The silence was broken only by the angry sizzle of grease from the stove.

As titular head of the family, it was up to Klaus to speak.

In fact, his tenseness suggested that he was about to say something definitive, but his rebuttal never came. In the end it was Lore who took charge. Leaning her hands on the table, she pushed herself up slowly. Her eyes met Siegfried's squarely. "Young man, you're a guest at my son's birthday party. It won't do for you to criticize the meal. If it doesn't satisfy you, the front door is open."

"I'm sorry," Siegfried said, and looked it. "I don't mean it isn't very good, and I love coming here. But if everyone were eating like this . . . Rules are rules." He muttered something about Stalingrad, the ghost which haunted them all. It had been less than three months since Paulus's great army had vanished, and the radio had played Wagnerian funeral marches for three days on end, three days of deep mourning for Germany's loss. The private announcements, "In proud mourning" for individual soldiers, had filled the papers ever since.

"Siegfried, I hope you're not misunderstanding," Klaus had said at last. "I may seem very unpatriotic, but this meal is all I have to give Hans on his birthday." He had apologized to Siegfried, going on to enumerate his own war record, his wife's factory work, Konrad's medals, even the patriotic zeal with which Gretchen discharged the household chores. This performance had seemed degrading to Hans. Yet when he thought of the "Night and Fog" decrees which had sent so many unsuspecting victims to the concentration camps, he realized that perhaps it was the wisest thing his father could have done.

The Amanns had half expected an investigation, but Siegfried hadn't reported them. He seemed more amused than anything else as he reminisced about it now in the bouncing truck. "Your father'd save himself a lot of trouble if he'd take up party membership. If my father had gasoline he could park a car on any street in Munich and the police would protect it like their own. Your father should think about that."

At last the truck was nearing the valley. A string of stray bombs had left craters all along the hillside. "God's footprints," Ernst called them, and was rewarded by an outbreak of nervous snickers.

"I remember your mother got angry at me that time. I was right, though, you know," continued Siegfried.

"Forget it," Hans told him. "That's all blood under the bridge, so to speak."

He didn't tell Siegfried that his mother had refused to have him in her house again. Other things had been said at that birthday dinner in 1943 which had forced Hans to agree with her. As usual, Konrad had been drinking—in contrast to their teetotaling Führer, Siegfried must have thought, disapprovingly. He didn't say anything at the time, though. He couldn't criticize a winner of the Knight's Cross, but the perplexity had deepened in his face as one glass of schnapps after another had been downed. "Here's to Moscow and Stalingrad. Here's to all those dear dead boys. May they rest in peace. Here's to death's deserters who came home covered with medals . . ."

"You don't mean that, sir," said Siegfried, shocked again.

"Oh, I do. In my case, it's quite applicable." He frowned greedily at his half-empty glass. "You see, Siegfried, there are heroes in the classic sense, like your brother, and there are others. I, for example, went to Russia with one purpose. I wanted to be killed . . . obliterated. I managed to arrange it for a good many less eager comrades, and here am

I, the very safe commander of a forgotten and entirely useless flak battery." He leaned forward, tapping the table. "If the rumors are true, boys your age . . . you boys . . . are going to replace those gunners." This was something new. There was noisy discussion. Konrad explained it was only rumor, but if it were true, if boys in their early teens were drafted, he would pull what strings he could to get Hans and Siegfried into his relatively safe battery.

Siegfried sat through it all biting on his lower lip as though he wasn't sure that he was being told the truth. He said nothing until later, when he and Hans were alone. Then he expressed his astonishment at Konrad's conduct. He added that anyone old enough to defend his country should prefer action to safety.

Hans became aware of a faint smell of charring which grew as the air itself developed a veiled and sulfurous cast. Swirling clouds of smoke and pulverized mortar were still screening the sun. Then a policeman stopped the convoy, directing them over a rough detour. The boys craned their necks to see what had happened. "Bombs must have hit the road," said Siegfried, but as it turned out, a plane had crashed there, burying itself in the asphalt. Its tail protruded, but the rest had vanished into the earth.

"That's our plane! That's the one we got last night!" shouted one of the boys from another tower.

"Probably hit by a night fighter," said Siegfried realistically.

Ernst held a handkerchief to his face. The smoke was awful. As though recently showered by random meteorites, the road and the fields on either side were pitted and scarred. Through it all, the caravan of trucks groped slowly, like a blind snake.

"How's that Jewish girl of yours?" asked Siegfried.

"What Jewish girl?"

"You know, the one at your house. That Gretel."

"If you mean Gretchen, she's fine," said Hans. He didn't feel like discussing her with Siegfried.

"She didn't like me . . ."

"Is that why you say she's Jewish?"

"I suppose so. She looks it, though. Listen, I haven't anything against Jews. But somebody has to do the dirty work. If some of them die in the process, it's better than Germans dying."

"I don't think it's that simple," said Hans.

"Well, if it isn't, it's the Jews' fault. For instance, that Gretel of yours. She's deliberately provocative. You remember the last time, when I asked her whether she was German or not?"

Hans remembered very well, for it was the same question he had once asked.

"You'd have to ask my parents," she had told Siegfried.

"No papers?"

"Nothing, unless you can pry information from a teddy bear."

"That's a queer name, Schnabel. . . . I wonder where you got a name like that," Siegfried had said just before leaving. Gretchen had offered no explanation, but when the door closed behind him, she had exploded. "I can't stand him. He makes my flesh creep," she had said. To a greater or lesser degree they had all felt the same. Even Hans had grown wary of his friend in the course of the evening. Nothing had come of it, however. And a year later there were worse terrors in the world than the Gestapo.

A yellow, sulfurous fog enveloped them. A church tower emerged briefly like a faded print and was swallowed up.

The trucks plowed forward toward the heart of the target. A few buildings stood intact, their walls coated over with the pulverized dust of those that had been demolished. Others had been split open, their insides vomited out into the streets, where an army of soldiers and works police was sifting the debris for signs of life. Corpses lay about with their limbs contorted in futile self-defense. Hans felt his own body stiffen with the rigidity of the dead. He tried to hold his breath against the smell.

Ernst sang in a shrill hysterical voice, "How the pussy-cats did mew. What else, poor pussies, could they do? They screamed for help, 'twas all in vain. 'So then,' they said, 'we'll scream again. Make haste, make haste! Me-ow, me-ow! She's burned to death, we told her so.'" Siegfried snarled he'd hit him in the mouth if he didn't shut up.

Hans swallowed continuously to keep from being sick. To think that a year ago he'd still been in school!

Konrad had been right. On May 4, 1943, boys of thirteen and fourteen had been called up as part of the "last levy." Still younger children had gone into industry. Hans hadn't learned much in those final frantic months of school, half the time reporting for Jungvolk duty instead of doing his homework. They'd been given the Einjährige exams at the last in an emergency matriculation test which was a joke. The principal question had been an essay on "The educational value of the Reich Labor Force." Old Mühlebach, the director, had lurched onto a platform crowded with flags and rows of black-clad SS men, hands on belts. He'd looked like an arthritic raven up there on that last day, calling them young heroes and extoling the virtues of death in the face of the enemy. He wouldn't have carried on that way except for the SS, stiff and unsmiling at his back. And when Old Mühlebach had lurched off through the swinging doors with all the other teachers behind him, the party speaker had gotten down to business.

They'd taken the oath as a body. "I swear by God this holy oath, that I will unconditionally obey the Führer of the German Reich and the German people, Adolf Hitler, commander-in-chief of the army. As a brave soldier, I will forever defend this oath at the cost of my own life."

A fine time was had by all, except of course by Ernst. He lacked the martial spirit, and the doctor's certificate and the X-rays his mother had produced had failed to win him an exemption. "Fresh air, lots of exercise . . . it'll do you good," Hans had told him, and for the only time that Hans could recall his friend had nothing funny to say.

Taking leave of his father had been a disturbing experience. Hans had expected a pat on the back and a word of old-soldier advice. He'd received a shock, one which had long festered and which had forced a gradual reappraisal of his father. Their last talk had taken place at his father's slaughterhouse. Actually, this was only a large shed, equipped with hooks and pulleys. A concrete floor, slightly concave, with a steel grate at the center, provided drainage. Hans seldom went there, partly from personal distaste, and partly because his father did not want him to be a butcher. On this occasion there was no choice. His father had received an order to supply a local party reunion. It was a big job and one that hinted of profitable connections, so Hans had to say his farewells at the slaughterhouse.

"I want to make something clear to you, Hans, before you go. This may be our last chance. Usually we talk around things, never saying what's important." But his father's reflections commanded less of Hans's attention than the sheep which lay on the cement floor. Its feet were bound, and it was bleating through its black mouth, turning its head from side to side in jerks of terror. Almost absently, his father held the creature in place with his thick brownish hands. "I've never liked this business, Hans, but a man can't grow old without funds. He can't be a poor musician and have a family at the same time." Hans stared at the sheep, conscious of its living, its blood, and its fear.

"If I could decide now, I'd have been a scholar, like your grandfather. Anyway, I want something better than this for you." Klaus took down a knife from a rack, its blade ground thin from years of use, and as dispassionately as a greengrocer slicing a melon, pressed the blade to the sheep's throat. Hans turned away. "There isn't much use talking about a future career, the way things are. You've no choice right now but to be a good soldier." The blood flowed from the sheep's body and its limbs trembled and relaxed. Klaus held it still while he searched for words, and the sheep, contemptuous now of all living, bared its teeth in a terrible grin. "Of course you must do your duty, Hans. You owe that to our Fatherland and to the Wehrmacht, which has given Germany a place of respect. But never mix with the Nazis. It's not all talk, Hans. I've been out near Dachau. Terrible things are going on there. If we win this war, the Nazis will be a disgrace to us. And if we lose, heaven help us all . . ." The lamb still jerked and shuddered. Again and again life revived, then retreated along the emptying veins. Hans could not keep his eyes away.

"In a year or two, Hans, the war will end . . . badly, I think for Germany . . . but I've been putting away a little at a time for your education. That's the one thing that never fails, no matter how old you get or how frightened or discouraged. Education is the only thing that will never disappoint you." As he talked, Klaus hung the lamb from a hook, its head down. Saliva dripped slowly from its mouth. He began the process of evisceration. Warm and glossy, the organs slid out over his wrists. "This is what I'm getting at, Hans . . . I want you to be a professor, like your grandfather. A poet, too, if you like. Maybe being in the war will do you no harm. Maybe a poet should see death and dying . . . but I'm not sure, Hans. Once another human being . . . even an animal . . . becomes a thing, a lump of meat . . . Maybe then the poet's dead, Hans. Dead for good."

His father seemed to have run out of ideas. They might have embraced, but Hans's uniform was fresh and his father would have soiled it. Hans went outside. He closed his eyes and took a long, sweet breath of fresh air. Then he was sick.

Little time remained for advice from his mother. At noon the boys marched to the railroad station. The town, which had already waved away its young men, awaited its boys with flags and pictures of the Führer. Gretchen was holding a flag. Hans laughed and called to her. But his voice stuck in his throat. He saw friends and neighbors, some of them cheering, some in tears. The boys marched awkwardly, feeling warm and nervous and bound together by a thousand invisible threads. There was Heime, good old Heime, frog-marching to get in step. There was Ernst, not even trying for cadence. There was his mother. She'd made him promise to wear clean underwear always, in case he got hurt and had to be undressed by strangers. She looked very old.

At the station the military police kept back the crowd. The band played "Deutschland über alles" faster than it ought to be played. "Victory or Ruin," "Victory or Bolshevist Chaos," read the posters on the walls. They'd see to victory, all right.

Relatives were allowed to pass through to the train. Lore held a handkerchief to her cheeks when she kissed him, and her eyes were red. Hans pretended not to see that she had been crying. "I'm really being quite good," she said, twisting her hands. She implored him not to catch cold.

"I know you'll come back," Gretchen told him with perfect tranquillity. Her face expressed complete confidence, as though she'd been given a secret guarantee. I could put my arms around her, he thought. She'd let me kiss her now. But he did neither. He boarded the train with the others.

"Don't get lost in the forest, Hansel . . . Come back," she called. Through the window, as the train began to gather speed, he saw his mother. She looked like an old woman in mourning. There was Gretchen again. She waved, a last white flutter. The train moved her hair as it went by. Then he was alone. His heart slumped off-center. His eyes began to burn. But with his comrades all around him, he could not cry.

Late that night trucks deposited them at the barracks. Lieutenant Rabbe had been there, along with a few gunners whose jobs they were to fill.

"What're the cots like?" Hans had asked.

"Like coffins, only not quite as soft," replied Ernst.

"You're familiar with coffins?"

"Don't be impatient."

Lieutenant Rabbe flattened the humor. "Now I'll tell you," he said, "and I hope you'll understand. You're not men any more." Men? Not one of them had a razor in his kit. "You're soldiers. Your comfort isn't important, and neither is your life. Your job is to take orders and to carry them out. If they happen to be unpleasant, that's not your concern. Dismissed." The barracks had been restless all night. Someone had sobbed into his pillow.

"Heime, be still!" Siegfried's voice rang in the dark. The crying had stopped.

In the morning, training had begun without delay. "There aren't any mothers here," Lieutenant Rabbe explained, "so you'll learn to make a respectable bed."

"Yes, Herr Lieutenant," Hans had replied.

"Shut up! Answer only direct questions." Lieutenant Rabbe lived up to the tenets of Frederick the Great, who had said that an officer's stick should be more feared than the bullets of the enemy. "Right turn, forward march! Left, right! Left, right! To the front, present! Halt! Order arms! Present and correct! By the right, number!" He marched them about with a shrill, commanding voice, which, it was rumored, could sound an uninterrupted "o" for as long as fifty seconds. Exhausted from drill, they went through more exhausting calisthenics. "Hands on hips—ho—stand up— arms out—ho—bend the knees, touch the floor—ho." It was several days before they were allowed to examine the flak guns. "I'll begin with the basics," Rabbe had told them. "A gun in its simplest form is a machine for throwing balls. Got that? All right." Before they were finished, they had to be able to take the machine gun apart and put it together again blindfolded, while the lieutenant timed them with a stop watch. The separating of oily steel parts sounded like the light collision of curling balls. "Try it again. Let's go . . ."

After dismissal, they rushed to seize brooms, buckets, and mops with which to clean the barracks. No one had delayed in this since the day Ernst had had to clean the place three times with a toothbrush.

In those first weeks Hans had neither time nor energy to write home. At least they were spared political indoctrination. Konrad even forbade the party salute, which had been

introduced into the army that year. He brought teachers
from the village so that the boys could continue their
studies. Hans was surprised to find himself looking forward
to classes as a relief from military routine. Only Siegfried
was displeased, frowning until his pale brows met straight
across his forehead. He was embarrassed by the safety of
this particular battery. He took to reciting "How-can-man-
die-better-than-facing-fearful-odds," until they began to call
him Fearful Odds Hellpack behind his back.

Their complete isolation from the war did not last long.
The English were already beginning to bomb Munich at
night. On such occasions, the boys were always up in their
towers. Then in mid-August the first American shuttle raid
passed over Munich on its way to Africa from Regensburg.
Every day after that they expected attack, but in October
the raids diminished. Clocks were set back and there was a
rumor that the raids would stop altogether so that Hitler
would not use his "reprisal weapon." Instead, the autumn
of 1943 brought overcast skies and the first haphazard
radar bombing. Real saturation raids began with the clear
spring skies of 1944.

As soon as the trucks had crunched inside the factory
grounds, they received orders to disembark. Here, concrete
bomb shelters had been built with loopholes to serve as SS
forts in case of riot. One of these shelters had been hit. All
that remained was a thirty-foot crater. Strewn about its rim
like the petals of some monstrous flower lay the bodies of
workers. A sweet vomitous odor pervaded the lemon-
colored air.

Shovels were passed out. For Hans, all chance of escaping into memory was over. When he saw Siegfried enter the
crater, he bound a handkerchief over his nose and mouth

and closed his eyes. No one else volunteered until Lieutenant Rabbe gave the order. "Don't stand there. Get busy!
It's not the end of the world." His voice was shrill.

"Look at Rabbe. He loves it," said Ernst.

The lieutenant dashed here and there among the dead.
He allowed no pause at the grim task save for a short lunch
break, but no one could eat. The afternoon was an eternity
of flies and smells and nausea which Hans endured silently
until Ernst said, "Hans, there's your uncle. He looks like
hell."

Konrad sat astride his motorcycle, his face terribly pale.
Stiff blond whiskers bristled from his unshaven chin.

"How do you feel?" he asked Hans.

"Sick."

"Well, you have to be alive to feel sick. With so many
dead, it seems almost indecent to be alive."

"I must get back to work, sir," Hans said.

"That's right, Hans. Strong and stupid to the end. There's
no place for the weak and intelligent in this world. . . .
Carry on, old man." He gave a disjointed salute and rode
off.

By late afternoon they were relieved. A train of cattle
cars had arrived, and from it the works police drove a crowd
of workers: a dozen foreign tongues, strange faces from
many lands, all marred by weariness and bad food. Hans
knew they were here not only to clean up but to stay on
until they died or the war was over. Well, that was their bad
luck. Silently he thanked God that he was leaving.

The young flak gunners climbed back into their trucks
like so many dummies. They sat side by side, rocking with
the motion. Hans tried to detach his mind from his body, a
body that was cold and tremulous, a body that had a bad
taste in its mouth. Heime looked green. He's going to be

sick, Hans thought. I hope he is before I am. Lord God in heaven, we can't be stopping again.

But they were stopping, on the road where the enemy raider had fallen. Works police and a crowd of workers were already there, and lines had been thrown about the larger fragments of wreckage. With the help of Hans and his comrades, the plane, or what was left of it, was to be drawn off into the field. A tractor had tried and failed, proving that it had to be done by hand. Hans struggled up to his ankles in mud. It reminded him of Jungvolk tugs of war, but this time he felt that he was on a losing team.

In the field other wreckage had fallen, including an aviator who had jumped with a defective chute. Siegfried had gone to look at the body, and back at the truck, he depicted the scene vividly. "His guts were strewn all over. All over." Heime looked at him with the blue-white expression of a nervous child at the zoo who expects the lions to roar. "I found some of his things. Look at this photograph. His name was Cliff. This must be his girl." He shoved the photograph into Hans's face. Hans looked at it dully. She was a little like Gretchen. Then Ernst took the picture from Siegfried and examined it closely. "Poor girl," he said softly.

"I only wish I'd had a camera," exulted Siegfried. "What I wouldn't give for a picture of myself with one foot on that plane!"

"Keep quiet, can't you?" said Heime, a mild but quite unprecedented rebuke.

"What the devil's eating you?" asked Siegfried in a low voice. Only his eyes seemed to shout. Abruptly Heime showed him, by being sick. "If you must do that, kindly lean out the back of the truck." Like a pawn compelled from one square to another, Heime moved to the transom, and there he clung, head down, his body jerking almost mechanically.

"Poor little toad," said Ernst.

When Heime returned to his seat, his eyes looked immensely round and wet and pitifully blue. Hans looked away, but Heime seemed to have no pride. He slumped down with his head between his knees until Siegfried tapped him lightly on the shoulder, saying mildly, "Take it easy, Heime. Get hold of yourself." Siegfried spoke kindly, but Heime mumbled back, "Go away. Leave me alone!"

Siegfried turned to Hans and shook his head. "I suppose it's up to me to get him straightened out again."

The rest of the trip passed in silence. Heime seemed to recover himself. He began to polish the grip of his dagger with a greasy rag, a procedure so common that the knife had entirely lost its inscription. Hans watched him idly. Gradually he became obsessed with his own filth and his need for a shower, for red-hot jets of water to scorch him clean. He saw the towers in the distance. There was never enough hot water, and the instant the word "dismissed" was heard, he would make a dash. But there was a surprise waiting for them all in the form of a Mercedes staff car. Behind the wheel sat a driver, straight and rigid as though he were riding a horse. At the sound of the trucks, two SS officers emerged from the major's office. The first looked quite pleasant, with a face like a big summer apple that had been deprived of the sun. The other, a full colonel, had a chest full of campaign ribbons. In his craggy, wind-gnawed face a pair of cold bleak eyes were set in a chronic squint.

Lieutenant Rabbe, without the slightest show of surprise, drew his charges up to attention before the barracks. "What's this?" whispered Ernst. Hans had no idea, but he did know that his uncle would be along at any moment in a disgraceful condition, and there was nothing he could do to stop him. The colonel of the SS, tough and savage, inspected their drooping ranks. Hans tried to meet his glance, but found this as impossible as staring at the sun. The colonel was in no hurry. He emphasized the increased importance of their job and hinted at the wonder weapons that would soon be under their protection.

How long must they stand here? Hans imagined himself running off to the shower in complete disregard of military decorum. So absorbed was he by this image that he did not at first hear the approaching mutter of a motorcycle. The sound rose and fell so irregularly that he had no doubt who was driving and in what condition. The motorcycle swung round the intervening trucks, turned sharply, braked screamingly, and rolled over. Major Wirth sat beside it, disheveled, dirty, and drunk.

"I must be dead," thought Hans. "My heart's stopped entirely."

Konrad got to his feet and with weary distinction set a zigzag course for the barracks door. The SS colonel, his body hard and flat, his manner youthful and alert, stood across the path of the oncoming hero. He looked frostily amused. Konrad advanced, limping, deliberately displaying his physical handicap. "Heil Hitler," said the SS colonel. He spoke with enameled articulation and threw up an enormous right hand. Konrad stopped, staring at the hand with bloodshot eyes. "Ah," he said, "Moses on the mountain."

"Do you regard this as a suitable example for these young men?" No response. "Tell me, Major. Why do you drink?"

"Disgust . . ."

"With what, Major Wirth?"

"With myself."

The SS colonel seemed to accept this. Hans could not

decipher the runes written on the colonel's face, but the interview, which in Hans's mind had ended with a gunshot, was going quite contrary to what he had feared.

"Let us assume, Major Wirth, that you are sober enough to appreciate my delicate position. We have been given your dossier. We know of your fine record in Russia and your Knight's Cross, but we are also informed that you have made repeated statements disrespectful to the war effort . . ." The colonel spoke without emphasis, his manner indicating neither suspicion nor condemnation. He seemed to be merely interested, in a detached, clinical way. "Particularly it has been reported that you have made disparaging remarks about our campaign in Russia."

"Hardly, Herr Colonel. How else would we have discovered vodka?"

The colonel gave a hissing laugh which he directed toward the ground. Hans noticed that his mouth stayed open after he laughed.

"There's something else, Major Wirth. I wonder . . . please give some thought to your answer . . . are you familiar with the expression, 'Rise up, my people; the signal fires are ablaze'?"

"Schiller. *William Tell,* I believe."

"During the summer of 1942 you attended classes under one Professor Kurt Huber."

"I did."

"Are you aware that he has since been executed for high treason?"

Konrad nodded. "And did you not know Hans and Sophie Scholl, two students at the university?" Konrad nodded again. "They were also executed in 1943 for leading the so-called students' revolt. Surely you came across their pamphlet, *The White Rose.* Very amusing, and full of

Schiller, I'm told . . . Tell me, Major Wirth, did you sympathize with their radical views?"

"A man has the right to speak his mind, surely."

"Once," said the colonel. The muscles in his jaw moved, but there was no expression on his face. "If this interview were reported in full, Herr Major, have you any idea what would happen to you?"

"Perhaps a promotion back into civilian life?"

"Cashiered? Come now, Major Wirth. For you, at least a court-martial . . . And, Major Wirth, what sort of verdict do you suppose they would pass?"

Hans knew. Every boy standing at attention knew. Lieutenant Rabbe, smiling like an open piano, knew. "But it need not come to that. I'm told you are an expert on .88's. If that's so, you are certainly wasted here with these machine guns. How would you like an opportunity to take part in the coming defense of Festung Europa? A posting to the Normandy coast, perhaps? I'm sure that would be more satisfactory, and I believe I can guarantee the transfer."

Through it all, the boys stood motionless, their eyes wide open as though the day's ordeal had given them a measure of dreamy immortality.

"Very well, Major Wirth. You may expect to receive the necessary papers within the next few days. I trust we meet again under happier circumstances."

"At Phillipi, Herr Colonel?"

"Heil Hitler!"

The interview was over. Konrad departed and the colonel addressed himself to the boys. Perhaps the scene had shocked them. Well and good. It might be hoped that with a change of climate the good Major Wirth would return to health. But let them ponder the consequences of such conduct to a boy who had won no Knight's Cross. He would be watching their performance carefully. From now on, they could expect more spirited leadership, a healthy orientation, and the Hitler salute. He expected great things of them. Very well, was everything understood? No voice was raised. It was understood, all right. As abruptly as he had arrived, the SS colonel and his apple-faced captain returned to the staff car. White-gloved hands grasped the steering wheel, the motor roared, and the car vanished.

"Dismissed!" yelled Lieutenant Rabbe. His shrill voice had an angry ring.

Hans took one step toward his uncle, then turned and disappeared into the crowd of boys rushing toward the shower. He was among the first, but there wasn't any hot water.

ELEVEN

DURING the three days that followed, the flak battery responded to one alert. From the towers they could see flashes
in the north; Nuremberg this time. On the fourth day
Konrad received his transfer orders and for the first time
emerged from his private quarters and spoke to Hans.

"I'll be leaving this afternoon," he said. "The Panzer
Lehr division."

"You're lucky it wasn't worse," said Hans. "I was afraid,
Uncle Konrad. You defied that colonel. You really did."

"Somewhat."

"Why did you take such a chance?"

"I suppose I couldn't find another way. It seems the
accuser always wears a halo now. If you'd known the
Scholls as I did, Hans, you might find it hard not to defend
them a little. Well, take care. I'll send you a postcard from
Normandy."

"Please take care of yourself. This won't be like Russia,
will it?"

"Who knows? I'm no longer suicidally inclined, if that's
what you mean, but it's a post of horrible probabilities.
Actually, I feel like Lazarus. Resurrected. If I had more

courage, I'd avoid the whole business. I'd vanish over those mountains. Instead, I'll impose on the family for a few days and then . . . well, who knows?"

"Give Gretchen my best. Tell her the witch hasn't devoured me yet."

There was no formal farewell, no drawing up of ranks or presentations for the departing major who had disgraced himself. Except for Hans, the only one who came to wish Konrad well was Heime, and even his appearance might well have been accidental, but Konrad seemed pleased. He placed his hand on Heime's shoulder with the same steadying gesture he had used in the tower. "Don't work too hard at this war, Heime, old man. The wages aren't good enough. They're all paid in counterfeit money." How Heime reacted to this, Hans couldn't tell. Whether he was squirming inwardly, or whether there lingered in the unattractive figure a spark of warmth and gratitude, this was Heime's secret, and he concealed it behind his unreadable froglike face.

Hans and his uncle embraced. Then the officer rode off on his motorcycle and was quickly lost among the trees.

The years can wear a man down as the sea wears down a shell, thought Hans, until that man isn't the same man any more but a stranger. He remembered the crisp decisive young soldier of the Munich beerhall. He still loved his uncle, perhaps more than before, but he could no longer respect him. Konrad had asked for this. He'd been lucky. Men had been shot for less, but he had gotten a leave and a posting to the west wall, which Hans knew very well the Allies would never attack. They'd crawl up through Italy like the comic snail on the war posters, if they came at all.

From this day forward, Captain Rabbe was in full command of the battery, and changes were made immediately.

Rabbe addressed them that very afternoon, holding his cap in front of his stomach in a gesture of shyness that was as insincere as a parrot's laugh. Hans could see that. "There'll be no more Sunday school classes up here," said Rabbe. "They aren't for you. They don't do a soldier any good. You're not here to think; you're here to be used and to want to be used, and that doesn't mean to be soft and civilized."

The teachers from the village were promptly dismissed, and Rabbe filled the gap himself with political and racial theory. Germans, particularly German Aryans, were human beings, he proclaimed. The English and the Americans were also human beings, but degenerate and cowardly. Most of the others—particularly the Jews, the Russians, and the black sons of Ham—were subhuman. They were animals. The wild ones should be exterminated, the domestic ones enslaved. These sessions, as frequent as the raiders would permit, began and ended with the party salute. The old Reichswehr salute was gone with Konrad.

Another innovation was calisthenics. Rabbe called the flak crew an unpromising bunch of weaklings and led galloping parades around the barracks compound. Those who shirked Rabbe's fitness drills, or were caught visiting the girls at the searchlight batteries, were publicly thrashed with a strap. Rabbe often acted purely on hearsay, without even asking questions. However good a soldier Rabbe might be, Hans despised him. Nothing could change that.

There was more to worry about than Captain Rabbe during that spring of '44. There were the Americans, the "Amis" as Ernst called them, who raided by day. Clouds of Liberators bombed the nearby towns and factories, but seldom came within firing range. There were no close calls at the battery, only the constant alerts and the cleaning up of the towns. Even that didn't matter much any more. The "stiffs" had become so much cordwood, and they were buried by tractor. Hans would tell himself that it ought to matter and he would remember his father's words. Life ought to matter, but he was drained of emotion and sympathy. To him war had become a butcher's business and nothing more.

They had returned from one of these errands, dusty and dirty as usual. Hans had done his best without soap in a cold shower. In the compound, he took a long draft of summer air. It was a June night, coming on full of stars and hidden colors. It would never get really dark.

The English would come, but Hans had learned to take one thing at a time. He strolled back to the barracks, where he found a much handled and smeared letter from France. There was the old-fashioned, monkish handwriting, and he seemed to see Konrad with his feet hooked around the legs of a stool. He'd been home, Konrad wrote. Everyone was well. Gretchen sent greetings from the gingerbread house. Hans wished she'd written herself, though he'd never been very conscientious about correspondence. Still, it piqued him to hear that she had already written to Konrad. There were a dozen years between those two, but their friendship bothered Hans.

"She completely restores me," wrote Konrad. "That girl, and the local Calvados. As officers, we're supposed to drink Chablis here in France. 'À votre santé' and all that, but the apple brandy is quicker. I'm joking, Hans. You won't believe this, but I've scarcely had a drop. Yes, your degenerate uncle is leading a healthy life for a change, and not without reason. In the first place, we're as busy as ants. General Rommel inspires us. We dig gun emplacements, we plant beach obstacles and 'Rommel's asparagus' wherever enemy planes might try to land. The French underground is beginning to stir in its sleep. We wear smiles, but carry pistols, and now and then one of us dies behind a hedge. The Maquis let fly carrier pigeons and we have squab for supper now and then, but on the whole our shotgun patrols are bad marksmen and the birds get through to gossip about us in England. So you see we work night and day building and protecting our sand castles. But what difference will it make to the anteater when he comes? And he *is* coming, Hans. I can feel his hungry breath. Then all this mad insect work will stop—a sobering thought and one which demands from me a reverential Amen. I hope all is well with you. Write if you have the time and the spirit moves you. Should you be lucky enough to get home, give Gretchen a kiss for me. One for Lore, too, and remember me to your father. I love them all. Yours faithfully, Konrad."

No raid came that night, or the next, and then the weather turned cloudy. Mysteriously, Rabbe sat brooding in his quarters, neglecting his political lectures, not even emerging for the physical-fitness periods. There was time for the gunners to play football in the compound or to sneak off and visit the girls if they dared.

One evening Hans had been helping Ernst collect lightning bugs in a glass jar. "I haven't done this since I was . . . well, since I was a baby," said Ernst, and that was exactly what made it fun.

"There's almost enough light for reading," said Hans, but Ernst replied, "They always die in jars." He unscrewed the lid and poured from the bottle a shower of sparks, bright splinters of childish happiness winking away.

"It'll rain tonight," said Ernst. "Smell the wind, how damp it is."

"It smells of the sea."

In the morning they awoke to rumors. The Allies were landing in France. "The anteater," said Hans gloomily.

"What's that, Hans? What are you talking about?" Siegfried was hopping mad, a puppet jerked on strings. "They must be out of their minds! They'll be flattened on the beaches!" But they were not, and as the days went by, Siegfried rationalized that Hitler had decided to let the beachhead enlarge. When the bag was full, an army of Tiger Royals would pull the string. "Biff, bang! Total victory!"

Worse rumors were soon to follow. An English broadcast reported that Hitler had been killed, that a bomb planted by fanatics had gone off in his East Prussian Wolfschanze. All the pots of geraniums along the window sills had been shattered in the blast of a 150 millimeter shell. Finally, the unmistakable voice of Goebbels, "Little Cloven Hoof" as some called him, announced over the radio that their Führer had been spared to continue his onerous duties. Still, rumors persisted that Hitler was dead, that the Wehrmacht was about to lay down its arms. The official reassurance was quickly followed by the rumor of whole army divisions in revolt. Hans and the other boys who had crowded around the radio hardly knew what to believe.

"Oh, Lord, here comes the Last Judgment," muttered Ernst.

It was Captain Rabbe. He herded his gun crews into the compound where a soiled metallic sky hurled down sheets of rain. "Hitler has been spared by divine providence," he said. The rotten core of army generals responsible for past failures had been purged. Germany would move on to victory with superhuman determination. Hans glanced at the other soaked boys standing quietly, their faces lowered from the rain as though brooding on the earth. "Further-

more," the captain announced dramatically, "you will re-
joice to learn that the rocket weapons of revenge have
already laid waste to London. Soon their range will include
New York as well."

"He's talking about the V4," whispered Ernst. "V5 will
go around the world and get us in the backside."

Rabbe's harangue was taking on a threatening note. "I
do not intend to lie to you. The English and the Americans
are still pressing forward, but they are paying a terrible
price. And the Russians . . . Let me tell you, I have
fought in Russia, and I know their savagery. Any man,
woman, or child who falls into their hands would be better
off dead . . ." Here the captain risked a pause, but his
unfriendly eyes dared anyone to break it. The silence was
filled with the voices of frogs and the drone of mosquitoes
from the swamp. When he continued, his tone was venom-
ous. "You have been here over a year and you have done
nothing. Now your test is at hand. The airfield you are here
to defend has been completed. The factories you are here to
defend are pouring jet planes into those fields. The Fatherland is about to use you. Remember, no matter what the
cost, Germany must win! No matter what the cost, this soil
must remain forever German!"

Then, with the order that they turn out for the Führer's
midnight declaration, Captain Rabbe dismissed them. At 1
A.M. they were still waiting, wondering if the Führer had died
of his wounds. Finally came the voice which had for so long
intoxicated them.

"My German comrades!"

"Thank God," said Siegfried. He grimaced painfully, and
Hans thought he was going to cry.

"If I speak to you tonight," came the voice from the
radio, "it is first in order that you may hear my voice and

know that I am unhurt and well; and second, that you may know of a crime unparalleled in Germany history."

"That isn't Hitler! That isn't his voice!" said Ernst. It did sound strangely hoarse and tired, but Hans had no doubt. He felt his spirits lifting.

The address ended with a promise of vengeance against the officers who had conspired against his life. If generals were to fall, what about small malcontents like Konrad, who had never veiled his views? Would he be crushed as well? The thought nagged at Hans, but the mood of the barracks swept him along. Siegfried was jubilant. "In years to come," he said, "we'll look back on this night and tell ourselves we were there at the turning of the tide." His pale cheeks seemed about to burst with pride.

In midsummer the air war, which had retired beyond the horizon, suddenly returned. The aircraft-engine plants and the Munich marshaling yards were attacked. Five times in one week the Munich area was bombed. The Americans came by day in their B-17's, the British by night in their cigar-shaped Lancasters. The jet airfields were carpet-bombed and the flak towers trembled. But the jets were up. They should have swept the skies clean, but the bombers only returned in greater numbers. Hans began to carry his pay book in his hip pocket, on Captain Rabbe's advice. He had told them that a body, no matter how dismembered, seldom lost its pants.

On July 11, Hans climbed the ladder hand over hand. It was one of those rare summer mornings. A fresh breeze drifted from the mountains, and the sky above was a bottomless blue well. Hans sat calmly behind his gun, thinking of falling up rather than down, of landing pain-lessly in one of the many puffball clouds that wafted over-head. Then came the infinite ribbons linking the clouds, led by the occasional silver wink of an American bomber, like sunlight on water. Too high . . . they were always too high . . . but on the signal he pressed down on the jarring pedal, and tiny streaks marked the upward passage of the bullets. All day the Amis were overhead, bombing Munich into a smoky fog, plowing up the airfield. Down below the towers, Captain Rabbe yelled at them: "We'll show 'em. Give 'em hell, boys!" But five thousand shells were not enough to bring down one bomber. Heime could cart shells all day until his back broke, until the barrel wilted with the heat, and Hans couldn't fire that many. Only the wounded planes ever came within range. Hans shouted constantly at Heime in a cracked voice and Heime scuttled quickly with the belted shells. He was crawling before the day ended, and the Amis left with the first violet light of dusk.

From the swamps, mosquitoes rose in silver streams into the eye of the dying sun. Suddenly it was beautifully serene. Fleecy red clouds sailed slowly across a dark purple evening, and Hans picked out mythical shapes in them: Heimdall with hand cupped to listening ear, the Valkyrie made out of cotton and pastel dust. Somewhere across the Channel, the English pilots were stubbing out their cigarettes.

A single gun spoke into the subsiding sky. One of the girls' batteries, Hans thought. So very female; just a little late. They ought to be making a wish on the first star instead. Oh, if only Gretchen could see him now: no brass-buttoned member of the Jungvolk, but a striped and steely warrior, grim and unflinching. If she could see him, she would surely love him with her whole heart.

As soon as supper was over, he would write her a letter in verse. But when supper was over, the twilight planned for wooing had turned dark and terrifying. Sirens were going off in the valley. In the intervals of silence, Hans heard only the whine of mosquitoes competing with the first distant murmur of motors. Searchlights began their explorations, followed by star shells which turned the deepening cloud cover into a pane of frosted glass. Against it, the raiders would be silhouettes for the German night fighters.

Moths fluttered around the flashing barrels of his gun. Hans tried to concentrate on the thunder of their wings, instead of on the rushing, jarring night and the subtle, deadly plunk of shrapnel falling back around him. Before the fight ended, they had blown the clouds away. There remained only the star-stabbed sky. He saw the Perseids, the shooting, lovers' stars of August, and an infusion of violet blue in the sky which meant that dawn was coming. Dawn. He crawled stiffly from the tower and stumbled wearily to his cot.

Weeks ran together as the raiders came day and night. The flak crews were either awaiting or recovering from attack, and when relief balanced anticipation, they tried to sleep. Hans was always too spent or too tense to read or to write letters. He would listen to Ernst confide for the hundredth time that in the next raid they'd be killed. When a soldier was killed, it would often turn out that he had told a comrade about having a premonition of death. But Ernst had premonitions all the time, and so did Hans, though he did not elaborate upon them. Ernst discussed self-wounding as a way to get home, but Hans told him not to be silly. How could you wound yourself and make it look authentic? Besides, their battery hadn't had one injury. Why worry?

Their first casualty came soon enough, during a night engagement. They were firing straight up into an empty sky because the raid was traveling through a barrage zone the corner of which was occupied by their towers. The shells went up and fell back, raining through the forest, spanging through a helmet in an adjacent tower. Then the planes were gone. It had been a short and very mild engagement. Hans had no inkling of the accident until he reached the ground. Around the base of another tower a crowd was gathering. He joined it, and saw a boy he scarcely knew lying on the ground, his eyes wide and unseeing, their gaze turned inward. His mouth, too, was open, yawning, but the corners of the lips were torn as if burst by the abrupt expulsion of life.

Hans heard Siegfried insisting: "Get a doctor! Somebody get a doctor!" as if it were possible to talk a corpse back to life. Captain Rabbe ordered them to carry the body inside. "Hurry up, boys, he won't bite." Hans felt saliva sharp and sudden against his tongue. He'd seen casualties before, but none so newly dead as this.

Hans experienced a mixture of emotions. "He's younger than I am, and he has nothing to hope for ever again . . ." Then sympathy changed to relief. "Thank God it wasn't me . . . Thank God they didn't drag him into our barracks." His body ached to do something, anything, and he rushed outside. In the fresh air he felt tired and sad, not for the boy, but because the warm shadows were full of the screaming of crickets and he knew autumn was coming.

The dead boy had been a stranger in life and in death. In a few days he would be forgotten. Captain Rabbe would do the right thing. He would write a form letter to the boy's parents. "I have the sad duty to inform you that your son was killed in action. I express my deepest sympathy to you in your great loss, etc." Then the captain would seal the letter, yawn perhaps, and go to bed.

Hans felt a sudden wave of superiority, greater than he had ever felt for the subhumans and degenerates of the world. He felt superior to the dead. He had been tested.

Death had whistled past him and he had survived. For some time this thought preoccupied him, and when he entered, the barracks was quiet. He looked at his friends, slumbering like infants with their knees drawn up, pillows clutched in their arms. He was acutely aware of the smell of summer and the sound of autumn outside.

As he lay unsleeping, his buoyant mood changed to one of fear. He was afraid of dying, afraid that death was waiting for him. Death was his grandfather, a fallen vulture in a casket. Death was a partridge with its eyes still bright and blood running from its beak. Death was a grinning, eviscerated lamb. Death was a yawning boy. Nothing in the world was worth dying for. In the dreams which finally came, death was a thunderous charge of eyeless horses, and his uncle saying drunkenly, "Did you ever notice that animals never kill themselves even when they're sure to lose?" The horses trampled over him and tossed him about. Then he was awake and Siegfried was shouting at him. "It's another alert. Hurry up! Get dressed."

Autumn brought a succession of Job's messengers. "Strategic retreat in the west" . . . "Shortening of the lines in the east" . . . "Paris fallen" . . . "Russians in East Prussia." Goebbels called for a new army, the Volksgrenadiers. But offices and shops were already empty. Were there any healthy men left who had time to test themselves against the mountains? With a few moments to walk idly in the forests of Bavaria? Forests which were bursting into color: reds and yellows that were more than pigments, glowing as though each leaf contained a tiny electric filament. From his high tower, Hans longed for the forests, but before the trees had completely turned, the rains came and stripped the limbs.

At first Hans welcomed the rain. It would hold back the

raiders and he would have time, at least in a letter, to be with his parents and Gretchen, to wax his skis in memory. Yet the bombers came through the worst weather, bombing by radar. No longer could the warning system be relied upon. Sometimes the raiders arrived with the first wailing of the sirens.

By mid-October, Goebbels's new army must have been exhausted, for a levy of men sixteen to sixty, the Volkssturm, was called up. That would include his father. At last Hans wrote a long letter home. He hoped it would make up for all his parents' letters and perhaps even bring a letter from Gretchen in reply. He heard nothing for days, and finally he asked Ernst, "If anything happened at home, do you think they'd let us know? Anything bad, I mean. If the house were hit?" Ernst tried to reassure him, but he worried until a letter came. He recognized the strong, straight shafts and the delicate transverse strokes, and he tore it open eagerly. It was a letter from Gretchen.

Her image glowed in his mind: the eyes slightly Oriental, looking darker than they really were; the long, breeze-rippled hair. Abruptly his vision was spoiled. She wrote of Uncle Konrad, saying how forlorn he had looked on his leave. For two days the Gestapo had questioned him. Then they presented him with a bill for board and lodging and released him in time to report to the front. Otherwise, the family was well. As yet the local Volkssturm had not been organized and Klaus remained at his shop. She had taken a factory job nearby, along with Lore, but it looked as if the plant would operate only parttime for lack of raw materials. "It's late," she had written, "and I think I hear the radio going 'kuk-kuk.' I'll write a little more down in the shelter if there's any light." Evidently there had been no light in the makeshift bomb shelter, for the letter ended abruptly with "Heil Hitler" for the censors, and the signature, "Gretel."

There was nothing lyrical or loving about it, nothing personal for him to cling to, no matter how he searched for subtle turns of phrase. Though disappointed, Hans found himself assailed by a wave of homesickness so sudden and overwhelming that he sank forward over the barracks' table, his face in his hands, his breath sighing between his fingers. He would write. He wouldn't move from the table until he had told her how lonely, how loving he felt. It was easy enough to write "I love you" on a sheet of paper, but how would it be read? And, most difficult of all to imagine, how would it be answered? He started one letter after another but was unable to transcribe his emotions into words. He blamed his inadequacy on Captain Rabbe, who censored all the battery mail. You couldn't have Rabbe snickering over love letters, so he ended up with a businesslike statement, full of ink stains and incoherence. How should he sign it? This was critical. With his pen pinched high and his eyes glancing from paper to ceiling, he pondered this, deciding at last upon "Love to all." Damn Rabbe, anyway, for reading mail. It was as bad as the way he'd listed up scars and marks of identification on the boys' faces and bodies. Always finding out things, prying so that you couldn't write what you wanted to. How could he say he intended to come home one way or another if things got any worse? That he would fight with the Volkssturm in his home town if need be, but not any longer at this godforsaken battery? He wouldn't dare write that if he wanted to keep the skin on his backside.

Creasing the letter carefully, he fitted it into the envelope. Inadvertently he almost sealed it with his tongue. Then, remembering, he carried it out into the gray November afternoon. His feet left squelching prints on earth that was no longer ever completely dry.

Captain Rabbe sat reading a field manual by the light of

a single candle flickering in a mason jar. Around it fluttered a gypsy moth, flirting with the flame. For a while the captain let Hans stand.

"Yes, Amann?" he said finally, not looking up.

"Mail, Herr Captain."

"Ah, mail. Give it here, Amann."

Captain Rabbe extracted the letter, read it through with an occasional loud bark of laughter that was anything but mirthful.

"You're not much of a speller, are you, Amann?"

"No, Herr Captain."

The captain had not shaved. His breath was foul, as though something were rotting in his stomach.

"Tell me, Amann, who is this Gretel? Your sister?"

Hans explained. Captain Rabbe did not seem to hear. He caught the big moth between his hands and broke it.

"May I go now, Herr Captain?" Hans asked.

The captain stuffed the letter back into the envelope as though it were a handful of excelsior. He looked at Hans searchingly, then held the letter out. "Here you are, Gunner Amann. Post it . . ." Finally, a belated "Heil Hitler."

Hans went outside. The compound was cold. A chill mountain breeze stirred the last of the autumn leaves. Soon the snow would come and silence would settle on the deep green of the forests. He longed for home and a fire and a girl with dark soft eyes.

TWELVE

HANS LICKED HIS FOREFINGER and tested the air. No wind; only a black shroud full of pin-prick stars, and a haloed moon that told of coming snow. November had been a warm gray shield protecting them from the raiders, but with December came deep frost and clearer skies. Weather was neutral, the old soldiers said, but the axiom did not apply in this war, in which the enemy commanded the sky in all but the grimmest weather. Before midnight the snow began to fall in big flakes, the kind Hans had once collected on black paper to examine under a magnifying glass. He began to think of Christmas cards, and horse-drawn sleighs, and the hiss of skis descending infinite slopes.

He wondered if he would ever ski again with Konrad. Konrad might be dead—but he wouldn't let himself think about that. He would keep on planning to climb those tall mountains as yet untouched by skis. If Konrad's leg was too stiff, he would teach Gretchen to ski, and Konrad would be there at the lodge when they got back.

Lost in this aching dream, he did not hear Siegfried's first joyous shout. Siegfried, with his air of withered childhood, came bounding, shouting, delirious as a mystic who after

143

months of failure has at last received a direct communication from God. "It's started! New weapons . . . the great offensive!" He threw his arms around Hans, almost toppling the sturdier boy to the ground in his ecstasy. From scattered bits, his news began to take shape. In the Ardennes Forest a great offensive to preserve the Fatherland had begun. Eight thousand planes of an entirely new and fearful design had swept the Allies from the skies. The Führer had launched new battalions of tanks . . . he had sprung his trap . . . at last there would be victory in the west. All over camp, glad tidings spread. The losing years were swept away. Even the radio confirmed the final victory.

Captain Rabbe assembled the battery. Hans and the others stood stiffly erect, directing their eyes at their captain's face as required by regulations. For a long time Rabbe stared back, his body tense, his hands, hard and rough as coconuts, clenched into fists. "Men!" he said finally. The word was a verbal explosion. "Men! You have heard the good news. The decisive weeks of the Fatherland have arrived. What you may not know is that your old commander, Major Wirth, is fortunate enough to spearhead this glorious victory. May we wish every triumph to our old comrade and the Panzer Lehr division. May the snow run red with American blood! May the Channel overflow with the blood of the English! Some of you may ask, what about the Russians? What is our Führer doing about them? Have no fear. He is waiting for the right moment. As a token of confidence you have all been granted a week's leave, starting this afternoon."

The silence was absolute. The boys had ceased to breathe. A moment ago a vision of the Holy Grail would have seemed as likely. Then someone shouted and someone broke into foolish tears. Captain Rabbe brought them fiercely to attention, dismissed them, and walked away. Hans and Ernst embraced. They were all half mad with joy, except Siegfried, who stood blinking, bewildered.

Without any luggage, Hans slogged down the long hill to the valley. Gas was so short, trucks couldn't be spared to transport them, but this didn't bother the long column of straggling, jostling boys. Songs were sung, snowballs were thrown. The column looked anything but military.

"If Siegfried were here, we'd march," said Ernst. "I'm glad he stayed at the barracks." Poor Siegfried. But the snow would have lost its sparkle if he'd been there, complaining in his sharp voice about their Christmas leave. It mattered not at all to Hans that the flak batteries were treated as superfluous in the hour of Germany's triumph. "I'm glad the Toad isn't here, either. Whenever I see him, I get depressed."

"Then don't talk about him," said Hans, tossing a lazy snowball at his friend.

There was much less gaiety when they reached the depot. Ernst was wheezing and Hans was tired. They discussed phoning home, but blitz calls were costly and invariably monitored by the Gestapo. They waited interminably beside a flatcar loaded with factory-new artillery. A crowd gathered, and a couple of black-robed priests walked by as though propelled on little wheels. "Good day, Fathers," said Hans, and the priests nodded silently.

"What did you want to do that for?" asked Ernst.

"No reason. It's funny . . . priests never seem to speak to you."

"Why should they? No one speaks to them any more. Not even God. Not in Germany."

"Why don't you shut up? . . . Hey, look! Some B.D.M. girls . . . pretty . . . Look at that big blond one."

A troop of Bund Deutscher Mädchen had come on the platform. "Be good and noble, German girl," said Ernst, quoting the Bund motto.

The train came at last with the sunset, seemed in fact to grow like a black canker out of the golden light which lay along the track. There wasn't much room on the train. People pushed and shoved. The engine breathed against the overhanging trees and made their branches shiver.

Ernst moved toward the rear of the train with his odd, traipsing run, and Hans had to look sharp to keep his small head in sight as it bobbed amidst a crowd of girls. The car had only third-class wooden benches. The priests had found seats and appeared to be absorbed in their prayer books. Ernst flung himself across the aisle into the last remaining space. Screeching with laughter, he held onto enough room for himself and Hans, in spite of the indignant stares of some of the girls.

"I wish we had little black books," said Ernst.

The girls managed to wriggle in among their companions as the train began to move. Hans leaned toward Ernst, his left hand unconsciously shielding his words from the two priests. "You know, I haven't had much to do with church lately. But at Christmas . . . when I see men like that, I wonder. Ernst, do you believe in heaven?"

"Of course. We call it the Thousand Year Reich."

"And hell?"

"The same thing. Germany is a complete universe." One of the priests looked up at them. "Remember the time Siegfried cut down the church bells?" Hans didn't answer. He was going home and he felt sorry for the priests. He put a hand up to quiet his friend, but Ernst's voice was louder than ever. "Are those two black mice bothering you?" Ernst had been a devout churchgoer as a child—but no more.

Why had there been no religious protest to Nazism? Hans knew that Ernst could not reconcile himself to the silence. Because he felt cheated, Ernst could not help demolishing his faith with ridicule, but Hans gave him no encouragement. He would hurt no one so close to Christmas.

At the other end of the car the B.D.M. leader, a broad-chested girl with fat legs pink from the winter sun, began to lead her girls in song. "Our flag leads us to eternity . . . Yes, the flag is more than death," they sang.

Hans felt sentimental and warm in the rattling coach. "Going home . . . going home . . ."

"Hey, you asleep?" said Ernst. His long body was loosely sprawled on the vibrating bench as though it were about to come apart. "You know, Hans, I feel like a Magi. We're almost there."

"Under an umbrella in the twilight," sang the girls, all stridency gone from their voices. Hans wasn't sure he felt like a Magi. His hands were empty of gifts, but there would be a star hanging over the end of the track. He felt safe.

"Look," he heard Ernst say, "we're passing a wreck." An engine and several cars, bombed or sabotaged, lay beside the tracks. Hans scarcely looked up. "I hate airplanes," he said.

"Would you hate them if Germany had any?"

"We have plenty. I hate them. Go to sleep, Ernst."

"Thank God, Heime isn't here, Hans. But staying behind was hard on him. Just because Siegfried wanted to spend Christmas shaking a spear . . ."

Hans didn't agree. Siegfried had stayed, and Siegfried was Heime's hero. Naturally Heime would stay with him, and the fact that Siegfried had insisted had nothing to do with it. The one he felt sorry for was Siegfried, who had said he wasn't going home because returning to army life would only seem harder by contrast. How could one go home to parents who like priest and priestess preserved the shrine of a heroically dead brother and say, "Mother, I'm home. The Fatherland doesn't need me in its finest hour." Hans couldn't help feeling sorry for the whole family.

Ernst spoke thoughtfully, with his head cocked to one side like an inquisitive child. "I don't think you know Heime very well. Our little toad has swallowed a wolf, and now it's gnawing at his insides. It isn't the same sort of wolf that's gotten into Siegfried, either. Wait till those two wolves notice each other."

"You're crazy," Hans told him. "Siegfried loves fighting, and Heime's a coward."

"Siegfried doesn't love anything. Well, maybe Hitler. If Hitler said the moon was made of cheese, he'd believe it."

"Believe it! He'd eat it," said Hans.

"I applaud that sense of loyalty in our friend Siegfried," said Ernst. "But why do we go on nibbling at the moon, Hans?"

"Now you've lost me."

"I mean . . . well, why do we still sit up in those towers? Why will we go back there after Christmas? I can understand Siegfried, but what about you, Hans?"

To Hans it didn't seem a matter of choice, but he was ready to play. "Go ahead, tell me. Why will I go back?"

"Very simple. 'Gott mit Uns' is stamped on all our belt buckles and you take it for Gospel. As long as God's on our side, we can't lose."

It had been a long time since Hans had thought about God, a longer time since he had entered a church, but the quiet black figures across the aisle made him whisper.

"I can't hear you," said Ernst loudly, and he went on to say that occasionally Satan tempted him to believe in God again. Ernst was rapidly moving into his element, but the priest did not look up.

With a mind as rapid and dexterous as the arms of an octopus, Ernst searched out every reason why Germany continued the war when it appeared to be lost. Perhaps it was fate, he suggested. Perhaps, as Dr. Goebbels said, it would go against the logic of history for an unknown such as Hitler to rise to such leadership and then be deserted by fate and his people. Perhaps Hitler was indeed Barbarossa, sprung from eternal sleep to restore the holy German soil to its dominion. Probably their comrades in the flak battery were fighting for less complicated reasons: for motherhood, for the Teutonic way of life.

"A man can fight simply for his friends," said Hans.

"Not I," said Ernst. "You're the only friend I've got, and I compliment you by supposing that you can take care of yourself."

"Well, duty and honor?"

"Hans, how old are you? There's a good and very practical reason why I fight. I'll be honest with you. It's the simplest reason of all. Cowardice. I'm afraid of Siegfried and of Captain Rabbe. I'm afraid of the SS. I'm afraid of losing my head."

"Every September is followed by May," sang the girls.

The train made a stop. In the steam-hissing silence of the station Hans heard the jingling of a horse-drawn sleigh. "We're near home," he said. The rest of the way he slumped with his eyes closed, affecting sleep for no other reason than to quiet his friend before they grew angry with each other. Despite the gulf in their thinking, Ernst had a trick of rousing Hans's mind to uncomfortable activity. It was Christmas, and Hans wanted to believe that victory was in the air, yet he could not overcome a sense of sadness at the heart of it all.

At the station they were the only ones to get off. The train went on up the valley toward Berchtesgaden. One of the B.D.M. girls waved to them. She was very pretty but she was not Gretchen, and that made all the difference.

"It's snowing." Hans held out his hands.

"Look . . . the station's been hit," said Ernst. All the glass was swept up in little piles. Hans wondered about his own house. A stray bomb, a misdirected letter . . . He would never have been informed. Fear took hold of him, subsided. "Don't be a fool, Amann," he told himself.

They trudged off through the blowing snow. Wind was piling it up against the statue of Bismarck. It wouldn't be possible to skate on the lake. By morning, the snow would be too deep.

Where their paths divided, they clasped hands.

"Sorry for the lecture," said Ernst. "Forgiven?"

"Forget it. Merry Christmas, Ernst."

"And a happy new year, Hans." Behind his glasses, Ernst's eyes were big.

Hans went silently through the dark streets. No footsteps rang on the pavements. All sound was suffocated by the same snow which had fallen on Varus and his defeated Roman legions, on Arminius with his victorious sword aimed westward as the Panzers were now aimed toward the English Channel. Anything could happen under snow, as long as it fell long enough and hard enough. Magical things could happen.

No lights shone from the houses. A dog howled, and then the sudden beam of a flashlight saved him from falling into a narrow splinter trench that had not been there before.

"What're you up to?" a voice said, and the flashlight

beaming into his face caught the snow like spilled iron filings. "Young Amann! Back from the crusades!" Müller, the block warden, whose cold face had the tint of blue meat, clapped him on the back. "Look out for these trenches," he cautioned, "and have a good holiday. Merry Christmas." It was the first time Hans had heard the block warden use any other salutation than "Heil Hitler."

Hans climbed the last slope. Around him the feathery flakes fell thickly. He couldn't see the house at all at first. Oh, God! Had it been bombed? Then it came vaguely, darkly into view. To the weary boy it was as lovely as a vision in a fairy tale.

"They aren't expecting me and they'll be asleep," he thought. "They'll think I'm the Gestapo or something." He tried the latch before knocking and found the door unlocked. In the musty hall he stamped the snow from his boots. There was still no response and he began to feel disappointed. What if the house were deserted? Then Klaus appeared, a hammer in one hand, a tiny dynamo flashlight in the other. "Who's there?" he demanded. The silhouette of his head and shoulders expressed a wary and tense concern.

"Father, it's me. Hans."

The hammer dropped to Klaus's side. "It's Hans!" he cried. "It's Hans come home!"

The house still had electric power and he switched on a lamp. Klaus looked as much frightened as surprised. "You haven't deserted?" Hans shook his head. "But you look fit," Klaus said proudly, laughing. "Dirty but fit."

"You too, Father. You, too." He could manage no more for the laughter and tears that competed inside him.

Klaus wiped his hand across his eyes. "I'm getting like your mother. Cry because she's happy, cry because she's sad. We must tell her." He seemed about to call out, then said, "Suppose I just tell her some refugees showed up out of the cold for a cup of soup. You stand here quietly and surprise her." His face was alive with excitement.

After some delay Lore appeared at the head of the stairs in an old bathrobe and without makeup. The bones of her face were stony slabs in the upward-slanting light, and her eyes were dark pits, ghostly. She flung back her dank hair and peered at the intruder. "Mother!" With a sob of recognition she descended upon Hans, embracing him furiously to make sure he was real. Holding him at arm's length, she studied her son. "Hans . . . how awfully tired you look! Your poor eyes, so red . . ." She sighed, as if replete. "Oh, but we've all changed . . . Hansel! To have you home! You must be starving. Come to the kitchen."

A suitcase waiting besides the front door disturbed him. "Where's Gretchen?" he asked, and was relieved by his father's reply. "Asleep. I'll wake her."

"Don't. Let her sleep."

"She'll want to see you," said his father.

But Gretchen appeared without being called. Her small pale mask of a face made her look to Hans like a figure from the stained glass of a medieval church. Her smile was radiant.

"Hans! How wonderful."

"I'm home for Christmas," he said, trying to empty his face of any expression that might reveal his feelings for her.

"Oh, now my face is all swollen up!" exclaimed Lore. Rubbing her eyes, she led them to the kitchen. There, she moved briskly and breathlessly, preparing a bowl of mutton broth with potatoes for the honored guest.

"There," she said. "There, Hans. Eat. You look so thin

. . . let me sit beside you. Have we changed very much? How long has it been? Since spring?"

"You haven't changed at all," Hans assured her, though inwardly he was shocked. She looked much older: harder, thicker, less beautiful. And there was more white in his father's hair. They seemed like strangers.

"Of course we have. All of us," said Lore. "Everything has changed, even this kitchen." Half the pots and pans had gone for war salvage. Hans looked about at the empty pegs on the wall, but most of all he looked at Gretchen. She was not as beautiful as he remembered her, but she had a loveliness that was rarer than beauty. He forced himself to look elsewhere, at the soup, at his mother, but always his gaze returned to Gretchen.

Without warning she rose from her chair, leaned forward and kissed Hans lightly on the lips, regained her seat with her chin cupped in the palm of her hand. So solemnly and unexpectedly had she moved that it was hard for him to believe she had moved at all. But his face must have foundered under the emotions that beset him, for she put her hand on his, and laughter wrinkled up her nose. Her laughter was candid and effortless and so utterly charming that Hans knew he would love her forever.

They all asked him questions about the battery. For the first time Klaus treated him as an adult, offering him beer, and granting his request for a drop of schnapps instead. Then it was his turn to ask questions. Things were as good as could be expected, they told him. At least they had food. There had been a bad air raid on the seventeenth. That's why the bag was packed, in case they had to make a dash for the shelter. He asked his father about the Volkssturm. Four times a week the old men put on moth-eaten firemen's uniforms and drilled with single-shot rifles left over from the Franco-Prussian war. Each man had been issued six bullets, which didn't fit in the guns. "You have to see it to believe it!" said Klaus. "Lore worries about my blood pressure. She ought to be worrying about my sanity." At the factory, lack of materials had put an end to the night shift. Most of the women employees, including Lore and Gretchen, were only working half time. That, and the blue ration stamps that Konrad had left over from his leave, were the most cheerful things they had to report.

Lore put bread on the table and a dish of cheese, the strong Bavarian cheese known affectionately as the country mailman's socks. Hans spread it thickly. The knife felt heavy in his hand. After the hours of anticipation, the excitement of homecoming, and the uncritical joy at the wonder of Gretchen, he was feeling the reaction. He was beginning to stagger inwardly like an overwound toy.

"I think you're tired, Hans," Gretchen said.

"Oh, he is," said Lore.

"I'm fine," Hans told them. He could feel his ears moving as he chewed. There was a very good chance he would fall asleep with a mouth full of crumbs.

"You're exhausted. We all are. And you're filthy, Hans. For goodness' sake, let's put some of the country back where it belongs." Telling Gretchen to put water on to boil, Lore went herself to prepare the tub. When the cupid-embossed zinc tank, a prize of his grandfather's early years, was ready, Hans entered it, naked and shivering, a sponge bag dutifully clasped in his right hand. There he settled, chin deep, as helpless as a drowned sailor, while the wind whined and whistled through the eaves and drummed like a brood of swallows in the chimney. After what seemed a long time, he pulled the plug out with his big toe, but the prospect of naked cold made him block the waste pipe with his heel. It was the start of another ice age, he mused, a glacial inundation that would bury everything, including the war. He imagined the house snuggling down into the yeasty snow. Outside, the storm was moving across Bavaria, falling upon all the small dark towns, filling in every foot-fall, every tank-tread track, every bomb crater. It had moved swiftly in from Russia. Deep and deepening lay the world.

Half asleep, Hans realized the water had turned cold and was sucking away around his heels. He crawled out, feeling scrubbed and clean all through. He was scarcely able to wrestle with the huge towel which seemed about to drag him to the floor. Towel-wrapped, he went shuddering down the short hall, shoving one foot in front of the other without his soles ever leaving the floor. On his old bed, the harlequin-patched feather bed was turned back. Again he shivered and yawned. It would be grand in bed with the cold sheets turning warm. With trembling fingers he pulled on his nightshirt. "I'm so sleepy I'm sick," he told himself. He took one uncertain step, caught his toe, stumbled, and fell onto the bed, where he lay with arms outstretched, mouth half open, fast asleep. Not even when his mother put out the light and pulled the feather bed over him did he stir.

Hans awoke early. He felt warm and satisfied, listening to sounds from the kitchen. He wanted to go back to sleep, but he could not command his foolish body, which had arisen early every morning for so long. He lay still, savoring the luxury of idleness. Finally he rolled out of bed, dressed, and began to rediscover the house, which he had not seen in almost a year. Instinctively he was drawn to the library. The door was ajar and he entered. When he trod on it, the carpet sent up a gray cloud. Dust lay everywhere, even on the seats of the chairs. He blew on the glass to see one of the pictures and then noticed a pair of feet sticking out of his grandfather's tall reading chair. Softly he went up behind and clasped his hands over Gretchen's eyes.

"You! Hans!" she shouted, half laughing.

"Do you read here often?" he asked her.

"All the time. I bring books up from the cellar. I know it's yours, but you don't mind, do you?"

"I'm happy. Anyway, it'll always be my grandfather's . . . It smells nice in here, of leather and cobwebs. But the dust . . . it's unbelievable." Gretchen explained that it was plaster dust from the last raid which she hadn't had a chance to clean up. "Well, plaster or not, the smell hasn't changed. I can't get used to the way the rest of the house smells."

"Poor food, too little soap, windows sealed up all the time against the blackout . . . War smells that way."

"But this room isn't shuttered."

"Because it isn't used. Well, except by me."

"Look out there. What a lovely day. Makes me feel young and hopeful," said Hans.

"Do you see all that stuff sparkling on the trees? It looks like icicles."

Hans saw that it was radar tinsel, dropped by the bombers to disrupt radar interception. The forest was full of it. "Have there really been that many raids? I didn't think they'd reach here."

"It hasn't been so bad," she told him.

"You know, you can see Berchtesgaden with a telescope on a clear day like this."

"I never speak of that place."

"You're funny," he told her. "You've got beautiful eyes just like his. Did you know that?"

"Like whose?"

"The Führer's."

"Don't make jokes. Not like that, Hans."

He had meant it as a compliment. He told her so, but she still seemed annoyed. Hans hunched over the telescope. "I can see the mountain where Barbarossa sleeps."

"You're impossible. I wish I could stay annoyed with you, for your own good."

"The story goes that he sits at a round table with his head on his hand, nodding away, with only his beard moving. It's grown twice around the table already, and when it goes around the third time, he'll wake up and take down his shield and a better time will dawn."

"Fairy tales. We're getting too old for them, Hans."

"I believe in fairy tales. So do you."

"Did Konrad write to you?" asked Gretchen. "He said he was going to."

"Once."

"Poor man. Loneliness is a terrible thing for anyone."

"He likes you," said Hans.

"Did he write you about the Gestapo?"

"He said they questioned him."

"I think they tortured him."

"Tortured!"

"Those little electrode things. You know."

"They have no right," protested Hans. But since the July 20th bomb plot, nothing was beyond the jurisdiction of the Gestapo.

"He didn't say much about it, but he looked ghastly when he came back. I asked a few questions, but he didn't answer. He just teased me about sailing away with him to the island of his dreams."

"I know he likes you an awful lot."

"You ought to hear Konrad on the subject of you," she said. "You'd think you were his son."

It was queer, Hans thought. She seemed so open on the

surface, but so much of what went on inside her was hidden.

"Would you like to try skiing?" he asked.

"I'd break a leg."

"Just out there. It's practically flat."

"Right now?"

"I haven't many 'nows,' " he reminded her. He couldn't stop time. It was the air he breathed, air with a rotten taste. "I wish you'd look after this clock when I'm gone. It's not good for the works to sit idle." Carefully he rewound the astral clock, turning the hands to the day and the month. One thousand years showed . . . The years of the Reich, thought Hans. The ancient clock began to tick, without urgency, without promise or threat. It was the pulse of infinity. Before it, they all were helpless.

Hans managed to find only one set of skis. They looked very small and something had been gnawing at the straps. "Look at this. It's not just rot. It must have been rats." It was a great disappointment, and he was moping about it when Lore marshaled her two young people. "We're having a tree this year," she told them, "and I want you to go out and fetch back a lot of that radar tinsel."

Hans pulled on his heavy jack boots. They had become such a part of him that in ordinary shoes he'd float away. Gretchen had unearthed an ancient pair of riding boots. "Ready?" Hans unlatched the door, and the first taste of winter air stabbed down his throat. Hunched over, arms hugged close to their sides, they went out into a white landscape where the snow lay very deep and as dry as sand.

"It's too pretty to trample," said Gretchen.

"You're not trampling," he told her. "You don't weigh enough." But each bootprint left behind was a small grave. "Hey, don't look up there . . . Don't look for planes on

Christmas Eve. They'll all be reading about Pickwick and Scrooge. They won't come." Hans knew where the Allied bombers would be on this first clear day. They'd be over the Ardennes, over the onrushing Panzer Lehr division and Uncle Konrad. If the Luftwaffe couldn't hold them back, that's where they'd be. He didn't say so to Gretchen, though.

Throughout the forest, on the bare limbs of the trees, on the surface of the snow and blown into balls by the wind, everywhere, the tinsel glittered. They collected it all afternoon, enough for ten trees.

"Look there! What a funny bird."

Like a stoop-shouldered little nun, a black bird pecked its way across the surface of the snow.

"It's a witch in disguise," said Gretchen.

"Our witch. Let's follow her. We'll nibble down her house. We'll take all the sugar cake home for supper. Don't let her get away." By the time the bird disappeared from their sight, Gretchen was lost. "The woods look eerie and strange," she said, and promised to scream at the first crack of a dry branch. Hans pretended he was lost, but with the first gold light of evening they stood on a hill above the Amann house. It was the long, smooth, swishing hill down which he had so often tobogganed into bedtime. Hand in hand they descended while above them the parapet of mountains turned rose red, iridescent in the late sun. Hungry, burning-cheeked, they arrived back to stand stamping and blowing in the front hall while the dusting of snow on their jackets formed into little silvery drops.

Lore already had the ornaments unpacked: wooden birds and animals from the ark with missing limbs and chipped paint, bells without clappers, and a disheveled angel for the top. "She belongs in a beerhall," said Hans.

"No," said Gretchen, "I think she's a chorus girl from an

asylum who's run away from her keepers. I like her. She belongs at the top."

But it was the radar tinsel that really made the tree. Klaus judiciously tested it with a match. It was safe enough, he proclaimed, for the lighting of their few hoarded candles.

Konrad's blue ration stamps had been squandered on the Christmas Eve dinner, which Gretchen and Lore prepared. They had learned to work well together, and Hans watched them, smiling contentedly. From the pots a rich aroma went up, seeming to overlay and quench the less lovely odors that were associated with wartime. "Oh, you merry, oh, you blessed," sang a boys' choir over the radio, and the Amann house snuggled down in the banked snow, its windows shuttered against the cold and the dark.

"I can't remember when I last ate like this. It's a Biblical feast," said Klaus. "Frau Amann, you've outdone yourself . . . You, too, Gretchen. Just look at that orange . . . where in heaven's name did you get it?"

"Magic." What other answer was there? And yet the goodness and the warmth of this family Christmas were as solid and tangible to Hans as a stone rolled away from his heart.

The party had officially done away with Christmas, calling it the "Festival of Jul," the celebration of the turning of the sun. But Lore sang the Lutheran hymns, all the old songs. She persuaded them all to sing, as if her encouragement were part of the lyrics. "You're not singing, Hans and Gretchen! You're not singing! Allelujah! Allelujah! Don't be magpies! Don't be magpies!" So they sang, his voice low and off-key, and Gretchen's so high and true it transported him. But it was Lore who supported them all, singing as though she were on a stage. Through vigor alone, much of her old beauty seemed restored in the candlelight. She sang lustily to the end. Then she let her head drop forward. "Oh, my," she said. "I'm too old," and she put her hand to her side.

"I've never heard you sing so well. I don't ever remember your voice as fine as it is tonight. That's the truth, upon my word of honor," declared Klaus, who had rosy cheeks and a carelessness of manner that was unlike him. They were all a little reckless and giddy from the warmth and the wine and a denied tension born of things in the future that could not be postponed.

A hammering at the front door cut short their singing abruptly. Nocturnal visits usually meant bad news, but this turned out to be a surprise.

"Mummers!" shouted Hans. "Come and see . . . the mummers are here!" Kings and queens and a tall Saint George were palely illuminated by the moon. A devil shook his horns and jabbed his long fork at the audience gathered in the doorway. Death was there, too, all in white with a bleached face and a scythe that caught the moonbeams. The mummers capered and sang. Hans would have enjoyed them, their old tradition, had he not detected in Gretchen's eyes the anxious look she so often wore when she believed herself unobserved.

Klaus called them all in for a drink.

"Honestly," said Lore, "that Death's enough to give anyone nightmares."

Klaus opened a bottle of Danziger Goldwasser, swimming with golden flakes. This was a ceremonial token, and one which the mummers sipped solemnly from small glasses. One of them coughed. As they were about to make their parting salutations, Death said his feet were cold and he was through with mumming. If it was all right with the Amanns, he'd warm up a bit—all this in a disembodied, gasping voice which Hans did not recognize until the crepe death's head came off.

"Ernst! How'd they ever get you into this?" Ernst shrugged and grinned. It was Christmas, after all, and they toasted one another in the rosy light of the candles that stood unwinking in the still air.

"Here's to Gretchen. Have they told you how pretty you look tonight?" said Ernst.

"You're teasing, Ernst, but thank you anyway," she replied. He gave what he called the optimist's toast: "To the losing of the war." And the pessimist's: "When?" This brought from Klaus an irresolute "Grrumph!" Perhaps even on Christmas and all in fun, this was too strong a toast.

Ernst finally left, disappearing quickly into the pale night. Over the surface of the snow, flakes were sent hissing by a wind from the mountains. Klaus bolted the door, and Lore started caroling again. She sang as she cleared the table, and Gretchen sang as she helped her. Reflectively, Hans ate the orange, which no one had touched. He had meant to keep half for Gretchen, but once he'd tasted it, he could not stop until he had eaten it all. This made him feel guilty, and he told her so.

"But it was meant for you. You're the honored guest, aren't you?" And to make him feel twice as guilty she presented him with a book. "It's Schiller's *William Tell*," she said. "The one Konrad likes so much."

He too had a present for her. "It isn't much. It's just something I whittled at the battery." At least he'd been able to wrap the thing. Gretchen held the package to her ear and shook it, acting out a pantomime of curiosity over its contents. "It's supposed to be a horse."

"Of course it's a horse. How beautiful!" She fingered the work with trembling hands.

He became embarrassed. "Look. Mother's lighting the candles on the tree."

"Thank you, Hans. I shall always treasure this."

The few candles on the Christmas tree burned with a wonderful golden brilliance, lighting the kitchen, the familiar walls, the faces that Hans loved. The family sang, comforting their hearts, while the thin candles burned down. Within a short while they were dangerously low, and Lore snuffed them out one after another, leaving only the melted stubs and the black vein that had stood at the heart of each flame.

Their throats had given out as completely as the candles before they went to bed. They were all reluctant to abandon Christmas Eve, yet it was over. Hans lay in bed listening to the old house creak and groan with the prying wind. Here childhood lingered, and a vision of life as fleeting and healthy as laughter. In the darkness he heard the solemn ticking of the astral clock, the pulse of the old house itself. As he listened, the mechanism whirred and gathered itself to chime the hour of midnight.

Hans awoke Christmas morning with the words already formed. "Why should I go back?" he said aloud to himself. "Just to listen to old Rabbe and wait around to get murdered." It seemed senseless to return to the battery. He could join the Volkssturm instead and defend his own home, if it came to a final fight. He'd fight harder and be worth more to Germany. It all seemed so sensible on Christmas morning.

Later he broached the idea to his father. Klaus didn't seem surprised. "So you don't want to go back," he said. "I don't know of any way you could be transferred. Still, there's always a way."

"What way do you mean, Father?"

"I mean you can hide," said Klaus.

"You mean desert? You wouldn't mind?"

"I've no sons to spare, Hans."

Hans was shocked. He was no deserter. Good Lord, no! And the idea was not discussed again, though it stayed in his mind. He had to play hard those last few days to keep the idea from growing. Three days to go, then two, then only one. His two worlds were like icebergs drifting apart.

The radio no longer told of victory in the west. The eastern front was dormant. But the bombers stayed away, and every day more children brought their sleds and skis to the hill above the Amanns' house. That last day Hans borrowed a set of skis and persuaded Gretchen to put on his old pair; he had mended the straps. "You know I'm certain to break both legs," she said, but she joined him just the same and took her spills. If only he could break a leg accidentally! He knew very well he could never do it deliberately, and the trees and fence posts flying by on either side never touched him.

Hans dug his poles in beside Gretchen, who sat in the snow with her skis standing up. Puffball clouds, radiant snow, a pretty girl . . . He wanted to say, "Isn't it all so beautiful," and "I love you," but what if she'd laughed at him the way she was laughing at her twisted skis? "What a skier you are," he told her. "What a mess." And he helped her up, an arm around her waist. She didn't laugh then. She knew. He could have said anything. He could have said, "Take care of me, Gretchen, tell me what to do." But tomorrow would come regardless. The planes would come. "Have you ever watched ice-yachting on the Chiemsee? . . . No? Well, you should see it. I guess they don't do it any more." They were standing close now, as nearly face to face as two skiers could be. "You know something?" a voice said, surprising him because it was his own. "You look great. Really beautiful!"

"You're a sweet boy, Hans."

"That's not fair, saying that."

"Well, then, I'll tell you what's wrong with you, shall I?"

"That would be better."

"Absolutely nothing." She gave him a lovely smile. If they had skied off together full tilt into the tree at the foot of the hill, he wouldn't have felt it at all.

With sudden resolution he said, "I want to tell you something, Gretel. I want your opinion about a talk I had with Father." And he told her everything. "But I couldn't desert like that."

"Why couldn't you, Hans?" Her eyes were brooding. Her mouth smiled a little without changing her eyes.

"You've heard of a soldier's honor?"

"Hans, there's something I want to tell you. Show you, I mean." Undoing the top of her jacket, she produced a locket that he had often noticed around her neck. "It's a strange time to talk about him, but look . . ." She pulled the chain over her head and opened the locket for him to see a picture of a dark, studious-looking boy.

"A sweetheart, Gretchen?" he asked. Though occasionally jealous of Konrad, he had never thought of the possibility of some other rival.

"No. Well, he was my cousin. I had a crush on him."

A flatness had entered her voice which reminded him of the night she had arrived.

"Did he die in the bombing?"

"No. Shot."

"In Russia?"

"In Dresden. By an SS firing squad. He'd been making

'Down with Hitler' posters. I never knew anyone with a stronger sense of honor than he had." Hans was at a loss for words. "Does it shock you? That I have had such friends, I mean?"

"I'm amazed, that's all. I can't be angry at you. Please smile for me." She did not lift her face, and suddenly, for the first time, he touched her. He put his fingers gently under her chin. "Smile, Gretchen . . . Are you thinking about him?"

"About him . . . and about Konrad, and about tomorrow. I can't bear to think of tomorrow . . ." It was a cry of pain. Hans couldn't bear it either.

"We'll ski," he told her. "We'll ski recklessly and end up together in the hospital." All afternoon they tried, but neither had a taste for self-mutilation. All they could show by evening was an assortment of bruises. Then the owner of the skis appeared on the hill to reclaim them, and there was nothing to do but walk slowly down, hand in hand, to the Amann house. With its snow-laden, icicled roof, it looked very much as though it had been fashioned in some magic confectionery to attract unwary children.

In the morning Hans would be leaving. No one spoke of it at supper and they conducted the evening with the accustomed ritual. Perhaps the laughter was false, the singing shrill, but they all tried hard. Klaus unraveled the old jokes. Lore fussed over her son, insisting that he take a hot bath. In bed, as Hans pulled his quilt right up to his nose and listened to the wind soughing through the eaves, there came the first suggestion that this might be such a night as the Amann family had never known. The cellar radio had reported a formation of heavy enemy aircraft in the Hanover–Brunswick area. The usual thing. Klaus made no mention of it until a succession of radio reports checked against his grid map of Germany showed the raiders moving steadily south. Finally he roused Hans from half sleep, made him dress. By this time the radio music had been replaced entirely by the alarm-clock ticking signal that meant a raid was imminent. The village sirens took up the warning alarm until the windowpanes trembled.

Hans was the last to dress. When he came down, the others were systematically opening the windows against the danger of blast. A cold wind blew through the house. "All right, that's enough," Klaus commanded, and they left for the shelter, suitcases in hand, as though they did not expect to return. Searchlights were already stabbing the sky, but the planes had a long way to come yet. Besides, why would they come here, where there was more history than munitions? "Slow down," Hans told Gretchen. He reached for her bag, but she clung to it and to her teddy bear with the force and fury of a young Medea.

"It's not only the raiders," Klaus explained. "But if you get to the shelter late, you stand, or you sit in sewage water."

Hans found out when he got there. The shelter was the town sewer, and it was already crowded when they arrived. Klaus pushed ahead and found a place under some warm pipes. If the pipes were full of steam and if they burst . . . well, it was an added hazard, but who would want to stand through what might be long hours of bombardment? Worst of all was the smell. There was no getting away from that. Hans tried breathing through his teeth. He was surprised to see a nun with a troop of little girls who were holding hands. He didn't think nuns were allowed to take charge of children any more. There was an organ, too, in this foul place, so old and creaky it might have done service in the catacombs.

Hans looked around for Ernst but didn't see him. There were other shelters in town, better ones, he hoped. He did see Siegfried's parents, and hoped they wouldn't recognize him. But they did. He tried to smile, and he lied when they asked about Siegfried, saying he was too valuable at the battery to be spared. He could see the lie had been transparent. Frau Hellpack looked hurt, and what she said surprised him. "He knows we're afraid of him. That's why he doesn't come home." Hans was seeking words to deny it when the bombers arrived and ended the painful conversation. Hans was aware of them before he heard the guns, as though a slow breath wafted over the town. The knowledge that thousands of others were at that moment listening to the first whispers of the imminent storm gave a ritual quality to the scene.

There were the guns, thank God. For the first time Hans endured the horror of waiting helplessly. The far-off bombs sounded like someone knocking on the outside of a tub. But the tub was the whole universe. Hans heard the drum of the bomb sticks hitting one after another. Convulsively he flung his arms around Gretchen. She was crying. "You'll be all right. You're safe with me," he shouted, but he knew she could not hear a word. With a sort of anguish they embraced, not kissing, simply pressing close, while a milky dust filled the air in the shelter and shrapnel tinkled and hissed in the street above.

The tumult diminished periodically, but there was no "all clear." The raiders came again and again. During the lulls, the people talked. A few ate sandwiches. The nun pumped the old organ pedal furiously and screeched out a hymn. Amid all the bedlam and discomfort, what Hans minded most was the heat—the heat and the smoke that came with it. Klaus had taken off his jacket. "It's hot as hell," he said. We're deep enough, thought Hans. He dared not remove his own jacket, for fear of disturbing Gretchen. Incredibly, she had fallen asleep. He looked at her defenseless face. The cold

drawn look had left it. How beautiful she was! Since he had
seen her cousin's picture, he had no doubt that she was
Jewish, but that no longer mattered. He felt pleased at his
own courage and independence, and he knew with sudden
conviction why he was going back to the battery. To make
Gretchen safe, to save the Fatherland, to share the fate of
his comrades; these were all noble reasons. There were
others, too: fear of the SS, and fear of another raid like this,
which was far worse than being engaged in combat, because
he was unable to strike back.

"It's over," Klaus said at last.

Other people were stirring, dusting themselves off. The
nun was calming her children. Up above, the sounds had
changed to shifting gears, racing motors, and the tinkle of
ambulance bells.

"Let's go home, Gretchen." For a moment it was as if
they had fallen in love from sheer relief. He helped her up.
In feather-trimmed hats and furs, in old homburgs, in ski
suits and overalls, the people climbed up into the roaring
inferno that had been their town. Tiny thermite bombs,
weighing two pounds apiece, had been sown by the raiders
as thickly as seed. The fire engines and the rescue squads
were helpless amid the fiery harvest.

"Come on," Hans shouted at Gretchen.

"Where are you going?" she shouted back.

He didn't know. He felt lost. People were scurrying in
every direction under a blizzard of sparks. Hans and
Gretchen ran through the burning streets wildly, turned this
way and that by demolition and by fire. "There's something
in the air," sang Hans giddily. This couldn't be his town. No
town could change so vastly in a few hours.

At last they were out of the fire, and they turned to look
back.

"I feel like Nero," he said.

"If they've bombed the train track, you won't be able to leave," she said.

They trudged up the hill, growing more tired and apprehensive at every step. Hans couldn't imagine the old house demolished, a smoking hulk, but that it might have vanished without a trace seemed oddly possible. It certainly didn't belong in this world. Yet there it stood, thank God, with no sign of change or damage except shattered window glass. His parents were already sweeping up and closing the shutters. There was china strewn about, and in his bedroom, glass fragments littered the floor. It was icy cold. He unhooked the shutters. Funny how the blast had left the snow on the window ledge undisturbed. Idly he packed the snow into a ball and was about to throw it out into the night. But the branches of the nearby trees all looked undamaged and clean. He left the snowball where it was and fell into bed without removing his clothes.

It was still dark when Klaus gave him a gentle shake. "Hans . . . Hans, it's time."

After breakfast they all slogged into a dull yellow morning that brooded heavily over the house and the town. They took the mill path, avoiding the smoldering fires. There the snow was trampled and old, flecked with soot, patterned and repatterned by passing feet and the urine of horses.

The station was still there. The track, too, and the train. Their parting was short.

"I have a feeling I'll never . . ."

Gretchen cut him short. "Nothing will happen to you," she said, as she had before, but this time her voice was imploring.

"I'll write. I'll write to you all. It's a promise this time."

"Be careful, Hans," his mother cautioned. She had her handkerchief in her hand, so he promised, a promise he would later remember with a faint smile. Then the station-master waved his baton. The train sighed and stirred, and without any consciousness of having made a move, Hans was on it. He was pulling away, and his future seemed to close about him as he went.

Ernst was probably aboard too, but he didn't want to see Ernst, or anyone else just then. He wanted things he couldn't have. He felt like crying, but that would never do. So in the end he slept. When they arrived at their stop, it was Ernst who woke him. "Hello, Devil," Hans said. "Welcome back to hell."

THIRTEEN

E<small>XCEPT FOR ONE BOY</small> who had been wounded in a raid at home, all the members of the students' battery had returned. Captain Rabbe greeted them with, "Now you're here for the duration," his voice brimming with impartial malice. "The fatted calves, so to speak, and I expect from you just what Jesus Christ would expect from his apostles: the whole man, body and soul, if any of you have a soul."

At first the alarms were few. Throughout January Hans wrote letters to Gretchen, full of phrases more fond and well chosen than he could possibly have managed face to face. Captain Rabbe no longer censored their mail, but he was emphatic in warning them that their time of repose was running out.

The radio had ceased to speak of victory, and was again using shopworn phrases: "regrouping of forces," "strategic withdrawal," "defense of the Siegfried Line." The Panzer Lehr division, with over a thousand armored vehicles in Normandy, had been decimated at Saint-Lô and reconstituted again for the Ardennes offensive. Now it had virtually ceased to exist outside Bastogne. There was no word from Konrad. Russian tanks supported by Tartar cavalry were within two hundred kilometers of Berlin. "Remember," Captain Rabbe told them, "it is up to men like you to gain enough time for the Führer to assemble new troops and weapons. If you fail in your duty, your families will be murdered by yellow Siberians and black Africans. They are coming, men, make no mistake. The jets you are defending are all that can stop them."

Hans waited and wrote anxious letters home. February came, and the first thaw. Hans sent Gretchen a letter with a love poem that he thought quite good and very bold.

Until the middle of winter the great Fatherland offensive which should have swept the Allies into the sea absorbed all bomber attacks. Then, less suddenly than it had begun, the offensive was over, dead. As a grim signpost of things to come, Dresden was bombed for three successive days until it was no longer an inhabited city. The Führer threatened a "death mist" in reprisal. As soon as the jets were ready in force, the death mist would end the war in one terrible hour.

How many rungs to Jacob's ladder? How high to the top of Babel's tower? No higher than Hans had climbed. Climbing had become his life, it seemed, and then the raids became so incessant that the young gunners seldom came down at all. For days on end they watched the American squadrons maneuvering like schools of silver minnows for their attacks on Munich. Sometimes they had to sleep on the towers, while Captain Rabbe, massively smiling, addressed them from below. This was the final test, he told them happily. The first sign of shirking was the first moment of decay. He expected no cowards among them.

"I don't know whether I'm a coward or not, but I'm too tired to worry about dying," said Ernst. "Rabbe's jolly mood is a sure sign not many of us will go home on two feet."

Not because he shared Ernst's gloom, but because their constant area firing, along with poor supply, had reduced the daily allotment of shells to a ridiculously small number, Hans began to reconsider transferring to the Volkssturm. A talk with Captain Rabbe would have to be the first step. There were only enough bullets left to keep two towers busy, not eight, he explained. Surely Captain Rabbe could see his point. But Captain Rabbe shouted him down. Ammunition was coming. In the meantime, he could throw rocks. Spitballs, if need be. Red-faced, Hans returned to the tower where they had been confined all day and the night before as well.

"My sinuses are killing me," groaned Ernst. "Oh . . ." His neck seemed to have grown longer, and he stretched it continually. "Hans, don't think I'm being morbid or anything like that, but I've got a few personal things. You'd see they got home, if anything . . ."

"Shut up, Ernst. Nothing'll happen."

"It's my head, I guess. Oh, Lord . . . it's the weather, too. I had a look at the report. This is the only clear area in Germany, just about. We're sure to have a night of it."

"I never knew the sun could set in so many ways until I came up here. Green, pink . . . What a sight."

"It looks like a severed head tonight."

"You really do feel bad, don't you?"

"Terrible."

"I've got a sort of empty feeling inside," said Hans. "I usually do."

"I've got that too."

The red sun lowered itself through a pillar of cloud, soft and full of magic, a stage set for an opera. Hans wondered what the weather was like in England. Rain and fog, probably. He could almost see the puddled runways, the pilots with their collars turned up, the propellers beginning to turn, fretting the puddles. In Switzerland, it would still be bright, on the highest peaks, on the last winging skiers. Farther south in Morocco, storytellers would be telling tales to lazy camel caravans, tales of princesses and thieves, in the smoky glow of lanterns. Back home, under the mountain's shadow, it would be dark by now. With Konrad there he wondered what his family would be doing. He'd received Gretchen's letter only this morning. Konrad had been released from the army as a convalescent, but not a whole one. He'd left a hand behind. Even so, Hans could not think of Konrad as unlucky. He was there with Gretchen, with his family, in the warmth of a home as night came on.

Hans wondered if he was a coward. Maybe his cherished courage was only shame at feeling afraid. But what use was courage on this fragile stilt tower, manning an outranged gun? He would rather be anywhere, even among those brown camel drivers of Morocco, than here, under the prying moon which spilled its thick honey light into the faces of his friends.

Down below, Rabbe prowled with his machine pistol crooked under his arm.

"Things don't look right," said Ernst. "My head's going to burst. I may faint if I have to stay here all night."

In the forest, the trees were motionless.

"It's a bomber's moon, all right," said Hans.

"We'll hear them a long way off. We'll be ready," said Siegfried.

"For what? To die? You know we'll never hit anything."

A cloud came, rained on them, and blew away. The drops gathered on the railing.

"I've a perfect right to be sick if I have to," grumbled Ernst.

"There's nothing wrong with you." Siegfried spoke with an air of authority which was lost on Ernst.

"My head! The pain's driving me crazy . . . Let me pass. I'm going down."

"You stay here and do your job like the rest of us, Ernst!"

"Everything all right up there?" shouted the captain from below.

"Yes, Herr Captain. We're short of ammunition, though," Siegfried called back.

"What time do you make it?"

"A quarter to twelve, Herr Captain."

Six, seven more hours of night. Three hours at most to wait for the raiders. If they came, two hours at least to endure them. Two hours: time for one good ski run and return, time to hear most of *Parsifal,* time to transfer supper from his stomach to his small intestine, time to read *William Tell.* As Hans sat waiting for sounds in the distance, each minute seemed unending.

"Listen. Isn't that something?" said Siegfried.

"Nothing," replied Ernst.

This was the momentary pause, the endless moment while the dark fiddlers raised their bows.

"He's right! They're coming!" cried Hans.

"We'll give 'em hell," said Siegfried.

"Remember our walking tour?" said Ernst. "Remember, Hans? When this is over, we'll go for a whole week."

"Of course we will."

Ernst held out his hand. Hans shook it firmly, though he considered the gesture unduly dramatic. "Agreed. That's a pledge."

As the raiders moved into their sector, Captain Rabbe

gave the order to fire. Like luminous oranges, the tracers went up to meet the ruin which poured from the skies. Hans had once imagined glory in it. Now a thousand million bare-armed housewives seemed to be beating their rugs against his eardrums. He felt the impact of every stroke, and was afraid.

Their ammunition was entirely spent on the first wave of raiders. Heime went down for more. When he did not come back, Siegfried followed him. "What about us?" said Ernst. "They won't come back."

Hans knew that they would. He tried to comfort Ernst. "We're as safe up here as anywhere," he said, but he really didn't believe it. He had no excuse to leave. The only escape was in his mind, to the mountains, home.

The two boys waited with the helpless terror of the condemned as the raiders passed over again, bombing the jet airfield. Flak opened up around them like pure white cascading flowers, and they had to cling to the jostling gun to keep from falling.

In the interludes Hans contrived a frantic conversation.

"I'll need a good hot bath when this is over. And listen, Ernst, when we go walking, what do you say to Innsbruck?"

"I wonder what they're thinking about up there," said Ernst.

"I've always liked Kufstein better."

"I'm sorry, Hans."

"That's all right. So you prefer Innsbruck."

"That's not what I mean, Hans. I'm sorry I keep thinking about the raid. I haven't as much nerve as you have."

"Do you know how to ski, Ernst? You look a bit fragile."

"I get winded . . . But walking . . . God, they're coming again."

The raiders burst out of the stabbing midnight. Their bombs fell. Hans felt as if the first one, which hit along the line of towers, had gone off between his teeth. He saw a jagged cloud, the star of an explosion, then a pandemonium of explosions and flames.

"We're falling!" screamed Ernst. Like a great tree cut through at its base, the eighty-two-foot tower fell, slowly at first. For a moment Hans was aware of Ernst's face embalmed by the fiery glare. Then his own bones and sinews were wrenched and unsocketed by the concussions. The ground hurtled up, faster and faster.

A tree partly broke his fall. It spun him like a rag doll to the ground, where he landed with dirt forced between his teeth. Hans tried to crawl away from the tower, which glowed white hot as it disintegrated. He thought he heard Ernst's voice, thought he saw him beating at his trousers and jacket, from which flames burst like red blossoms. Then there was nothing but darkness and a pulse that kept beating slowly. When he awoke, everything around him was quiet and gray, and he could feel each deliberate breath. There was smoke in the air, and the honest smell of heartwood laid open from the felled trees.

"Why am I lying here?" he asked himself. "I mustn't lie on the ground. I'll catch cold." But he didn't move. Was that Ernst's voice again? "I've hurt myself, Hans, I've hurt myself." He turned his head but he couldn't see Ernst. Slowly memory returned. Even more slowly he realized that he was badly hurt. He felt no pain, but he knew about the swift anesthesia of shock which followed a severe wound. When he had enough strength, he'd yell for help. When he had the strength. The sun came up. A butterfly in February? Or was it March? Surely it was too early for butterflies. It seemed like a sign of some sort sitting there on his chest. He watched with a kind of horror as it waltzed in the air. If it came back tomorrow, would he be able to see it? Or would it flatten its wings across eyes that couldn't see? Hans cried out for help until his voice gave out.

"You . . . water . . . help me . . ." came an injured voice. It sounded small and plaintive, pleading for dignity amid the solitude of pain. The boy crawled slowly toward Hans, his features rigid and his upper lip distorted.

"Water . . . water . . ." said the boy again. With his mouth still open, he made a gurgling noise. Then great ropes and clots of blood poured from his mouth. He collapsed to the ground and Hans watched him as in a dream. He had no water and he said so, but the stranger didn't answer. He rocked to and fro, saying his name repeatedly: "My name is Fritz Dressler, my name is Fritz Dressler, my name . . ." as though trying to prove to himself that he was still alive. The words became halting, indistinct. Then he was still.

Hans was alone. A small red squirrel stared at him from a broken tree, and they shared a momentary joy at discovering another living being. Throughout the morning, consciousness came and went like the sky above, which opened and shut, sun and cloud and sun again, exploding into knives of gold and silver. If Gretchen would only come. "Gretchen," he said to a dim shape hovering there. He needed the girl's steady heart and light touch. "Gretchen?" A figure knelt beside him.

"Hans, you're alive."

It was Siegfried, smeared with soot. Words tumbled out of him. Not a tower was left standing. He'd sent Heime for help, and he'd searched through the ruins. Everyone else was dead except for Ernst. Ernst had been burned and was barely breathing. "Where are you hit?" he asked. Hans didn't know. His head felt full of chipped rock. His left arm had no feeling at all.

"I want some water," he said. Siegfried brought it, brought blankets, too, and a waterproof. He said it was going to rain or snow. "You were lucky. Our tower was the only one that didn't get a direct hit."

Siegfried brought hot liquid from somewhere and carefully held the spoon to Hans's lips. "I can't get Ernst to eat either," he said.

Before morning it snowed lightly, great winged flakes, better than rain. The pain was coming. Hans felt it in waves, but now and then he slept, and tossed in an ancestral nightmare. Hackelblock and the furious hunt trampled over his body, an endless stream of equine fury, with great hoofs and annihilating pain. He dreamed of his father, too. "Take this hammer," his father said. "See where my hand is? That's where to strike." Where his hand was, Hans saw the head of a lamb, and he struck with all his might, uttering a loud grunt like a woodcutter, and feeling the pain of the felled lamb in his body, feeling the bubbles around its lips around his own. He was the lamb, and his father stood by, telling him never to give a name to the animal one has to butcher, never even flick a fly from its back. Then the lamb grinned at him, a lipless breathless grin. All the lambs grinned. He was on the top of a vast pile of lambs stacked up in neat rows like firewood. He began to worry about those underneath, those at the bottom, but when he looked they were flattened. They were just wool, neatly pressed on the ground. Somewhere the wool began to burn. He smelled it, felt the roaring and the flaming inside him and heard Siegfried, soothing. "It's just a bad dream, Hans. You're all right. Any minute now, Heime will come with help."

Heime did not come the second day. The raiders came

instead. Fighters this time, but there was nothing left of the flak battery for them to attack, so they flew away.

"Heime'll come once it's dark," said Siegfried.

Hans slept intermittently. From time to time he heard Siegfried's voice. Ernst was still alive, the voice said, but Hans was too full of pain and exhaustion to care. He did not even open his eyes.

"Captain Rabbe!" shouted Siegfried. "Hans is alive! We're over here . . . Captain Rabbe!"

Hans stirred. The sun flamed in his eyes.

"Thank God he's all right," said Siegfried. But Captain Rabbe was not all right. His red-veined eyes gazed about vacuously while his mouth gnawed hideously on nothing. Even Hans could see that Captain Rabbe was mad. Siegfried offered him a can of soup salvaged from the barracks but Captain Rabbe did not seem to hear. He fumbled through the ruins until he had reached a spot where the burned tower supports formed a loose cage about him. Here a single, inexpressive shriek tore from his throat. As if in obedience to this signal, the captain immediately sat down, drew up his knees, rested his head upon them, and did not move as long as there was light to see him.

Hans could not sleep at all the second night. He had one thought, one sensation: pain. It filled the world. His body cried and groaned in pain, yet he seemed able to view his own suffering from a dispassionate distance as though he had not one body but two. The hurt body was delirious, calling for water, calling for Gretchen, while the other observed it idly and longed for sleep. Vaguely, even rather gratefully, it was aware of Siegfried's concern and his attempts to help. It wanted to say thank you, but the first body closed its lips and rolled back and forth.

"I guess it's no use," Siegfried muttered. "I guess it's no

damn use . . ." Then louder, "Don't die, Hans . . . We've been through such hell together. Don't die."

He hadn't thought of dying for a long time now. It no longer frightened him. If he could die like a hawk that goes to sleep under a folded wing, that would be all right. Even the hurt body did not seem to mind. It no longer screamed, but groaned rhythmically, the sound of an old man dying, while the dispassionate Hans tried to make each groan into a prayer.

Night came again, and a little after dark a motor stuttered up the hill. An electric torch bobbed through the clumps of debris.

"Over here! We're over here!" cried Siegfried.

The torch shone in Hans's face.

"He's dead. I'll bet you fifty marks," said a stranger's voice. Then Hans heard his own voice piping, "I'm still alive. Can't you hear me? I'm alive." The stranger laughed. "We'll take your word for it, old man. Stretcher bearers, over this way . . . two stretchers. Look after that burn over there, medic. I don't know what's keeping him alive, poor devil."

Hans felt someone cut off his boots. He thought he heard Siegfried crying, but he couldn't tell for sure. He tried to tell Siegfried everything was all right. He couldn't because they'd shoved a needle into his arm before lifting him onto a stretcher. "Siegfried . . ." Then the pain of motion closed over him.

FOURTEEN

SOMETHING was making a squealing noise like a run over dog. Hans wanted to help the animal or to shut it up, but he was making the noise and he couldn't stop it. Two nurses looked down on him. With them was a doctor in a rubber apron. "They never make a clean hole, those bomb fragments. . . . More ether, nurse." The scene dissolved as Hans departed into another world where pain was conquered. It was very still. Death was there somewhere, but it wasn't the terrible rider on the pale horse. Death wasn't strong at all. It was weak and quiet, like a mist. It could be pushed aside as easily as cobwebs.

Hans thought he had died. Then pain and the stench of sepsis and anesthetic convinced him he was alive and in a hospital ward. His bed was screened off and his left arm was immobilized in plaster. It smelled horribly, and he called for help. "Gretchen! Gretchen!" He sank back exhausted. When he came to again, a nurse was standing beside the bed. She had Gretchen's Byzantine eyes, full of sadness, and the same acceptance of man's inhumanity. "Who's Gretchen? She must be very nice."

"I think I'm bleeding," he managed in a weak frightened voice.

The nurse answered him reassuringly, "What do you think I'm here for? I'll have a look." There was a brief silence. "Well, so you are. Just a moment . . . That's all right now. Rest's all you need." She looked at a card attached to the cot. "Yes, Hans, try to sleep. There's nothing to worry about."

Within a couple of days the nurse had pillows behind his back and was threatening to get him into a wheelchair. "We've much more serious cases . . . not half enough beds." For the first time it occurred to him to ask where he was. To his amazement he learned he was in his own town, what was left of it. Then why hadn't his parents, why hadn't Gretchen come to see him? "They have come," the nurse explained, "when you were asleep. You've been sleeping almost twenty-four hours a day. Sleep's the best cure. Don't be impatient."

When his parents came the following day, he was awake. His father was very controlled, his mother just the opposite. Tears kept trickling down, making marks on her powdered cheeks. "Hans . . . Oh, Hans!"

"Listen to her," said Klaus, blowing his nose and twisting his hat in both hands. Awkwardly he leaned over and rumpled his son's hair.

Questions followed. "Are we tiring you by asking so much?" Lore was still drying her eyes with the back of her hand, like a child.

"Your soldiering is finished, Hans. You're a civilian," said his father. "The school sent a petition to Himmler. No more fighting." Hans noticed that Klaus now wore the Volkssturm band on his arm.

"How many of us are left, then?" Hans asked.

"You and Heime and Siegfried. Ernst, too. He was badly burned, Hans. He needs a special room."

"Some of the other boys must be here . . . They weren't all killed."

Klaus turned his hat half round in his hand, studied it.

"We were so fortunate, Hans, that you were spared to us." His mother seemed on the verge of tears again.

"They died instantly, Hans, without pain," said his father. "Forty-two boys. Besides the four from your tower, only the captain . . . Captain Rabbe . . . survived."

"I saw him there, under the tower . . . I remember . . ."

"He's here in the hospital. The doctor calls it catatonia. He hasn't uttered a sound or moved a muscle since he arrived. They don't think he ever will."

Hans asked about Gretchen and Konrad.

"You've heard about Konrad's hand?" asked Klaus.

"Yes, but I mean, why haven't they been to see me? Why's Mother looking so strange?"

"They've been wanting to come. Gretchen sends her love, and now that you're able to see visitors . . ."

In midsentence a determined-looking nurse appeared and over Hans's protests ushered his parents out. The patient needed his strength, she explained, for the following day would mean an introduction to the wheelchair.

The wheelchair required all his strength, but it was good to move about with the ersatz rubber wheels rolling silently down corridors smelling of beeswax and turpentine. He wanted to see Ernst, but was told his friend wasn't allowed to have visitors.

Back in the ward, his bandage was changed. "Wonderful," declared the nurse. "You're healing perfectly. The doctor will be delighted." But at the sight of the high welted ridge along his arm, stitched as by a cobbler's thread, Hans felt sick. "None of that," she told him, "or I shall have to send your guests away. You have a young lady visitor today."

"Gretchen!" He recognized her footsteps before she appeared around the screen. "Gretchen. I thought you'd never come."

"I'll always come when you need me."

"Will you?"

"Always. Konrad is here, too."

Hans expected to see a veteran broken in his country's wars. His uncle was far from that. Emaciated, with a bandage for a left hand, he still gave the appearance of great strength. His very thinness somehow made his vigor more striking. "Hans, thrice welcome. This is a wonderful moment." He held out his hand. Hans took it. "How's it been, old man? They say the first hundred wounds are the hardest." Laboriously he helped Gretchen take off her jacket. "I'm something of an expert."

Hans watched him pull a cigarette from his breast pocket, put it between his teeth, and find a match. Gretchen moved as though to light it for him, but he struck the match against the plaster cast on Hans's arm.

"I hear the war's over for you," said Konrad.

"That's what Father tells me."

"The Americans crossed the Rhine at Remagen yesterday. Very soon it will be over for us all."

"I wish you meant that," said Gretchen.

"I do. How long can it last, Gretel? The army's crumbling at the edges like stale cake. We've nothing left but Cossack deserters and horse artillery. Instead of Panzers we're sending out bicycle boys to face tanks. This is sunset and I say amen."

"He doesn't mean amen at all," said Gretchen. "He means to become involved. I hate it!"

Hans was confused. He turned to Konrad, who made a joke of it. "Gretel, if men listened to female advice, we'd live out our lives basking in cradles with bottles of luke-warm milk between our gums. And believe me, women are right. I mean to suck at life through that lukewarm bottle."

The exchange was entirely between Konrad and Gretchen, and it seemed an extension of a longer dispute. Hans did not understand it, and he felt uneasy.

"This girl's done me good, Hans. She takes care of me, all right." Konrad put his arm around Gretchen's shoulder, appearing to hang there for support.

It was Gretchen who finally brought Hans back from isolation. "Is there anything you'd like from home the next time I come, Hans?"

"A book . . . maybe Schiller."

"Here? In this place? They wouldn't allow Schiller," said Konrad. "You can be shot these days for reading Schiller. Listen, Hans." He sat down on the edge of the cot and spoke confidentially. "You know Captain Rabbe is here."

"He's crazy, isn't he?"

"Yes, but you don't know why. You probably didn't like Rabbe. He wasn't very likeable, I know. But once he made a confession to me, and afterwards I think he hated me for knowing his secret. He was in the SS . . . Action Squad C, in Russia, near Kiev. He told me that he sat on the edge of the Babi Yar ravine there and for two days did nothing but machine gun women and children. It took thirty thou-sand bodies to fill that ravine. You may have thought of Rabbe as some sort of iron puppet, but he wasn't devoid of feelings. He broke down, and they drummed him out of the SS. Now all that Germany has left on the field is the Waffen SS. They can't win the war . . . they can only create ruins. There won't be any men left in Germany except on crutches. God in heaven, the more I hate this war, the more I find growing in me a terrible need to kill."

Gretchen pressed her hand over Konrad's mouth. "Hans, he rants like this from morning till night. If he doesn't drive himself crazy, he will the rest of us."

Konrad pulled her hand away. It remained in his grasp as if he had forgotten all about it. "If you'd been listening to the radio, Hans, you'd know who's crazy. There aren't many people I can talk to as freely as I do to you and Gretchen. Do you know that more and more soldiers are taking independent action?"

"Desertion?"

"Hardly that. They're thinking of the welfare of Germany. There comes a time to stand fast, even at the risk of being dead heroes. Perhaps that time is already past. But there is a group in the Munich area called the Anti-Fascist Committee. Mostly regular army, a few civilians."

In a kind of panic Hans thought, I don't really know my own uncle. With one spike of confidence after another he was being nailed down.

"I don't want to hear any more, please," he said, hoping Konrad would stop before he had made Rabbe's mistake of revealing too much.

But Konrad continued. "We aren't trying to lose the war. It's long been lost. All we can do is make the end less horrible. Call it a mercy killing, Hans. The SS are like so many rabid dogs. They must be disposed of before they infect the rest of us. Hans, look at me. Is it such a glorious thing to fight in a lost cause? It is if that cause is just, but to fight for a criminal cause that has already been defeated, Hans, that's idiotic."

Hans lay in bed with his eyes closed, but he did not, like the Oriental monkey, stop his ears as well. His uncle had more to say. Lies? Fantasies? The truth? He no longer knew.

"Hans, the Nazi curse is worse than criminal. A criminal sometimes turns up with a conscience, like Rabbe—but this? This is like fighting for a mad dog. It never considers its victims. You may think I'm bitter, that I lost my judgment along with my wife, but I know now that Astrid was lucky. She went quickly, with a little dignity. Have you any idea what would have happened if she had survived in this country? First the yellow star to kill the soul, then the work camp, starving, and killing the body. Open your eyes, Hans! For God's sake! It could have happened as easily to Gretchen. It's happened to millions like her. You know that. You do. No man in his right mind owes any loyalty to a mad dog. His moral duty's to humanity. Surely you can see that, Hans?"

"Let him alone, Konrad," said Gretchen. "Can't you tell he's exhausted? I'm sorry, Hans. We shouldn't have come."

"Think about what I said, Hans. We need everyone we can get," said Konrad.

Was he being asked to fight against the SS? Against his oath and against the Führer? Hans closed his eyes. Only the reappearance of the nurse saved him from commitment one way or the other. She said that he had two more visitors. He had expected his parents, but it was Heime and Siegfried.

"Hans, this is good," said Siegfried. Then he stopped short and clapped his heels together. "Herr Major Wirth!" He gave the Hitler salute.

"Just Herr Wirth, thank God."

Heime looked nervous. He mumbled greetings all around. Konrad warmly shook his limp hand.

"Well," said Siegfried to Hans as if they were alone, "I

see your Gretchen's here." He continued not to address Gretchen directly, but in the third person. "She's the one you kept calling for when you were wounded. Yes, she ought to be flattered."

Konrad placed his hand on the back of Gretchen's neck. "We'll be going," he said. She rose under the pressure of his hand, light as a kitten. He held up her jacket. She helped him adjust it around her shoulders so unobtrusively it did not seem to be help at all. She must have practiced, thought Hans, and suddenly he was jealous of the fondness between these two people he loved. The unfamiliar emotion burned in him so hotly for a second that he felt like denouncing them as traitors. Then the knowledge that he could harbor such a thought, however briefly, filled him with shame.

"I'm sorry about your hand, Major Wirth," said Siegfried.

"And I'm sorry you haven't won a medal, Siegfried. You're welcome to mine . . . stop by the house any time."

"You're very generous, Herr Wirth. Until the war's over, I'm not giving up hope." Between the two there was a conspicuous antipathy, as fundamental as between a cat and a mouse.

"Take care, Hans. We'll see you tomorrow," said Konrad.

"Heil Hitler!" from Siegfried.

Very slowly, Konrad shook his head. "To every dog his day—Hitler's is over."

Siegfried's face turned ashen. He struggled for words but managed only a moist, inarticulate sound. Wrinkles of good humor radiated from the windburned corners of Konrad's eyes. Siegfried glared at him, seemed to waver, then spat ineffectually in Konrad's direction. Konrad flung his head back and laughed. He seemed to have grown suddenly younger. "Come, Gretchen, we must go. You boys . . . I advise you all to ponder. And good luck." He took her arm and drew her away.

Hans was frightened. "Your uncle should be reported for that," said Siegfried.

"Uncle Konrad is never serious, Siegfried. He was only baiting you."

"Well, he'd better learn to keep his mouth shut."

"He doesn't mean any harm."

"He hasn't enough courage to mean harm," said Siegfried. His fingers, thrust up into his hair, were rigid with the effort of restraint.

"Stay friends with me," said Hans.

"Always. You know that. I only hope I don't run across your uncle again."

"That sounds like a threat. Do you mean to be dangerous, Siegfried?"

"I mean to do my duty."

Heime offered not a word to the conversation but sat looking anxiously back and forth.

"Listen," said Siegfried, "in three weeks we're to be honored at the Academy. Presentation of medals by the Gauleiter. Speeches."

"You mean they haven't closed it down? I thought all the schools were shut down."

"The Academy's being run by the party. Special courses. We're to give the students a kind of graduation pep talk. And Hans! We're to be given medals!"

"Medals? For what? For being alive? We didn't get credit for shooting down a single plane."

"Don't you suppose that's preyed on my mind? Not one plane! Well, we're going to have another chance. That's what this ceremony's all about. You've been in here too long. Haven't you heard about the Alpine redoubt, about Werewolf? There are great events just ahead for us." Siegfried's pale eyes seemed actually to beam out light.

"But that's all done with now. We're out of it."

"Done with! Not while a German lives. Done with, Hans!"

From Heime came a series of equivocal throat noises which Siegfried took to indicate agreement with Hans. "Heime," he said, "you always look at the dark side. Always. Besides, you've got no guts." Siegfried gave Hans more studied attention, seeming cautiously to circle his friend's mind with his own. "You've changed since our last talk."

"Hasn't everything changed since then? Our friends are all dead." Forgetting that several excuses are always less convincing than one, Hans went on. "I'll probably still be here three weeks from now. Besides, I'm tired . . ." Here Siegfried interrupted with skeptical grunts as though he disbelieved everything that was being said.

"You'll feel differently, Hans, when you get your strength back. You don't understand what great missions we have before us. Listen, I'll explain . . ." His passionate talk devoured the afternoon. It sapped Hans's strength and resistance, even though he suspected its logic was built from evidence as substantial as moonbeams. Siegfried talked of the national redoubt, that natural fortress of mountains which rose behind the town. One hundred German divisions could fall back there, mostly SS divisions, the best equipped and most determined. With them would be new weapons, and the Volkssturm, the old fighters like Hans's father and boys like themselves. He talked of a new citizen's organization called Werewolf, dedicated to the principle that every German would try to take five enemies with him to the grave.

Hans had been as close as he cared to get to his own grave and he said so. Siegfried stared at him in disbelief. "Could you stand there and watch your family overrun by a horde of Mongolians?" No, Hans admitted, but as he understood it, the Americans were more likely to invade the Munich area than the Russians.

"Exactly! That's the whole point." Siegfried was triumphant. "The Americans are coming with their black troops. What are you going to do about it when a mob of cannibals begins to batter on your front door?" Hans said he had not heard about the proximity of Negro troops. "Because you've been in the hospital. Everyone's talking about it now. Hans, it's up to us to make a stand. That's why we've got to go to the school exercises."

"Let up on me for a while, Siegfried. I'm tired out."

"I will if you've made up your mind to go."

"I think it's made up, all right."

"Think about your speech, then. We won't lie to them. We'll tell them they may have to live in tattered tents in the rain. They may have to eat rotten food. They may be wounded, even killed. But they'll stand up proud and tall because they are the last hope."

Hans settled back on his pillow. "When you go out, tell the nurse I'd like her to come." He shut his eyes. Against such tactics, Siegfried finally subsided, promising to return with Heime in a day or two.

"Fine. That'll be fine," said Hans in a weak voice, but he uttered a strenuous curse after the pair were gone. It was not clear in his mind to whom it was addressed: his beloved uncle, who had aroused his jealousy; Siegfried, who troubled his sense of loyalty; or himself, whose helplessness he despised.

Two roads lay open. One, no matter how rational and noble the argument, was to turn traitor to a lifetime of faith. The other was the patriot's way, but surely the mad dog's way as well. Between such alternatives Hans only wished to hide, to languish in the hospital indefinitely; but his body would not cooperate. Day by day it grew stronger. It left the wheelchair and walked. It was ready to go home.

All along, Hans had been refused permission to visit Ernst. On the morning of his departure, however, his nurse asked if he would like to say goodbye to his friend. "I think he'd appreciate a word or two. He talks about you a good deal. About a walking tour."

Ernst's room, its shades drawn against the bright sunlight, struck him as cold and barren, like a grave without a cross. There was a small white table on which were a glass and Ernst's spectacles. In the bed was Ernst; at least Hans assumed it was Ernst, for his friend was wrapped almost entirely in gauze, with only one arm, his eyes, mouth, and nose showing through. The scene was clean and unfrightening. Only the fearful smell, and the sharp breathing like a knife sliding in and out of its sheath, hinted at the ruin the flames had left beneath the mummy wrappings.

Ernst did not seem to see Hans at first. Like a surprised snowman, he appeared to watch the nurse disposing of his pillows. Then the nurse left them alone. The huge silence of the whitewashed room and the strangeness of the figure in bed filled Hans with an acute embarrassment.

The patient opened and shut his mouth.

"How are you?" said Hans finally.

"How's . . . the . . . battle going? Hans . . . Any . . . nearer . . . final . . . victory?" Even now there was irony from beneath the gauze, but it was not Ernst's voice. It was not even a human voice, but rather the hoarse croaking of an animal, which, in its dying, had finally

accomplished speech. "I hear . . . all . . . all the croco-
diles . . . in the Berlin zoo . . . have been bombed.
What . . . do you think of that?" Still the last awkward
prancing, the last flicker of Ernst's world, where heaven and
hell were equally extraneous.

"I'm going home today," Hans said. "You'll be going
home, too, before you know it. I hear you're coming
along." He was in trouble already, and Ernst's next question made matters worse.

"Why me, Hans? Why me?" Hans wished desperately
that the nurse would return.

She entered with a glass of liquid and a bent straw, which
she held to Ernst's lips. He pushed the straw away with his
tongue. "Your friend tells me you're a great walker," she
said. "If you want to get well and climb in these mountains
again, you'll have to be more cooperative . . . very well,
you're not hungry." She produced a syringe, the contents of
which she injected into Ernst's unbandaged arm. "For
sleep," she explained to Hans. "I've never done much
hiking myself, but I expect it must be very thrilling when
you get up near the peaks. I'd enjoy the view more than the
climbing, though . . . there, now you'll rest." She pulled
out the needle and turned to Hans. "He'll sleep now. You'd
better say goodbye."

Suddenly the air was charged with emotion. Hans grabbed
Ernst's free hand. "I'll be back. I'll bring a map. We can
talk about our hike together."

"Why, Hans? Why me?" And again "Why?" as though
he were about to answer his own question. The lips parted,
moved without speech. There seemed a kind of urgency in
the eyes; then this, too, faded.

"Come along," said the nurse. "He's asleep." In the hall
she raised her voice. "He'll be up and around in no time."

Then more softly, after the door was closed, "We keep him under sedation as much as possible. All we can hope is that he will never completely wake up."

Hans went slowly down the hall. Frequently he stopped to rest, his hand against the wall. In one of the rooms a patient screamed.

FIFTEEN

THERE WAS no fuel for private vehicles and the streetcar tracks were smashed, so Hans went home on foot. Five miles uphill took him the better part of a day, with constant help from his parents and Gretchen. Even a butcher's family dined on turnips these days, and all of them looked very thin. Klaus's shoulders looked more hunched than ever, and Lore's hair had a silver sheen. Halfway home, Klaus left them to join a Volkssturm detachment that was working on a barricade in what was left of the main street. The old men had spent six days putting it up, and now an SS officer had them tearing it down.

With the steepening grade, Hans needed support on both sides. "Oh, what a sight. What a stupid awful sight," he said.

"Nonsense." His mother's voice was sharp. "Anyone who sees us will be jealous. A mother with her son home alive!" She bore most of his weight without any sign of fatigue. The house looked fine, Hans thought. From the outside you'd never guess it had been almost six years at war. Inside, it was different. There was a smell of damp rot. The radio constantly brought news of ruin and hysterical defiance.

That first afternoon Hans lay on his bed, too tired to

read, too discouraged to listen to the radio, too confused even to talk. He was intensely aware of a need for privacy, and the next morning he found the place. His library. The door opened under his hand with explosive suddenness, as if in excitement at being disturbed after such a long repose. It even smelled better, of mothballs and leather. Gretchen had forgotten to wind the great clock. Hans wound it now and reset it, and Gretchen brought him the books he wanted from the cellar. She started to open the windows, but he told her not to. He didn't want to look out at the mountains. He preferred the room closed. "Why?" Gretchen asked him. "You must feel like a butterfly stifled in a bottle."

Other than Gretchen, Hans welcomed few visitors and emerged only for meals. Through his connections with farmers, Klaus managed to keep a small supply of bread and turnips on hand. The Volkssturm called him away more and more frequently. Given the chance, Klaus would have shut himself away like Hans. "When you don't know what to do, the best course is to do nothing," he said. Apparently seeking some solution to his dilemma, he would hunch over the radio, hour after hour, spreading the news of each disaster about the house while Hans, curled up in his grandfather's armchair, searched through brittle pages for a more satisfactory world.

At such times his grandfather lived vividly in his memory, even to the scent of pipe tobacco and the crunch of his stick on the floor. Hans would move lightly and effortlessly into the stream of images the library evoked around him. Once again he would hear his grandfather's voice in the many underlined passages in the old books. Once again they would debate. "The duty of every patriot is to hate his country creatively." What did that mean? "To want power is corruption already." And, "The stronger the state is established, the weaker is humanity." That was Nietzsche speaking. "Where races are mixed, there is a source of great culture . . . Just now I am having all anti-semites shot": also from Nietzsche. He could hardly believe it. And written in his grandfather's familiar hand: "Fanaticism means redoubling one's effort after the goal has been forgotten." Yes. He could see his grandfather writing that, a kind of modern Moses, tired after the wilderness, discouraged perhaps and dying, but undefeated. There was no argument between them any more.

As he reread these and other passages, it all seemed so clear. He felt like Aladdin lighting the darkness with the gleam of an antique lamp. How could he have been so simple? How could he have given his entire devotion to another man's dream, only to discover the dream was mad? He'd spent his boyhood trying to rhyme those seductive words: fatherland, blood, soil, sacrifice, the Aryan race, honor, homeland, the Führer. Now someone inside him was shouting: not a simple soldier, not a patriot or a moralist, but someone new whom he did not entirely recognize. He waited patiently. "I am no longer myself. I am something new being born."

The greater world made frequent intrusions into his private domain. Out there a sun was setting which would not rise again in his lifetime. Out there was violence he could not face again, and rumors of evil too ghastly to believe: Auschwitz, the perpetual smoke from human fires, a race extinguished. The German conscience would never cleanse itself entirely. Out there were hatred, deception, cruelty too ghastly for conjecture. He tried to exclude them from his thoughts, but Klaus kept up his perpetual radio reports. Another camp full of living dead had been liberated, Hans was informed, and the leprous company of his country's sins closed about him again.

Occasionally it was Gretchen who brought agony into

the library. "I don't know how you can breathe in this closed place."

"It smells better than anywhere else," he would grumble. Even Gretchen came as an intruder now, letting in the world, letting in a sense of guilt that he might be responsible for the annihilation of a race she very painfully represented. "I just want to think. I want to be left alone," he would tell her, and she would leave, not understanding.

This time she stayed. "I'm sorry, Hans. You needn't listen, but I must tell you something."

He looked up. "Well?"

"Ernst is dead. He died last night."

He should have felt glad for Ernst. Whatever death was, it could be no worse than the gauze-wrapped agony he had seen at the hospital. Still the news came as a shock, and left him with nothing to say.

"I'm going to pick some wild flowers for the funeral," she said. "It would do you good to help me." Hans shook his head, and she left him. He tried to lose himself again in the books, but on every page appeared that bandaged snowman's face.

On other occasions Gretchen came to discuss Konrad. This was an uneasy topic at best, and one which caused Hans's sense of duty to pinch like an ill-fitting shoe.

"It's important," she would say.

"Nothing's that important. Nothing at all." But it was important. What Konrad was doing in Munich was of concern to the whole family. Was he really active in preparing a revolt against the SS? Gretchen thought he was.

"I can't believe it's come to that," Hans argued. "Anyway, he's a grown man. What can I do? You have more influence with Konrad than I ever had."

"But Hans, he can't even hold a gun. He hasn't a chance."

"Don't appeal to me, Gretchen. I'm through. I don't want to die until I've read all these books. Maybe written one or two." This was becoming his dream, the more important because he felt certain it would never happen. "Do you blame me for feeling this way?" In the gloom he couldn't see her expression and had no idea how she was reacting.

"Of course I don't blame you, Hans. You've been through so much. But I can't help feeling the way I do about Konrad."

"You love him, don't you?"

"Of course I do. You're all my family. I worry about all of you."

"But Konrad most of all."

"Yes," she said, "I suppose so. He's more alone than the rest of you. I can do him more good. We're both casualties in a way."

"And I'm not?"

"Yes, Hans, you are; but with you the wounds will heal. With us . . . Don't you see, there's a difference?"

He didn't want to understand just then. "You're a better person than I am, Gretchen. I see that."

"Don't be silly."

He didn't want to be concerned about anyone, but concern smoldered like decay in his heart. Even his books could not save him. On the day following the news of Ernst's death, there came a brisk rapping at the library door which was to destroy completely his artificial haven.

"Come in. Door's open," he said impatiently. He expected his mother, who was forever dusting and polishing. Instead, Siegfried entered. He wore his uniform and looked very brushed and pressed. "How do you feel?" he asked abruptly.

"Well, I guess I've felt better. What's the good news?"

"You haven't heard? The Americans have just surrendered. It will be the Russians tomorrow."

Humor was so unlike Siegfried that Hans almost believed him. "You're in a good mood."

"Actually, I'm not. You heard about Ernst. What a shame! He's a great loss." As Hans knew perfectly well, Siegfried had never had anything but contempt for the living Ernst. "He's to have a funeral, you know."

"It's the usual thing."

"I mean a special funeral, like General Rommel's. A big affair with a speech by the Gauleiter at the Academy. That's when you and I are to get medals and say a few encouraging words." Siegfried took out a pocket comb and ran its teeth along the edge of the old desk. "There's to be a fine marble monument in the cemetery for Ernst."

"What on earth for? All he did was die."

Siegfried seemed completely unaffected by his friend's unreceptive manner. "His life wasn't wasted, Hans. It was a triumph and an example to all the boys in the Gymnasium."

"It doesn't happen to be the way I see it."

"Hans, what the devil's happened to you? We've talked about the national redoubt, haven't we? You know the Führer is going there any day. Things may be desperate for a time, but you know it's always darkest before the dawn. Put your faith in the Fatherland, and in the Führer. Hans, we're going to make a stand." Siegfried's faith was no longer exuberant. To Hans it seemed grim and rather terrifying.

"I'm sick of the whole business. This isn't the pass at Thermopylae, Siegfried, and I'm not interested in a Viking funeral. If Hitler wants one, that's fine. Good riddance. I don't want to burn on his pyre."

Siegfried swayed as from an actual blow. His pale face

flushed scarlet and he drew in his lower lip. "Hans, someone's corrupting you. It's that Konrad . . ." Hans denied
it. "Then it's that Jewess, that pig of a Gretchen." Hans shot
out of his chair so violently that his book slid across the floor.
He caught hold of Siegfried's shirt. "Let go, Hans. It's
clean." Hans almost struck him then, but it wouldn't have
made any difference. Siegfried would have gone on arguing
from the floor. Hans let him go.

"All right, Siegfried. What do you want?"

"You. At the Academy. Day after tomorrow."

"No, thank you."

"Don't make me threaten you, Hans. You owe me this
much as a favor. I kept you alive after the tower came
down."

Hans turned his back. One way or another, Siegfried
managed to probe until he drew blood. "Telling lies to
school kids won't do you or anybody much good."

"Listen, Hans. What I know about your uncle could put
him in front of a firing squad."

"You don't know anything about my uncle," said Hans.

"Perhaps not. But I know your uncle. He's into something up to his scrofulous neck. Then there's your father,
with his radio and his illegal meat. Not to mention that
Jewess. It's only our friendship that keeps me from doing
my duty. A Gestapo investigation can be a messy process.
But we are friends, aren't we?"

"We're friends," said Hans bitterly.

"And you'll be with me day after tomorrow? Yes or no."

"Yes, if you'll leave me alone after that."

"Good." Siegfried held out his hand. Reluctantly Hans
grasped it. "Unless you want to bother, I'll write out a short
speech for you."

"Just as you like," said Hans.

"Fine. I'll take care of it. No hard feelings. I'll let myself out. Oh, and here's your book." Siegfried picked up the spilled volume, smoothing back the rumpled pages. "Poe? What a funny thing to read, Hans. American horror stories, aren't they? All about black apes stuffing mutilated women up chimneys. Exactly what we'll have here, Hans, if people like you don't buckle down." He pressed the volume into Hans's lap, and left, closing the door emphatically behind him.

They came for Hans in a Mercedes staff car. In the front was an SS driver with an SS Obersturmführer beside him. Pale and frightened, a captive unsure of his future, Heime rode between them. In the back were Siegfried and the district Gauleiter who would give the funeral oration.

The Obersturmführer was resplendent in his black uniform, the German gold cross and the hand-to-hand fighting clasp emblazoned on his tunic. The Gauleiter, also in black, looked more like a grocer. His fat red face hovered behind a large black cigar and a little black mustache. He talked at the top of his lungs, apparently on the theory that a soldier never listens to a civilian unless he shouts.

They turned onto the Reich Autobahn, the center of which had been cleared for an emergency runway; but it had been cleared, used, and bombed again all in the same day. The craters drove them back to the side roads, where finally they reached a wooded stretch that led to the Academy. Here all was familiar and unchanged. The three-story red brick buildings were frescoed, like steepleless churches. Except for the uniforms, war had not touched the place.

There were Ernst's parents. His father looked self-contained, but his mother was taking it badly. Hans was relieved that his party didn't linger. They marched through the oak doorway into the vast lobby with its brass chandeliers and granite fountain. They trod ringingly along the white corridors, past the gymnasium full of leather horses and climbing bars. Hans waved at a teacher he knew. It was old Wilhelm Frey, but they'd called him "The Greener" because his flesh was the color of bad meat. He wore an SA uniform now, with stiff collar lapels. Most of the teachers did.

An SS corporal saluted, flinging open the door which led to the auditorium platform. The front rows were packed with young boys. Immediately the crowd leaped to its feet. "Heil Hitler! Sieg Heil!" they roared. Hans had forgotten that such zeal still existed in Germany. "Sieg Heil!" He saw admiration in their eyes and he felt ashamed.

The director was calling for attention. It wasn't old Mühlebach any more, but a younger man in uniform. He thumped on a large flag-draped lectern until the shouting ceased. Then the Gauleiter was introduced and took his place behind the lectern. In the springy manner of a sports-man he raised himself a couple of times on the tips of his boots, then settled back to deliver a funeral oration which Hans found totally in keeping with an insane world. He spoke of the dark rune that Woden, wise father of battles, had carved for them, "the roll of heroes, on which the boy who lies flag-draped before us is one of many. He is a young Atheling called home to the great Ur in the east."

A woman in the second row of mourners began to weep. Hans couldn't see her face. No one else seemed to notice. They listened enraptured as the Gauleiter's words rattled down like hail on the coffin, which Hans had mistaken for a lectern. Didn't they realize how ridiculous it all was? Why weren't they laughing? Ernst would have laughed like a hyena.

Presently there was laughter. The Gauleiter had been talking for ten minutes, his round naked head glistening in a halo of sweat, when he began to choke and gasp. His words became thick, and there was a gust of laughter from the back row. "Peace be to his ashes," lisped the speaker, his false teeth bumping up and down on his gums. The laughter spread. An SS officer raised his hand, demanding silence. The Gauleiter struggled to go on. "May his soul rise to Valhalla." The SS officer walked threateningly down the aisle of students while the Gauleiter finished hastily and indistinctly with an image of Ernst gone to join the Horst Wessel Brigade in the sky.

So far the occasion was only a partial success. Even during the award of Iron Crosses second class to Heime, Hans, and Seigfried, laughter continued sporadically while the woman in the second row sniffled audibly.

Hans felt that any moment he would laugh or cry. It was both ludicrous and tragic. Even with the medal around his neck, a prize long coveted, he felt himself part of a madman's joke. The realization that he was about to be called upon to speak sobered him at last. Taken alphabetically, he would be the first. He looked out from above his friend's casket into the faces so eagerly awaiting his heroic utterances. There were of course the lines Siegfried had prepared for him. He had them in his hand, but he shrank from using them. He wanted to call out loud to whatever God there was, listening and powerful, to guide his words so that these children might understand that all of this was false. "Ernst, old friend, you who can't hear us or see us, we honor you. We're alive and you are dead, and you don't care any more about this nonsense." This would be suicide, and he was afraid. Head down, in a voice too low for the large hall, he pronounced the words that Siegfried had written; and low as his voice was, he felt himself deafened by the patriotic pomposity of his utterances.

They drummed their feet in approval when he retired. That made it even worse. They're all of them doomed, but they don't know it.

Siegfried was speaking now in a strained falsetto voice which was meant to sound pious. He was talking about a youth brigade to be formed from the student body which would hurl back the "black hordes from America." "He's not dragging me into that," Hans told himself. "Not on my life or his." When Siegfried turned away, the students stamped until the room trembled.

Heime came last. Poor timid Heime! He'd make a mess of things. Standing there behind the coffin, he was so short his blond head looked like a white ball resting on a table top. While the shuffling of feet subsided, he did not try to speak. In the silence that followed, he did not utter a word. Every cough, every scrape of a chair was horribly magnified as Heime stood stiff and silent. He seemed about to fall. The SS captain took a step forward, and then Heime made a queer wrenching motion with his mouth. A hoarse cry escaped him. "Soldiers!" On the paper prepared by Siegfried, Hans knew it said "Students," and the speech that followed was Heime's own. After the first croaking spasm, his voice rose earnestly, high and enduring. He spoke of a battle upon which depended "our German way of life." "They must break us behind the Rhine in our Fatherland or lose the war . . . Let us brace ourselves to our duties, and so bear ourselves that the German Reich shall last for a thousand years. Men will say, 'This was their finest hour' . . ." Hans realized that these were Churchill's words. He'd taken it all from Churchill! This was the biggest joke of the day, but no one laughed, for there was something in Heime's delivery that gripped them all. It was like martial music. Hans felt it, too, the same hypnotic appeal he remembered in Hitler's speeches years before. It seemed impossible, coming from Heime . . . from the little toad.

Heime had reached the end. He stood erect, his cherished dagger raised, a Viking chieftain in miniature. At first the audience was silent, as though they expected him to continue. Then the hall went mad with applause. Nothing else could equal it—not the SS captain's announcement that guns and ammunition would be issued after the funeral; not even the hint that a new and deadly poison gas was on its way by train. Until the casket was carried out to the waiting truck, Heime was the center of attention. But it did not seem to Hans that he enjoyed the adulation. He seemed as frightened as before, like a medium unconscious of the voices which had spoken through him.

The truck that carried the coffin and the three bemedaled boys was the usual open-backed personnel carrier. Many others who didn't want to walk the six miles back to town climbed aboard. There weren't many seats, and a few boys had to stand, until the jolting of the truck forced them to sit down on the casket. Hans was pushed up against the cab, next to a sign offering ten day's furlough to any soldier shooting down an enemy strafer with his infantry weapon.

They would have done better on foot. A convoy of military vehicles clogged the road: tanks covered with straw sacks and mattresses; guns like long-necked gray giraffes pulled by skeletal horses. There was even a troop of prisoners being evacuated from Dachau. Workers for the national redoubt, Hans supposed, but they didn't look strong enough to get there, let alone do heavy work. Within a few days they would surely become an army of ghosts to haunt his land forever. The troop parted raggedly as the truck plowed through, and Hans could not look at the prisoners.

He stared at his feet until the truck stopped on the outskirts of town where the Volkssturm had erected an antitank barricade.

"Halt!" cried a bewhiskered old man wearing an arm band instead of a uniform. "Traffic prohibited." He waved an antique gun.

The truck driver shouted back. "Grandfather, get that broomstick out of the way or I'll run you down." The truck lunged forward, pushing aside all of the barrier which the Volkssturm men had failed to remove. In what remained of Hindenburg Square the truck halted again so that the funeral procession might proceed on foot to the cemetery. A few villagers were waiting. The body of a soldier was hung there as well, a gruesome but somehow fitting sentinel. A placard was attached to the rope around his neck: "Lieutenant Schmiedemann, 226 Res. Inf. Regt., was a defeatist." With such encouragement the Volkssturm were kept at their posts.

Hans saw Gretchen. He would have liked to walk with her, but he was obliged to follow Ernst. Eight boys carried the coffin, and the others drew up behind in solemn procession. Hans managed to achieve a pace of slow piety, head inclined, counting the fresh imprints that the weighted feet had left in the warm tar of the road.

A gaunt pariah dog watched them from the ruins of a house but disappeared hastily when a small detachment of Volkssturm passed at a trot. They carried picks and shovels, and a couple of drab banners inscribed, "Bavaria Stand Firm," and "Better Death Than Slavery." "Nice day for a funeral," shouted one. Hans hadn't thought of the weather before. He hadn't thought of the weather for a long time, but it was a fine day, tasting of spring. Everything seemed painted in primary colors: blue sky, white mountains, and the red, white, and black casket up ahead. It didn't seem possible that Ernst could be dead on a day like this.

Hans felt strangely disembodied, neither dead nor alive. Nothing could truly surprise him, not even the figures up ahead banging a gong. It seemed to have frightened the others. The coffin swayed, then ran for the side of the road on sixteen legs, its skirt of a flag flapping. Then the legs became individual boys, and the coffin fell with a hideous splintering of wood. Only the high incisive note of a fighter plane coming with the unnatural speed of its kind brought Hans to his senses. The sirens had been destroyed. The gong was the only warning left. He fell flat as the plane went over, saw the saber flash of its twin propellers, saw Siegfried planted in the middle of the street hurling stones. A moment later he heard the raider's guns go off as it reached the main road and the military convoy.

The coffin lay in the street. No one stirred. When Hans started to get up, a voice warned him there was another plane coming. Hans rolled over on his back. There it was, a bomber this time, a Liberator. As he watched, it dropped a bomb, one solitary bomb which fell slowly toward them in endless, dreamlike flight. Someone screamed. Hans curled himself up, arms over his head, awaiting death. There was only a popping sound high in the air and then a volley of laughter.

"It's snowing," someone shouted.

High in the sky a canister of leaflets had opened, and thousands of tiny scraps of paper were falling. The procession re-formed, moving on toward the cemetery path before a single sheet reached the ground. A few landed in the trees and on the coffin. Hans picked one off the ground. The heading read, "One minute which may save your life." It was a Passierschein, a surrender pass.

SIXTEEN

THE MONUMENT honoring Ernst and the other dead of the
flak battery depicted a lion about to spring. Some said it
had been originally planned by the War Graves commission
for General Rommel but had been rejected by his widow.
In any event, Ernst had it now. The bearers moved on, their
faces rigid. Hans stared at the box. He thought of the
honored dead who populated the romantic labyrinths of his
youth. But here was no field of honor. There were no
Valkyrie here, no generals with unsheathed swords, no
priests, no altar boys, no tolling bells. Only Ernst, scorched
and forever dead.

Someone handed him a spade; one ceremonial clod of
mud, and he was finished. He ought to have stayed until the
job was done, but he walked away with the beat-beating of
the thrown mud drumming on the pine box behind him.

Gretchen was waiting for him. She took his hand. "Don't
worry about me, Gretchen. I'm all right."

"Why do people seem to enjoy that sort of thing?"

"I'll tell you why," he replied. "I think they imagine
they're the one in the coffin. At peace. All their troubles
over . . . When you think about it, it's a very democratic
and peaceful society in this cemetery. My grandfather's here.

There are Jews here, too. The party never got around to chucking them out."

Some of the upright stones marked Jewish graves over a hundred years old. One with a copper tablet was dedicated to those who gave their lives in the Great War.

On the other side of the small cemetery the crowd was already beginning to break up. A flight of raiders moving from the northwest hastened the withdrawal, sending some members of the funeral party running into the woods. Hans laughed. "I guess they think there's so little left of Germany that the Allies have given cemeteries first priority. Look here, you're not frightened, are you?" Gretchen had closed her eyes. Lashes like crescents of black pollen rested on her cheeks. "Gretchen, they won't come here . . . Look, they're passing over. Lancasters, I think. British. Don't worry, they're heading for the mountains." This puzzled him, but then it came in a flash. "Berchtesgaden!"

"Will Hitler be there, Hans?"

"He should be. He was coming south after his birthday. What day is it?"

"April twenty-third, I think. Saint George's Day."

"Then he'll be there," said Hans. "His birthday's the same as mine."

"I hope he is. I hope they kill him."

For the first time it occurred to Hans that his birthday had gone by and nobody had remembered it, not even himself. Such a small thing, and yet it increased his unhappiness.

No one remained in the cemetery now. Lower down the hillside, a few people who had guessed the bombers' mission silently watched. The planes moved with what seemed ceremonial restraint. When the first bombs fell, their descent was invisible. There was only the flash, the tiny pillar of smoke, and later the concussion and report. Under the impact of ten-ton bombs, Hitler's Berghof was disintegrating, its white stucco walls blown out, its picture windows shattered, its green tile bathrooms scattered like playing cards. The distant thunder of the bombs seemed to Hans like a roll of drums sounding the death march of the Third Reich.

"Do you think that finished him?" asked Gretchen.

"Unless he's still in Berlin." What did it matter? The god had vanished with the falling of the towers. The dying was left to the ordinary people, and Hans wanted to keep himself and his family from being a part of it. "I wish there was some way to get out of the whole business, right now."

"There is. Take off your uniform. Go home."

"And be hung?"

"Your father threw his arm band down the toilet this morning. He said a lot of the Volkssturm were fed up."

"What about Konrad?"

"Oh, Hans, I don't know." With her finger she drew a little brown furrow along the soft ground.

"Don't." He laid his hand firmly on her wrist. "Don't dig graves. We're all worried about him. Do you think he's with the Engineers in Munich?" There was a rumor that the regular army was fighting the SS there. There was also a rumor that the inmates of Dachau were defying the Tötenkorps guards. That would account for the prisoners on the road.

"I suppose someone must make a stand," she said. "With Konrad, it's a kind of expiation, you know. Making up for all the things he's had to do, the things he hasn't been able to prevent."

"Honor, duty, loyalty . . . what grand words they are, Gretchen, but I'm beginning to wonder what they mean.

Anyway, I'm no longer willing to die for them. I just want to get through this alive."

"I couldn't expect you to go with Konrad," said Gretchen, but the very statement suggested that she did. She looked so solitary and small among the tall gravestones that Hans could not bear it. "He's terribly important, isn't he?" She nodded. "Would it do any good if I filled my pockets full of pebbles and wandered off to help him? Would it?"

"Don't be silly, Hans. I only wish . . ." She began digging at the ground again with her finger. "I wish he needed me."

"I'll be lucky not to be fighting on the other side. I mean, with Siegfried and his private army."

"Hans! You don't have to listen to Siegfried."

"I know he's crazy," said Hans, "but he half convinces me sometimes. He keeps telling me we're going to be overrun with American Negro troops." He did not mention Siegfried's veiled threats against Gretchen and Konrad.

"How does he know?"

"I've no idea, but he seems sure."

"Even if he's right, what difference does that make? They have less reason to hate us than the Russians have."

"What difference . . . Gretchen!" Though Hans no longer trusted propaganda, he had heard what the Moors had done during the Spanish Civil War, and these men were darker, stranger still . . . completely alien.

"Hans, you don't know anything about them . . . you don't."

"I know they're one reason I might go along with Siegfried."

"As long as you never fight against Konrad," she said.

"Of course . . . I couldn't do that. I just meant . . . I don't know."

"What will you do?"

"I wish I knew. I've lost my way. Even if the witch is dead, I'm still lost."

"Then go home, Hans. If you don't, you'll regret it by and by."

"A woman always wants you to be in the place where you were last. My grandfather said that."

Two feverish spots of determination had formed on Gretchen's ordinarily pale cheeks. "It's the last time I shall ask you for anything."

"All right," he said. "And when Siegfried comes with his little army?"

"Hide in the woods with your father for a few days. The Americans are already in Nuremberg. It can't last much longer."

"I can't think, Gretchen. Tell me what I ought to do."

"Come on, then, let's go." She gave him her hand and pulled him up.

They went by way of the new monument. The grave was covered with wild flowers, and over the freshly turned earth a black fly hovered.

"Goodbye, Ernst," he said. "I wish it had worked out . . . our walking tour." He took the ribbon from around his neck and dropped the dark metal cross on the ground—not as a tribute, for it had no value any more, but as a first step in cutting away the past.

It was late afternoon when Hans and Gretchen descended from the cemetery hill. Swarms of ravens, returning from a day's scavenging in the ruined town, flew overhead. Suddenly Gretchen clutched his hand. "Hans!" she whispered. "I think we're being watched."

"Not Siegfried?"

"I don't think so. Pretend you're talking to me, but look over my shoulder."

He saw nothing at first. Then at the edge of the woods he saw a collection of rags. The forest was alive with scarecrows in tattered stripes. "Prisoners," he whispered. "Keep moving. They must be the ones I saw this morning. They must have escaped during the raid."

"Shouldn't we help them?"

"They might kill us. Keep going," he told her. Besides, what was the use? It was a miracle such cadavers could still move at all. Getting this far must have killed some already. Or were they perhaps immortal? Merely to survive in Dachau seemed to affirm a certain immortality.

They saw no more prisoners, but encountered a mixed detachment of SS and Volkssturm. The SS were armed with machine pistols, the Volkssturm with scythes and pitchforks. Grechen was concerned with what Hans and his father would need if they went into hiding. She would scour the house for food. "Just a couple of blankets," Hans told her. "We'll forage for our food. There are any number of streams." Through the roar of his own hungry saliva he made it sound like a picnic. How could he take food from Gretchen, with her wrists like the bones of a wren? She looked like one of famine's children. And his mother was more gray and gaunt every day. He couldn't take food from either of them.

"No matter what happens, you'll go today," she urged him.

"If Father will join me."

As they approached from the hill above, the Amann home seemed wrapped in the sleep of centuries, untouched by the war. A shock awaited them by the front door: sitting on the steps, as singular and deadly as two-headed Cerberus, were Siegfried and Heime. There was no use turning away. Siegfried had seen them. He stood up, extraordinarily tense and self-possessed. Crooked in his left arm was a short, bulky machine carbine.

"Hans! Where have you been?" He hailed them genially, as if sure of his welcome, emitting sounds resembling mirth. "I can guess. You look very pretty, Gretchen. What pink cheeks!"

"No more! We're not listening any more to you," said Hans. Siegfried's laughter, if it had been laughter, ceased. "Do you know what the Russians intend to do with girls like Gretchen? Those that aren't killed?" asked Siegfried. "And if you think the Americans are any better, why do you suppose they're sending their black troops here? You'd be better off dead."

"May God forgive you for your hatred," she said.

"May he forgive me for not hating enough. Come on, Hans."

Hans didn't move. "The war's over, Siegfried. Can't you see we're beaten?"

"Beaten? We've a great army! Haven't you seen it?" As if to emphasize this point, a machine gun rattled from the forest. Hans had seen nothing but the remnants of an army, a last handful rubbed raw. Some were retreating in slow orderly columns up the mountain roads. Their trucks and horses were laden with furniture and sacks of clothing instead of weapons: a gypsy army in full retreat.

"They call it Operation Götterdämmerung," said Heime.

"Shut up!" Siegfried warned him. "Listen, with some rest, with the new poison gas, we'll hold the mountains forever. I'll stake my life on it."

"Well, don't stake mine. I'm sick of all this," Hans told Siegfried. "Move out of the way and let us inside."

Heime complied, but Siegfried barred the door. "Listen, I'm not a complete idiot," he said. "Let me explain." He described an army of schoolboys. "You can't expect them to sacrifice their lives without some sort of leadership." Hans didn't expect any sacrifices, but Siegfried held the door, his hands on either side of the frame. "And there's more. This is the thing . . . The railroad passes near the airport, and that's where we'll be, with our army, waiting . . . Don't you see what I'm getting at?" Hans put a hand on Siegfried's arm to move it from the door frame, but Siegfried shook him off. "Hans! I'm talking about the new secret weapon, sarin! We'll intercept that gas. It's overdue from Berlin. With it we'll be invincible!"

Hans gave a despairing laugh. There was no use talking to Siegfried; that was plain enough. What could it lead to but endless ranting and procrastination? Before Hans could decide on his next course of action, the door behind Siegfried opened so violently that the boy was almost thrown to the ground. He whirled and crouched, the gun clutched as though he meant to use it. "Ah, Herr Amann! It's you . . ." He lowered the barrel.

"Hans, Gretchen, come inside."

"Herr Amann," Siegfried said, "shouldn't you be down at the firehouse? I heard the Volkssturm alert signal."

"Go home, Siegfried. Comfort your mother. Losing one son is enough," said Klaus.

Siegfried took a backward step, then halted. "Herr Amann, I don't see your arm band."

Klaus pulled the door shut behind him. He stood with his back against it, and his hands were fists.

"If the SS military police knew about this," said Siegfried, "you know what they would do." Hans knew all right. Lampposts and trees along every road in Germany were festooned with the bodies of those who had done less. "Hans, I don't want to force you. We've been through a great deal together. We need you."

"And if I don't come, Siegfried?"

"I'll make you sorry you ever drew breath." Siegfried's face was full of unexpressed fury. I'm beginning to be sorry now, thought Hans, who had no doubt that Siegfried meant every word he said. For a moment he had a terrifying impulse to kill his former comrade. He knew exactly how he could do it, with both hands clasped together and raised over his head. Using the full strength of his back, he could bring them down, smashing the frail boy's neck.

In a hoarse whisper Klaus ordered Siegfried to leave, and without looking to right or left, Siegfried marched down the path, Heime trailing behind him. For an instant Hans hesitated. If he didn't catch up with Siegfried, the SS would surely ransack the house, hang his father, do unspeakable things to Gretchen and his mother. And then, suppose Siegfried was right about the dark tattooed migration descending upon Bavaria. That was the final spur.

"I've got to go with Siegfried," he said.

"You'll not," Klaus ordered, grasping his son's shoulder with a muscular hand.

"Do you want to be hung?" Hans half hoped his father would not let him go, but the words struck home. As slowly and painfully as a paralytic, Klaus lowered himself to the step.

"We can all hide in the woods," Gretchen begged him. "For God's sake, Hans, nothing's changed. Only we must hurry!"

Hans's mind was finally made up. Gretchen stared at him, a hand over her mouth. "Father?" Klaus said nothing. He fumbled in his pocket for his pipe, and his hands spilled tobacco all over the steps. "Take care of Mother. I'll be back. Gretchen . . . take care." She was mute, her eyes almost closed as if she expected a blow. "Gretchen, I will be back . . . I'll bring Konrad." Softly he smoothed back her hair. Then he squared his shoulders and went down the road, loyal, it seemed, to the nightmare of his childhood.

A poet had once said, "If this is Armageddon, one had better be in it." If the poet was right, he might as well die fighting for Bavaria. If the poet was wrong, then he was a bigger fool than Siegfried. In any case, he no longer had any choice.

At the end of the path he began to run.

SEVENTEEN

THE DAYS of Siegfried's army were few. It was a time when German fought against German through a fog of rumor and false report. Munich had fallen to the Wehrmacht and the radio called on Bavarians to rise against the SS. Some did, and many died. The SS, the Hitler Youth, a few isolated detachments fought back, while the great army of Field Marshal Kesselring dissolved on the alpine roads. An endless procession of soldiers and refugees moved through the exquisite springtime, a living artery of suffering, despair, and defeat. Behind them were left the relics of Nazi rout: burst haversacks and cartridge boxes, baby carriages loaded with kindling wood, scattered letters and lockets, burned-out tanks, and horses dead in their traces. Only here and there armies, reduced to company size and company command, remained to fight. These were brief, spasmodic struggles, followed on no battle maps, recorded in no histories, written only on grave markers and in women's hearts.

Never had defeat been so obvious, so complete. Yet Hans was waiting now for his first real fight on a small airfield at the foot of Hitler's Obersalzberg. A troop of SS had supported Siegfried's army at first, in the expectation that the Führer would arrive from Berlin. Now it was rumored that Hitler had died at the head of a youth battalion. The SS were gone, leaving Siegfried to receive, if not the Führer himself, at least the poison gas from Berlin.

Hans saw his comrades as they really were: an absurd little troop, tired, dusty, and afraid. They lacked the monumental courage and the taste for history needed to check for one moment that black horde from across the sea. They would be trampled in the dust. Still they waited. It seemed the appropriate ending to an insane dream.

This was Siegfried's hour. Frail of body and weak of voice, he addressed his phantom army with a passion that held them together. What honor was theirs! When the wonder weapon arrived in its gleaming cylinders, they would bear it to the national redoubt. Like descendants of Prometheus, they would rally round the Führer and repel the hordes. Siegfried spoke with the certainty of history remembered, and they all labored together, straining to cut free a dual-purpose .88 millimeter cannon from the traces of dead horses as though this one gun might replace armies. Laboriously, they rolled it into a natural depression where its field of fire included the airfield and a short stretch of railroad track.

Someone called it the "Siegfried line," and this was repeated one to another. Hans laughed until there were tears in his eyes. I'm hysterical, he told himself, and he tried to concentrate seriously on Heime's small platoon, which was dragging what looked like picnic baskets. They contained .88 millimeter shells, and Hans read the labels: "For practice use only." This also made him laugh dangerously, as did Siegfried's proclamation that a dead and bloating horse was just as good protection as several bags of sand.

It must have been one of the airfield horses, Hans

thought. A few had been kept to help pull the planes off under the trees as they landed. If they didn't pull fast enough, they were strafed. That was how the horse had died.

All day, planes streamed into Bavaria from the Russian front, weird fauna fleeing a forest fire. There were Italian trimotor bombers, big Junker JU52 transports, bizarre machines escaped from a museum, of purpose and type unknown to Hans. Some were jets barely out of blueprint; others belonged to the First World War. From all of them poured passengers as remarkable as the planes themselves: a general wearing the Knight's Cross around his neck and carrying a baby in his arms; women in costly furs; a frightened dachshund that ran in circles. The complete chorus line from a nightclub appeared, and one of the girls carried a caged canary.

How Ernst would enjoy all this, Hans thought.

Against the evidence of his eyes, Siegfried insisted that the shipwreck from the skies was really a great armada assembling for a decisive counterblow. No one tried to dissuade him, until the second night, when he and Hans asked one of the Luftwaffe pilots for news of the front.

"What front?" The pilot was blunt. He had obviously been drinking. "Are you from the little Nibelungen circus over there? The ones with the eighty-eight? Listen, my advice to you kids is to go home, change your diapers." Naturally Siegfried could not let it go at this. He spoke of the army massing in the mountains, and the pilot spoke of surrender at Saalfeld. Siegfried spoke of dying for the Führer, and the pilot replied that the Führer was already dead.

"A false rumor," declared Siegfried. "He escaped by plane. He'll never die."

The pilot shrugged. "You poor idiots," was all he said.

Siegfried posted a double guard that night over the .88. It wasn't only the drunken pilots that bothered him. He had heard that in the village some rowdies had dumped a Jugend ammunition truck into the sluiceway. "They're not doing that to my gun," he said, and all night he hovered near his sentries, mumbling to himself.

"I'm going to get that pilot," he told Hans. "He's a defeatist. I'll kill him." But all military planes which lacked the fuel for further withdrawal were set afire during the night, and by morning the pilot and his cohorts had gone, carousing down the road to oblivion.

Twelve of the thirty-odd soldiers in Siegfried's army had disappeared for unknown destinations during the night. Heime was among the deserters. While Siegfried was searching for him with mayhem in his heart, Heime returned. He'd been home, he told Hans, and he had news of Konrad. He was still alive, though the SS had nearly finished him. Only the arrival in Munich of American and French tanks had saved him.

"In Munich already?"

Heime nodded.

"Then they'll be here today," Hans said.

The last day was beginning.

"Konrad's here. In town somewhere. He's armed a lot of prisoners from Dachau. Some university students, too."

So Hans and his uncle were finally on different sides, and at a time when more than ever before they were in agreement. How would it end? Would they meet in a sunny field and shoot one another and lie side by side among the flowers for their women to lament? The old ballads would end it that way.

A thin voice, sharp as a razor, cut through his lugubrious musing. Siegfried had raised his fist to Heime's face in an

ugly brutish gesture. "Back, are you?" He called what was
left of his troops together. "Look at Germany's hope!" he
shouted. Heime submitted to it all. His froggy eyes behind
their steel rims, lips drawn tight in a mirthless grin, gave him
the look of a still-born child. "I don't want cowards here! I
want comrades who are willing to die for their Fatherland!"
Siegfried's gun was in his hands and it was plain that anyone
who moved to depart would not get far. "You must all have
faith that our great Führer will come. At any moment his
plane will appear from the sky . . . Or his train will come
up those tracks. We will be here to greet him. We will
receive the terrible weapon he brings us, the sarin, the
poison gas." Siegfried ranted on about filling the valleys
with gas, filling the cities . . . If it had not been for his
brandished gun, Hans would have broken into nervous
laughter. Siegfried's sinewy hands moved as he spoke, and
his delivery was almost a chant. Death, he made it clear,
was simply a weakness of character, something to be overcome, submitted to if need be. Only surrender was forbidden. They would fight to the last man.

The valley curved eleven miles in each direction. Already their allotted time was running out, for somewhere
amid the trees, the towns, and the hills, a cannon had begun
to fire. Its voice was singularly unterrifying. It hung lazily in
the air, which seemed worn out from carrying loud sounds
for so long.

A cloud ceiling rested like a piece of parched earth along
the mountain ridges, but as the day wore on, it began to
crack and melt away. It was going to be a fine day, Hans
observed, very warm for the first of May. A gun sounded
closer now, and a plane came over. The boys dove for
shelter in a strangely polite way, speaking to each other in
low, considerate voices. The plane turned out to be a

German fighter, and when it landed, Hans, half persuaded by Siegfried's eloquence, awaited the emergence of a deposed and fleeing god. There was only the pilot. Siegfried tried to question him, but the man impatiently began to pour gasoline over the plane. Siegfried then tried to interrogate him at gunpoint, while Hans and Heime stood by. The pilot failed to recognize the passion of the small person who was annoying him. He pushed Siegfried down, touched a match to the plane, and carelessly walked away. Siegfried struggled to his feet and fired just as Hans gave a shout of warning. The pilot sank to his knees, then to hands and knees. Finally he rolled over on his side, his movements slow and ponderous.

Siegfried ran back to the .88 millimeter gun while the other boys watched his every move. Hans went to examine the pilot, but he could see that there was no use feeling for a pulse, so he followed Siegfried. Steadily the noises in the valley were growing. The cannon were accompanied by the familiar rumble and clank of tanks moving through forests and gardens like a grazing herd of monsters. Morning became afternoon, and still no enemy showed himself. There were occasional planes, of course: an American reconnaisance plane, at which Siegfried discharged an errant shell from the .88, and later a plane that looked like a single-engine trainer, trailing smoke. The trainer swung in toward their field. The .88 fired a shell, and the plane, skating from its course, nosed over into the forest. Hans had barely time to recognize the German cross on the plane's wing before the forest absorbed it. Smoke rose in a dark column, to be skimmed away gradually by the wind. Siegfried was jubilant. He either did not know or did not care that the plane was German.

Tanks had now reached the village road. Hans could

hear them just beyond the trees. Toward the far end of the airfield moved the striped figures of prisoners. Siegfried racked down the long barrel of the .88 until it squinted out across the field almost level with the grass.

"Our Führer's plane isn't going to come," he told Hans with what seemed a breaking through of sanity.

"Then what are we staying for? You can't stop tanks for long with that thing."

"No, but we can hold them up while you have a look at the train track."

"What for?"

"The gas, you fool! At least we'll find the gas."

"All right." Hans made the words sound like a curse. "How long do you expect to last here?"

"Until you return with the gas."

Siegfried had reached the edge of his world, the Nazi world, which had all along been flat. Now he was prepared to wait upon the brink with his most fanatical supporters. Rather than submit to a despised enemy, he would have them take that final step backwards into extinction.

Hans seized the opportunity to guide some of his comrades back into the world of reality.

"I'll need a few men," he said.

"As many as you want . . . And Hans, take care! Stay alive. As long as a single one of us survives, the spirit lives. If there's one good German left, the Führer will come again. He will!"

Hans named his companions, and they stepped beside him with all the alacrity of prisoners receiving pardons. Among them was Heime, but Siegfried put his hand on Heime's shoulder. "Stay with me," he said. Heime turned to Hans with a wild look of pleading. He did no more than that.

"Hurry, Hans," Siegfried urged him. "Go round by the trees." He looked pale as the death that faced him. He held out a hand, and Hans seized it, a hand that was damp and hot.

"Good luck, Siegfried."

"They'll remember how we fought today, Hans."

Siegfried gave him a parting shove. Once his legs were in motion, he could not stop them. He was a child again, chased by a nightmare; he could not stop running. His small troop followed. He could hear the shuffle and clink of their equipment, but he did not look back until they had rounded the far corner of the airstrip. Through a fringe of trees he could see that the field was clear. It was beginning to tremble in a haze of rising heat. He knew where the gun was, but he could no longer see it.

"Come on. Keep down, and hurry." He counted them as they went by. Sheep, he thought. Not one had vanished. Couldn't they use their heads? From the trees across the field emerged an American tank. It was ponderous and slow, the barrel moving in its turret like the clumsy feeler of a terrible insect. Either it did not see the entrenched .88 or it relied upon the paralyzing effect of its own presence. In any event, it did not fire. With seagull cries of joy, the prisoners ran toward it, waving. They surrounded the tank. Flowers were thrown on it. Its hatch came open, and what must have been emergency rations were passed out.

Then the concealed .88 went off. Its shell racketed across the field and into the woods, exploding there. The clang of the tank's hatch closing was followed by a much louder clang, like the sound of a church bell cracking. It was the second shell from the .88. At first Hans thought it had glanced off the tank, but the long cannon swung abruptly downward in its turret, and there was a rumble of explosions, deep and muffled. Smoke wisped from the hatch and from the driver's slit. The tank looked as deadly as ever, but it was finished. The harlequin crowd of prisoners rushed to and fro, then crouched behind the huge iron skeleton. From their salvaged weapons, irresolute bursts of fire began to spray the woods opposite, plucking down leaves and tearing up plumes of dust.

"Down! Get down!" Hans shouted at them, and none too soon. A lash of tracers hummed overhead. They opened tree trunks, left them smoking, and came down on the other side of the field where the .88 was concealed.

Hans herded his comrades on again. They crept down the slope that led to the railroad tracks. There they stood up. They were out of the battle's range. "All right, everyone," said Hans. To his surprise, he found that he was trembling all over. "All right. We'll walk along the track until we find that train. March!" He didn't count, but he knew very well they weren't all there. They were coming to their senses, then. When he saw another going, he didn't try to stop him. They hadn't been reprieved from death to seek death again, and he didn't blame them. Yet there was something about Siegfried's last fight, a kind of Wagnerian sense of consecration, that had won his cheap loyalty. Mindlessly he would follow the bomb-ribbed track looking for a nonexistent train, with its phantom passengers and its boxcars full of mythical poison. This was the easy way, without decisions, jogging along in the sun, and he would keep at it, alone if need be, until exhaustion or some unforeseen event intervened.

They were far from the airfield now. No shots interrupted the busy undertone of the spring morning. The routine process of simply following the bright pebbles of the railbed must have sobered the little flock of sheep following him. It had allowed their brains to picture homes and families not far off. Most of them had already disappeared into the woods. Hans guessed the others were keeping up simply because they knew the iron tracks would guide them home. Why not? After all, it was only a game, this search for a train full of deadly poison gas. A child's game. An adult would have laughed at them. They were children who at any other time or place would have been punished for carrying firearms, children who were supposed to turn the tide in the most terrible war the human race had fought. Presently he would have scurried off into the woods himself, had he not rounded a long turn and seen before him on the track the train from Berlin.

EIGHTEEN

THE BERLIN ENGINE, its boiler burst and hissing, stood less than a hundred yards ahead of him, its wheels no longer churning. Behind it ranged the boxcars. Hans had enough comrades left, enough guns among them, to force open the train. Siegfried would have been tearing at the boxcars already. Just as surely, Konrad would have been burning the train to destroy the poison, killing or being killed by its guards if need be. Both inclinations stormed inside Hans. He was at once the banner bearer of past glory and the prisoner breaking through the barbed wire. There was another way. He could go home, he could hide. But to do so was to make no commitment to past or future. It would never silence the voices that called aloud in him.

Hans gave a signal. He took the first step forward, unsteadily. His young comrades followed, moving more surely as they went. Keeping well below the crown of the embankment, they had reached the engine when the sound of splintering wood came from far down the line of cars. There were shouts, the sound of an ax or heavy hammer delivering frantic blows. Hans crept to the top of the embankment and finally stood erect under the shelter of the

231

engine. Figures were appearing from the woods and running toward the boxcars. They looked like prisoners. Crossing fearfully to the other side of the engine, Hans peered
out upon the long inner crescent of cars. The scene made
no sense at all. He closed his eyes hard, looked again. Then
he began to laugh.

"Come on, everybody. Come on! It's a joke!"

He could no longer support his gun. Laughter seized
hold of his comrades. They, too, threw down their rifles and
shouting with joy ran off to take part in the fun. The path
that led to town was jammed with people. The woods
spilled them out in growing numbers: German hausfrau,
men in uniform, prisoners from Dachau, Belgian and Dutch
prison workers from the cement factory. Some Russian
farm girls were trying on blue denim overalls. An ex-
prisoner in stripes bore away on his head a great tower of
felt hats. It was a goods train, bombed and abandoned, and
now yielding up its treasures car after car. Wine and cheese
and delicacies for generals who would win no more victories, heavy clothes for a Russian winter that would not
come again. It all poured from the train into the arms of the
crowd. Hans and his troop dissolved into the struggling
mob.

Hans pushed toward a car from which canned goods
were spilling. They hadn't had meat at home since Christmas, not even a can of sardines. But the crowd overwhelmed him. He tried another car. He was shoved back,
but managed to grapple a very large carton tied with cord.
He ran into the fields with the box in his arms, skirted the
Russian farm girls who were still outfitting themselves in
blue denims, and fell at last exhausted in a patch of
meadow grass not far from the forest's fringe. There he lay
panting, still clutching the parcel. Specks swam before his

closed eyes and he was aware for the first time of a weariness and a hunger that was close to complete collapse.

"Someone's after me!" He felt around for a gun that wasn't there. "They won't get this box." But the running was inside him. It was his heart beating in his ears. He felt that if he waited any longer before eating the contents of his prize he would certainly faint. The string was tough. It tore his fingers, but he kept at it doggedly until the box was open. Its contents spilled out before him: sixteen feathered Tyrolian hats in assorted colors. He looked at them in wonder, as one might study a still smoking meteorite. "Happy birthday, Hans," he said out loud. Very thoughtfully, he tried on one hat after another, then several of them at one time.

"Happy birthday, Hans," he said again. Then he began to laugh, and the laughter got out of control. It went on and on until its tenor changed and with a groan of relief came to an end. It was the end of what had started at a Munich street parade. The boy's shoulders began to shake. His lip quivered and he whimpered and gasped for air.

All the emotion that for so long he had kept in check drained out of him as he lay on his back in the tall grass, with the sun beating on his closed lids. Shouts and the crash of rending wood still came from the train. The sunlight burned into his face. It hurt but it was good. After some time he opened his eyes and gazed in wonder at the sky. It was as bright as glass and filled with small clouds like puffs of breath. Life shone about him. For a long time the desire to live had failed in him, and now he felt renewed, ready to be part of the world. This was the day of his birth. He felt like Ymir, out of whose body the human race was born; a medieval Adam whose flesh was soil, whose blood was the oceans, whose bones were the mountains of the earth. He was all the dead and all the wounded and all that was newborn. He was a spring butterfly, tremulously unfolding damp wings in the sunshine.

Slowly he got to his feet. The afternoon was almost spent. Shadows were lengthening on the meadow, and the crowd around the picked bones of the goods train was reduced to a few stragglers like himself. Battered boxes, empty bottles, shreds of paper were everywhere. His friends had disappeared. They were home, he supposed. He was about to collect his hats and follow them when a voice called out his name.

"Hans . . . Is it you?"

He turned, squinting into the bright light. Then he saw her running toward him. "Gretchen! Gretchen!"

"Hans, I thought you were dead . . . Oh, Hans!" Like a husband and wife of long standing, they embraced.

"Hans, are you all right? You're not hurt?" Her hands were on his shoulders; she was studying him.

"I wounded myself on a bit of string." When she noticed the hats, he told her he was celebrating his birthday. "What are you doing here, Gretchen? You ought to be home, with the doors locked."

"I was at the airfield. I've been looking for Konrad . . . and you."

"Is Konrad all right?"

"I don't know. I couldn't find him." She stared at Hans as though she hoped desperately to see news of Konrad printed on his face.

"Gretchen, don't cry. Konrad's indestructible . . . Did you see anyone else? Was Siegfried there? Or Heime?"

"I saw Siegfried. Hans, he was dead. There was a knife in his back. So many boys were dead, and so many prisoners . . . I kept expecting to find you or Konrad among them."

So Siegfried was dead. Hans was not able to grieve. What other ending could there be for Siegfried, whose only life was a dying cause? The only strange thing was not finding Heime beside him.

"Let's go home, Gretchen, before it gets dark."

"I want to find Konrad," she insisted.

"He'll come home," Hans replied. "He'll look for you there."

"You don't know . . ." she began.

"Lean on me," he told her. "We'll help each other home. Konrad will be there, twice as worried as you are. You'll see."

They went up the road together, following the tattered paper and empty gleaming cans the villagers had strewn behind them. Otherwise it was a deserted road. Hans trod heavily upon it, as if he expected to find at its end the first dawn of the world.

The town, as they passed through it, was only vaguely familiar. It was a ruined town and very still. White flags, some the size of handkerchiefs, others like bedsheets, hung from every inhabited building. It looked as though all the housewives had decided to do their washing at once. A few dead lay in the streets, already swollen, their faces tinted yellow, green, black. Paper moved in the streets. There were pictures of Hitler, and a pile of *Mein Kampf* hastily set afire and only partly burned. There were the winter-aid notices still flapping on the shell of the town hall. They were faded now, and Hans noticed beside them a more recent publication: "Attention, Eaters of Cats!" It stated that cats ate rats and therefore as a matter of health were unfit for human consumption. Hans hadn't seen a living cat in weeks. Everything alive or worth preserving was behind locked doors, waiting for the Americans.

There was no time to stand and stare at wreckage. The Americans were coming. Like a lumbering, grumbling herd of metal elephants, their tanks were moving up the road to town. They had reached the outskirts when Hans and Gretchen reached the mill bridge. A shot, followed by a series of shots and the crash of a tank butting through a half-demolished building, indicated the presence of snipers. So there would be a little more killing after all. It would take the Americans a while to work through town, but they would eventually find their way to the Amann house.

There were the usual signs of rout and disorder on the road as Hans and Gretchen climbed the hill. There was a dented helmet, the flattened tire from a Volkswagen, and a trail of horse manure ending in a dead horse. Hans's father knelt beside the body with a bucket and a butcher's knife. When Hans saw them first, his father's profile was on such a level that horse and man appeared to be united as in the ancient myth. Then Klaus sprang up to hug them together in his arms. "This calls for a real family celebration," he told them. "Fresh meat for supper." Gretchen, as though she feared the answer, asked hesitantly for Konrad. No answer came from Klaus. There was no need for one. Konrad hobbled toward them down the path and as he moved he appeared to grow stronger with every stride.

Gretchen gave an inarticulate cry. She took one running step, then stopped, perhaps because he could not run. With odd dignity she held out her hands to him. They embraced. It was an ungainly, unromantic picture, honest and completely private. Hans tried not to feel the sharp pain in his heart. They looked so happy, so really happy.

"Hans, old man! Thank God you're safe." Konrad gave him a crushing hug.

Hans asked if he had come with the demolished Ameri-

can tank. He said he had. In fact, he'd rallied the prisoners
against the .88 and the rifles that had supported it from the
forest. The carcass of a dead horse had saved him from a
shellburst. There'd been no shelter after that. He'd limped
the last hundred yards armed only with rocks, relying on
the hope that the boys had all run away. Only one was still
there, Siegfried crouched behind the muzzle of a cocked
carbine.

"Don't shoot! It's all over!" Konrad had shouted, but the
boy had taken aim, and as a last insult had stuck out his
tongue. What a stupid way to die, Konrad had thought, at
the hands of a crazy boy. He had stopped in his tracks,
waiting for the bullet, but it did not come. Instead, Siegfried's open mouth had seemed to widen, and the pink
protruding tongue had disappeared in a rush of blood.
Siegfried had swayed forward, and the gun had discharged
into the ground.

"It was Heime. It must have been Heime," said Konrad.
"He stabbed Siegfried in the back and ran. He disappeared
into the forest before I could get a good look at him, but it
was his knife all right. Well, Siegfried was born for trouble.
It's just as well."

Siegfried was gone, demobilized for eternity. And Heime
. . . Had his knife made his final statement? Hans would
not forget the speech he had made. Only time would tell
about Heime.

The Americans did not reach the Amann home that day.
Hans's fear abated, and he awaited the invaders with growing equanimity. They did not come the following morning
either. Though Hans no longer believed Siegfried's tales of
black cannibals, he kept a gun loaded just in case. "From
now on," his father told him, "the only killing done in this

house will be with kindness. The only thing we'll aim at the Americans is a bottle of schnapps." Still, for the sake of his mother and Gretchen, Hans saw to it that the gun had bullets, and they were not from a box marked "For practice only."

When there was no sign of the enemy on the following day, the household began to relax. It was a bright spring morning, and Hans stood with the front door wide open. Later it would grow hot, raising each blade of grass a fraction of an inch, hatching the droning flies. When the first fly came to sit on his arm, Hans wouldn't kill it. The cool of morning filled his nostrils and he felt like someone awakening from a sleep of centuries. Many things had happened during the long war which he regretted. Perhaps he should be full of guilt, but where guilt should be there was in him only an emptiness. He felt hunger, hunger in his stomach like a clenched fist, and hunger in his soul. Horse meat and the Red Cross would probably fill the first need. The second void would take longer to fill, but it could be done, with books and poems. With luck, he had fifty or sixty years before him, a treasury of living, and yet it seemed short for everything he had to learn. Learning to live with himself would take time and then, too, he'd have to learn to live with others. Such thoughts made him giddy. He pressed one hand over his stomach.

"There's too much oxygen in the air this morning," he told himself, and he sat down to let the feeling pass. Once recovered, he began moving his grandfather's books up from the cellar. Each one felt heavy as lead, but he bore their weight lovingly. There hovered about him the aura of a new self-possession.

He threw open the shutters of the library, unmasked the windows. "There," he said. "There, that's better." Dust swirled around him, and the imperturbable astral clock ticked away the minutes of waiting.

The bowl of thin potato soup he had eaten for breakfast wasn't enough to sustain him. He sat down in his grandfather's chair. He didn't even feel like reading. He simply sat and listened to the house. Konrad and Gretchen were sweeping out the hall. They sounded like children at play. He managed to smile to himself. One never made a clean sweep of anything, it seemed. There came the clatter of pots and pans from the kitchen. His mother would hold the house together with her bare arms if need be. It was funny about his mother. The war had changed her more than anyone else. Only her concern for food was the same, and she was cooking now. None of them would have touched horse meat before the war, but hunger had changed all that.

Lost in these speculations, Hans did not hear the alarm when it was first given. Then Gretchen bolted into the room. "The Americans are coming!" He stood up as though the chair was electrified. "The Americans!" He heard nothing, but from the window he saw them: two solid khaki-clad figures looking somehow immortal in their bulky clothes. The dark men showed no seed of decay or sickness in their flesh. They must pass by! It would be too absurd to be killed now, when the war was over. "Oh, God, make them pass by!"

Even as he said this, the two soldiers wandered from the road and up the front path, as cautiously as two children approaching a gingerbread house. One was a coal black giant, too black to show the tribal tattoos Hans knew must surely be there upon his face. The other was also dark-skinned, a bear of a man with wirespring hair and a cigar clenched between his teeth.

Resigned to die for his home and German womanhood, Hans ran for his gun. He was caught in the hall by his father, who held a bottle of schnapps in his hand. In their collision the bottle fell and broke. "Now they'll know we're here!" Hans said.

"Yes," Klaus agreed, "and we'd better smile and open the door before they do."

Hans's eyes were glued to the door, the last barrier. He could not move. His mind clambered for phrases with which to begin. "Welcome." But the word would stick in his throat. Perhaps, "What can we do for you?" If they didn't attack at once . . . if they understood German, if they were at all civilized.

Klaus had his hand on the door. Hans moved to stop him, but he was too late. A pressure from without flung the door open, and, guns foremost, the two soldiers prodded into the hallway. "A firing squad! We're going to be shot down!" thought Hans, but Klaus was saying in his best Gymnasium English, "Good afternoon. Will you please come in?" They were already in, but Klaus was trying hard.

The taller soldier, whose face showed at closer quarters a curious hint of undersurface copper, broke into a wide gash of a smile. "Ooooo-wee!" he exclaimed, almost whistling.

Less relaxed, the shorter soldier shifted his cigar from one side of his mouth to the other. His face was shiny with sweat. "Where'd you pick it up?" he asked suspiciously.

"Pardon?" replied Klaus.

"English. Where'd you learn it?" said the soldier, as though his language from a German mouth was a form of treachery.

"In the Gymnasium."

"Gymnasium?"

"How do you say . . . school."

In more laborious English than her husband's, Lore invited them to stay and eat. The tall Negro gave her a wide smile. "We're always hungry. I'm hungry enough to eat a horse." His companion agreed, which seemed to obviate an explanation. While dinner was being prepared, the shorter man explained their presence. "Quick now, we'll have a look around. For snipers," he said. They went through the house. Hans didn't see them take anything, but even if they had, there would have been nothing to say. It was the victor's right.

The books in the library didn't interest them, but the cigar-smoking soldier fixed his eyes on the old clock. He examined it. "That sure is pretty." Opening the little glass door in front, he hefted it. "Heavy! My, oh my, that sure is a pretty clock."

His companion seemed displeased. "Get your hands off that thing before I give you a clout on the head."

Hans overheard all this, but didn't understand. Perhaps they thought the old clock contained a bomb. In any case, he felt easier when they were called to the dinner table. Horse meat, stale bread, the heavy waxed boxes of K rations the soldiers drew from their kits: hunger made it all taste wonderful to Hans in spite of his nervousness.

The tall soldier sat majestically. "Any of you folks been to the States?" he asked.

"Ach, no. But my father . . . he was there," Klaus explained.

"When was that?"

"A long time, yes. He was in New York, and Boston. Lecturing."

"Didn't get down to old Tishabee, Alabama, I reckon?"

"No, no, I do not think so."

"He missed a swinging town," said the shorter soldier.

The meal came to an end all too quickly. Only a little chocolate from the K rations remained, but all seemed reluctant to leave the table. Klaus brought the radio up from the cellar and tried to find a news broadcast. Instead, over the B.B.C. came "God Save the King" and the triumphant ringing of Big Ben. "Victory, man, victory." The Americans' friendly laughter was full of a promise kept.

Konrad produced a small flask. He and Klaus drank a toast to the Americans as though together they had won the war.

"This is fine liquor," said the shorter soldier. "Mighty fine."

"Schnapps," Konrad corrected him. They drank toasts to liberation and to freedom, to Eisenhower's health and to Truman's, to the good German soldier, gone but not forgotten, to the Allies of World War II and the comrades in arms of World War III. It was all done with good will and conviction.

"Would you like to sing?" Lore asked them.

"Blues, ma'am?"

She led the singing of "A Mighty Fortress," singing with her whole face until her eyes disappeared and her wrinkles deepened. Their guests sang along in their deep bass, and finally, for Hans, they sang the birthday song, "Let Us Thankful Be." It had never seemed so fitting.

Lore asked them to sing again, but the tall soldier said they had to be getting along. His companion glanced once more in the direction of the library and remarked, "I've never seen such a fine clock."

"You would like the clock?" asked Klaus.

"It'd be the only one in Tishabee," said the short soldier.

"Take it. Please."

Hans was distressed. It wasn't his father's clock to give.

"We don't take anything we don't pay for. At least I don't," said the tall soldier. "Come on." He pulled at his friend's sleeve.

The short soldier hesitated. He was no scavanger, he said, but could they do a little transaction? For the promise of rations to come? Finally, the short soldier went off with the clock in his arms.

Klaus insisted they could not take anything for the clock, but they'd welcome the soldiers back any time.

Hans watched them go. Strangers, surely, as foreign to Bavaria as men from the moon. Yet they were kindly, and undemanding as conquerors. Like rusty armor, his malignant prejudices had been stripped away, and he stood now unburdened of illusive threats. To be sure, the clock was gone, but he would try not to miss it. It belonged somehow to times that were dead in Germany. A few K rations were worth more than any clock these days, though he didn't really expect their guests to keep their bargain. He went back to his books.

Toward evening he stepped out for some fresh air. It was with real surprise that he found a huge crate of K rations sitting on the path.

"Gretchen! Come look!" he shouted. "Come help me!"

She came, and Konrad with her. Hans guessed it would always be that way.

Together they moved the crate into the front hall. Gretchen began removing the green packages and stacking them tenderly like books. Konrad carried them into the kitchen. Hans saw that they could manage without him; they worked well together.

He walked slowly outside. The clouds were drifting toward the mountains where Barbarossa slept forever. Vast cavities of blue sky were opening up. Slowly he started up the long hill. When he reached the crest above the house, he paused to feel the wind blow against his face. The spring night came on quietly over Germany, the blood-red colors fading, becoming brown, then black. The long Nazi night was over, and he had survived with only superficial wounds. Some were already healing into scars. Others were not the stuff of surgery. He had left the night behind him, but it had been long, and full of bad dreams. Many of his friends were lost in it, along with part of himself. All that remained of them—of Heime, of Ernst, and of Siegfried—breathed only through him. He would not let them die entirely until he had made some sense from their living.

The earth had been scarred forever, but the sky remained serene. Lost in those stars were his mountains, the refuge he had loved so long. But the refuge had been also a prison, defended at terrible cost against a menace that had never come. Each man has his Jew, his Negro, his enemy from beyond the mountains. The towers of Golgotha hill which Hans had climbed in fear and despair were gone, but only the eroding centuries would level the surrounding peaks. They were high, those mountains which stood between men, but he was not afraid. He knew them now. There was time to climb them, a whole lifetime.

GLOSSARY

Action Squad SS There were several such "squads" in Eastern Europe. Their function was the mass elimination of Jews and Communists.

Alien Blood Laws "Laws to protect German blood and German honor," put forth at Nuremberg's "Party Day of Freedom" in 1935, and designed to deprive German Jews of the privileges of citizenship.

Alpine (or national) redoubt A dream of a few fanatical Nazis to make a last stand in the Alps. Though no Alpine redoubt developed, the rumor about this stand became a very real concern of the American Army.

Austrian Anschluss In March 1938, Germany absorbed Austria into the Reich by quasi-political means. The army was on hand in case of resistance.

Barbarossa's Cave According to legend, Barbarossa (Frederick I, King of Germany and Holy Roman Emperor, twelfth century) sleeps in a mountain cavern, awaiting the time when he will awaken and lead Germany to victory. A parallel to the legend of King Arthur.

Battle opera house Underground center where the German fighter command coordinated defenses against United States and British air raiders. Called "opera house" because of its steeply tiered seats.

245

B.D.M.   Bund Deutscher Mädel, League of German Girls. Organization within the Nazi Party for girls, rather like a political Girl Scouts.

Berchtesgaden   Literally, garden of the goddess Berchta. A popular mountain resort town; nearby, Hitler erected his Berghcf (mountain villa) as well as other living quarters and military buildings. The place served as a retreat and administrative center.

Blockleiters   Block leaders; Nazi Party members in charge of a block area.

Blood Flag   A flag carried by the Storm Troopers in the 1923 attempt to seize power in Germany. Once the Nazi Party was again ascendant, oaths of loyalty were sworn before the blood flag.

Corresponding member, Gestapo   A party informant, often an air-raid warden, but not a full member of the Gestapo.

Dachau   The first (1933–45) of the infamous concentration camps. It was designed for political prisoners, as distinguished from the later "extermination" camps where mass murder was the express policy. Thirty thousand prisoners died at Dachau, mostly from malnutrition and disease, particularly typhoid, which killed 15,000 in the last five months of the war.

Death's Head SS   Branch of the SS in charge of prison camps.

Deutschlandsender   The official Nazi radio station.

Eagle's Nest   Kelstein House; Hitler's mountaintop lodge near Berchtesgaden. It is now a tourist restaurant.

Einjährige exams   Matriculation exams, a sort of low-level college-board exam which became almost meaninglessly easy during the war so long as the politically oriented questions were answered patriotically.

Ein Volk, Ein Reich, Ein Führer   A Nazi Party slogan: "One people, one Reich, one leader."

Fenrir   In Teutonic mythology, a gigantic wolf allied with Loki against the gods.

Fortress Europe (Festung Europa)   A term, synonymous with Germany itself, which was used late in the war in an attempt to give Germans a sense of security and the conviction that their land was safe from conquest.

Gestapo   Geheime Staats Polizei, Secret State Police. Originally Reichsmarschall Goering's private police force, gradually expanded under Himmler to enormous power.

Goebbels, Joseph   Nazi Minister of Propaganda.

Goering, Hermann   Head of Luftwaffe, German air force.

Götterdämmerung   "Twilight of the Gods," a cosmic Armageddon.

Great War   Until World War II, a reference to World War I.

Gruppenleiter   Group leader.

Guernica   Town in Spain savagely bombed by the German Condor Legion during the Spanish Civil War, 1937.

Gymnasium   In Germany, a boys' private high school. These schools were not as imbued with Nazi doctrine as the party-run schools.

Heimdall   A god of Teutonic myth who guarded the rainbow bridge to the abode of the gods and who at the approach of danger would sound his horn in warning.

Horst Wessel Lied   Nazi Party rallying song, written by Horst Wessel.

Jungmädel   Nazi Party organization for young girls up to fourteen years of age.

Jungvolk   Nazi Party organization for young boys ten to fourteen.

Knight's Cross   Medal awarded for bravery, akin to United States Medal of Honor or British Victoria Cross.

Last levy   Drive to increase the war effort in 1943, characterized by propaganda as the levy that would win the war.

Lederhosen   Bavarian leather britches worn traditionally with waist-length green or gray lodencloth jacket.

Loki, Vengeance of   One of the oldest Teutonic gods, Loki became the superior demon of that pantheon working against the benevolent gods until he brought about their deaths as well as his own. His vengeance thus brings about destruction of vanquished and victor alike.

Maquis   Member of the French underground movement.

Mischling   A half Jew; one of mixed blood.

Night and Fog Decree   "Nacht und Nebel Erlass," issued by Hitler on December 7, 1941, for the purpose of seizing persons endangering German security. Under this decree, persons were seized without notice to their families; they disappeared literally into the night and fog.

Night of Broken Crystal   November 9, 1938. Following the assassination of the third secretary of the German embassy in Paris by a refugee Jew, allegedly spontaneous reprisals in Germany resulted in the burning and wrecking of countless Jewish shops and synagogues.

Nuremberg Laws   See "Alien Blood Laws."

Obersalzberg   Mountainous area above Berchtesgaden where Hitler established his villa and Eagle's Nest.

Pfennig   Small coin.

Pilot of Africa   Joachim Marsaille, who shot down more than a hundred Allied planes in the Mediterranean area. A great hero in Germany.

Pimpf   Little fellow; a Nazi Party organization, part of the Hitler Youth movement, incorporating boys six to ten, from which they would graduate into the Jungvolk at age ten and into Hitler Youth proper at the age of fourteen.

Pimpfenprobe exams   Exams given on graduation from Pimpfe status.

Putsch   In Munich in 1923, the Nazi Party tried to seize power by force and failed disastrously. Nazis killed in the fiasco later became party heroes.

Reichswehr   The small, regular German army during the days of the Republic, after World War I. In 1935, Hitler changed the name of his revitalized armed forces to the Wehrmacht.

Rhineland   German territory west of the Rhine River that was demilitarized as a buffer zone by France after World War I and occupied by Hitler in a first show of strength in March 1936.

SA   Sturmabteilung, the Storm Troopers, or Brown Shirts, as they were called, the strong arm of the early Nazi Party.

Purged of leadership in the early 1930's, the SA became subordinate to the SS.

SS   Schutzstaffel, or Black Shirts. Originating as a small group of Hitler's personal bodyguards, the SS under Himmler attained power rivaling the army itself.

Stahlhelm   Steel helmet; a militant political group that was eventually absorbed into the SA.

"Strength through Joy"   A program of mass entertainment whereby German workers were provided with cheap and well-regulated diversion.

Third Reich   Term used by Hitler to indicate the supremacy of Germany, which would last a thousand years. The First Reich had been the Holy Roman Empire, whose power was centered in Germany; the second, the empire established by Bismarck. Hitler's was the Third Reich.

Thor   Teutonic war god. His emblem was the swastika.

Tötenkorps   SS in charge of concentration camps.

Uhlan (or *Ulan*)   Heavy Polish, later Prussian, cavalry.

Valhalla   In Teutonic myth, a paradise for warriors fallen in battle.

Valkyries   Warrior goddesses who dispensed destiny to warriors in battle, deciding which must perish and which would be admitted to Valhalla.

Volksgrenadiers   A final recruitment of office workers into the army. Unlike the Volkssturm, they were equipped and trained, but lacked the fire and optimism of the formal German army.

Wehrmacht   See "Reichswehr."